E TAMER:

S RIDE

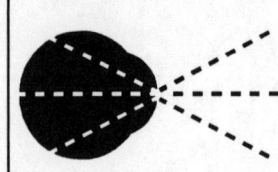

This Large Print Book carries the Seal of Approval of N.A.V.H.

THE MULE TAMER, BOOK 2

THE MULE TAMER: CHICA'S RIDE

JOHN C. HORST

WHEELER PUBLISHING
A part of Gale, Cengage Learning

GALE
CENGAGE Learning

Copyright © 2012 by John Horst.
Wheeler Publishing, a part of Gale, Cengage Learning.

ALL RIGHTS RESERVED
This edition of Mule Tamer II: Chica's Ride is designed to provide entertainment for the reader. It is a work of fiction. All characters, organizations and events portrayed in this novel are either products of the author's imagination or are used fictitiously.
Wheeler Publishing Large Print Western.
The text of this Large Print edition is unabridged.
Other aspects of the book may vary from the original edition.
Set in 16 pt. Plantin.

LIBRARY OF CONGRESS CATALOGING-IN-PUBLICATION DATA

Names: Horst, John , author.
Title: The mule tamer : Chica's ride / by John C. Horst.
Description: Large print edition. | Waterville, Maine : Wheeler Publishing, 2017. | Series: Wheeler Publishing large print western
Identifiers: LCCN 2016043638| ISBN 9781410494030 (softcover) | ISBN 1410494039 (softcover)
Subjects: LCSH: Large type books. | GSAFD: Western stories.
Classification: LCC PS3608.O7724 M847 2017 | DDC 813/.6—dc23
LC record available at https://lccn.loc.gov/2016043638

Published in 2017 by arrangement with John Horst

Printed in the United States of America
1 2 3 4 5 6 7 21 20 19 18 17

Still for Peggy and Kate

Be kind, for everyone you meet is
fighting a hard battle

TABLE OF CONTENTS

Chapter I: Heartbreak 11
Chapter II: Getting Ready 63
Chapter III: Resolution 74
Chapter IV: Captive 84
Chapter V: Hunting 102
Chapter VI: Healer 106
Chapter VII: Down Mexico Way . . . 115
Chapter VIII: Marta 123
Chapter IX: Arvel 142
Chapter X: The Mexican Cossack . . 171
Chapter XI: Subterfugio 176
Chapter XII: Gentle Will Panks . . . 200
Chapter XIII: Nemesis 212
Chapter XIV: Fiesta 229
Chapter XV: Chica's Ride 245
Chapter XVI: Sappers 266
Chapter XVII: Tarahumara 275
Chapter XVIII: Attack 280

Chapter XIX: Coming Home 319
Chapter XX: Wedding Day 374
    EPILOGUE 379

Chapter I: Heartbreak

Alice Walsh watched her girls sleep as the train puffed rhythmically east. A man watched her watch her only granddaughter, Rebecca, and the young woman who had given her everything she held dear in the world, Rebecca's mother, Maria. She was happy. He watched her until she acknowledged him; he was eager to talk. She looked at her hands, hoping to avoid the inevitable, as she did not like the man.

He was dressed too busily and did not seem to care enough to maintain a kempt appearance, despite his obvious means. She never held anyone in contempt and, like her son whom she taught from a young age, was tolerant and kind to everyone she met, even oafs and simpletons. The man persisted and she finally gave him a smile, looked him in the eye, and let him proceed.

He grinned, baring incomplete tobacco-stained teeth. He rose briefly, assuming a crouch, ape-like, and tipped his hat. He looked on at the lady's sleeping companions. "How's she working out for you?"

"I'm sorry?" Alice was genuinely confused.

"How's the Mexican working out for you? They're usually better than the darkies if you get one that's not too lazy."

"I beg your pardon?"

"The servant girl. I am sorry, madam. I should properly introduce myself. I am . . ."

"That won't be necessary, sir." She waved him off dismissively, in the superior attitude she'd known all her life but only rarely used. "I believe you have mistaken my daughter-in-law for someone else."

The man retracted his hand. "Humph. There's no telling what will be in first class these days."

"I could not agree more, Sir."

He stood up abruptly and made his way to the lounge car.

Chica woke, shifted little Rebecca's head to a more comfortable angle and smiled at her mother-in-law, speaking through a yawn into the back of her hand. "Abuelita, who were you talking to?"

The old woman smiled at her daughter-in-law. Abuelita: she loved her Spanish name. "No one, daughter. Absolutely no one."

Chica smiled and stretched, looked at the watch pinned to her blouse. They'd be in Tucson soon. She yawned again and pressed her daughter's shoulder. "Wake up, Cielito."

The little girl smiled at her mother and grandmother. "I was dreaming of Daddy. I miss him." She suddenly looked anxiously into her mother's eyes.

"I'm not sure I want to go back East, Mamma." She looked over at her grandmother and down at her own lap.

Chica smiled and hugged her, straightening the child's hair. "I know, my darling, but it will be all right. Abuelita will make everything nice at her home and you will make many friends and learn many wonderful things and Daddy and I will come to see you many times."

"That's right, Rebecca. And I have a lovely pony waiting impatiently for you there. I have told her all about you and she can't wait to meet you."

"Sí, and you will ride like Umberto taught you. Like an Englishman. And Abuelita will ride with you all the time, and you can even ride at school."

"And dress like the people in the picture over the mantel, in the red coats, Mamma?"

"Sí, sí. You will find out. It is a grand place and there are many trees. It is so green Rebecca, greener than up north in Flagstaff. You will love it, I promise you." She patted the girl and felt better now that the child was smiling.

She, herself, felt as if she might cry at any moment and she never ever cried. Her little girl's anxiety was the hardest thing to take and she was not certain she could stand to let the child leave. They were constant companions, but it was Chica's idea to send her away and she bore the burden heavily.

She thought Rebecca was growing up wild. The child was nearly eight years old and, despite the tutoring by Uncle Bob and the nice young woman who'd been hired as her governess, it did not seem enough to her mother. Chica wanted her girl to be prepared for a new world, a new century, and she knew that living back East would be the right thing.

Chica stood up and looked at her reflection in the window. She put a strand of hair in place. "I am going to find the porter. I will be right back."

As she wandered through the coach car, looking for the old man who'd been so helpful when they left California, a red rubber ball bounced across her path and she deftly caught it as a pretty little boy with blue eyes and sandy hair lunged for it. Chica smiled and pretended to take a bite of it, as if it were a fresh apple. The boy looked up at her, mouth agape. She cast a spell over even miniature versions of men.

She held out her hand as if to present the ball to him and his mother snatched it away, ignoring Chica and scolding the child for playing too aggressively. Chica moved on, looking over her shoulder at the unpleasant mother and feeling sorry for the little fellow.

"If you do it again, I'm throwing it out the window!" The pretty redhead spoke at Chica's back. She looked out at the landscape as they rode on. She was thoroughly miserable, the seats were terrible and she could not wait to get up to Flagstaff. Her sister promised her there were mostly whites up there. She was full up with these Mexicans, like that one who had just passed by; in their fancy clothes, putting on airs like a white. She hated them all.

The little boy squirmed but dared not look up from the ball. He knew when she got into these moods that it was best to try to be invisible. He stole a glance at her now. She was watching something off in the distance. He looked in the direction she was peering and saw a gang of men high up on a hill. Mexicans. No wonder she was in such a foul mood.

His father had left them that winter. He dragged them to the farthest point south in California and she hated it. Then the money ran out and his father ran out of steam and then he ran off with a damned Mexican. She hated him for it and every time she looked into the boy's blue eyes, his father's eyes, she thought of how she'd been mistreated, how unfair it was that she was in such a predicament, stuck with the boy and no means and no prospects for the future.

She, herself, was a fine looking woman: big, big-boned, nearly six feet tall. She had big features and big breasts and flaming red hair and fair skin and freckles all over.

She still remembered when it all fell apart. He used to be smitten with her, used to fawn over her. Then that one night, when they were intimate and she was lying on him, he pushed her away, told her she was suffocating him. That's when she knew what he had been up to and later she saw her, a little woman, tiny, like the one who'd just passed them on the train: Her own polar opposite.

The Mexican woman was coming back.

The redhead looked at her, looked her up and down and felt the twinge deep in her gut; it bothered her even more that the woman walked along so proud and confident.

She didn't even acknowledge her. Here she was, staring the Mexican down, and the woman didn't even have the presence of mind to notice that she was being stared at. That's what she was like, all dark with the black hair and pretty shape. She was ten years younger. Oh, she hated him so much for leaving her.

She looked back at the hill where the Mexicans were, but now the train was coming around a bend and high hills obstructed her view. She thought more about her sister. She was lucky. She married a much older and ugly man. He had money, though. Her sister had told her to marry well and not for love and she didn't pay heed; she'd gotten the handsome man and now she was paying for it.

She'd chosen Willoughby and she should have chosen Colonel Brandon, but Jane Austen had not written her story and that ship had sailed long ago. She had one chance and she blew it. Now she was damaged goods, with a child, abandoned by her husband, over thirty, and not even divorced and all the eligible men her age were gobbled up.

They had lasted six years together and of

those, only the first nine months were good. Then the boy came and then his wanderlust took hold and he began dragging her around from one stupid idea, one hell-hole, to the next.

She had nothing to show for it except a boy she never wanted in the first place, one who looked too much like his father, to boot. And on top of all that, she'd let him have her dowry. It wasn't a huge fortune, five thousand dollars, but it was her money and she stupidly let him have it. He promised to return it a thousand fold; they'd be rich and never want for anything again. They'd travel all over Europe, live well. It was all going to happen, soon. The next town, the next opportunity, the next venture. But it didn't. Nothing happened but the loss of her fortune, youth, beauty, and the love of her life. All lost in the span of six years.

Well, at least her sister had a governess and the boy would be taken off her hands soon enough. Then in a year, just one short year, back to Michigan, to school. She'd not have to deal with him at all then.

Chica wandered through the car and into the next before she remembered her task; Rebecca was on her mind. She suddenly thought of the old bandit, Sombrero del Oro, and she did not know why. She felt a chill as she walked between the next two cars, despite the heat of the midday sun. The hair on her neck stood on end and she had goose bumps on her arms.

The smell of something familiar, cordite or burning fuse suddenly assaulted her nose. She looked off to the south and a rider could be seen, galloping hard, closing quickly. He wore a big sombrero and bandoliers full of cartridges crisscrossed his chest. He carried something in his hand, smoldering, dangerous and Chica immediately comprehended.

She wheeled and ran back to the coach trying desperately to reach little Rebecca and Abuelita. She heard the explosions behind her and knew she had little time as she burst through the door of the car. No one but Chica seemed to know what was going on.

"Go to the back of the train!"

Abuelita looked up, confused. "What is it, daughter?"

Alice had never seen the young woman so agitated. Rebecca knew to take heed when her mother gave orders. She jumped to her feet and grabbed her grandmother by the hand.

"Come, Abuelita, come."

She dashed to the back of the car, which lurched and shook, bobbed one way, then the other, like a great serpent being pecked by a flock of diving crows.

The engineer saw the attack coming and pushed the throttle to full despite the fact that they were coming to a bend. He tried to outrun the bandits and only managed to make matters worse. The train was now out of control.

The little girl flung open the door as the explosion ripped through their coach, tossing her like a ragdoll into the lounge car, tearing her away from her grandmother's grasp. Everything turned sideways and she found herself thrown into a corner; what was once the ceiling was now plowing into the desert floor beneath her.

There were more explosions and now gunshots and screams of fear and pain and panic welled up, as if all the passengers were singing a chorus of agony as one.

She lay there, half conscious as the train skidded and burned up and broke apart all around her. She could feel the heat of the friction and wondered if this is what it was like to die. She wanted her mother and grandmother. She wondered why this was happening.

∎ ∎ ∎ ∎

The redheaded woman stood next to the boy in the hot sun beside the crashed train. Bare-headed, they had already begun to burn. She held a small fan and waved it, but it just moved hot smoky air and the labor required to operate it cancelled out any cooling effect.

The bandits rode up on them and two dismounted. The boy had dropped his ball when they looked at him and dared not retrieve it. One bandit kicked it, like a football, manipulated it deftly and bounced it off the toe of his boot. Another and then another joined him and soon they were playing about like school children, deftly passing the ball to one another in a loose circle.

One bandit, still mounted, unwound his riata and put on a show for the little boy. Around and around he spun the rope until the loop was big enough to encircle his horse. He spun it again and again, first left, then right. It was a spectacular feat, and the boy stood mesmerized by the man's skill and momentarily forgot his predicament.

Despite this distraction, the outlaws had their eyes on the pelirroja de grandes. One bandit approached her, leering at her breasts. He reached for them and was soundly cracked on the knuckles with the folded fan. The man jumped back dramatically and smiled at his companions.

"Oh, she is a spirited one." They all cackled like a flock of grackles. He bowed to her apologetically and she was able to relax just a little. Maybe their predicament wasn't so dire, after all.

She looked on at the men playing with the ball and the one spinning the rope; they did not seem so terrible. She'd made it clear that she was not to be trifled with. Maybe they only wanted the loot from the train. Maybe they'd be gone once they'd extracted anything of value.

She looked at the boy who had the beginning of a smile on his face. He was enjoying the men. It looked as though he was primed to start in playing with them, his body erect, leaning forward, just waiting for the invitation.

Just then another bandit rode up and began to mirror the actions of the man twirling the rope. It was quite the choreography and she too was enjoying it a little. Suddenly the first one reeled the riata in a bit, then threw it at the boy.

He looped it around the child's shoulders

and the boy stood, smiling. It was nice the man was giving him so much consideration. The bandit just as quickly adjusted it up and, like a snake wriggling up the boy's body, it settled around his neck and suddenly tightened; a death grip. He wound the end in his hands around the big saddle horn and casually turned away, knocking the child off his feet and dragging him away through the dust and rocks and thorny brush.

The redheaded woman screamed. She demanded they stop it at once and the bandit who'd had his knuckles rapped walked up to her. He was not smiling now and he punched her hard in the nose, opening a stream of blood and causing her pain unlike any she'd ever felt before in her life. Even the pain of childbirth was not as intense as the pain she was feeling now.

She fell back on the ground and grabbed her face. The pain shot through her, searing, and then she felt the other bandit's stiff rope hit her on the shoulders. Like her son, she too, was now dragged through the desert; the friction burning her thighs as she tried desperately to get fingers between her windpipe and the strangling line.

Chica awoke to darkness. The train engine

was wheezing like a dying giant, far away. The air was thick with smoke and dust, the smell of burning oil, blistered paint and wood, and gunpowder. She called out to Rebecca. Abuelita answered, somewhere above her, seemingly off in the distance yet only just inches away. Chica felt as if her eyes were closed. All was in darkness, yet she knew they were open.

She tried to reach up in front of her face, but her arms were pinned by something hard: wood, splintered wood. She focused and realized wood was covering her eyes. Something dripped, wet, on her face. It tasted salty, metallic. She called out again, more carefully, quietly.

"Maria, you are buried under debris, child. Stay still, I will help."

Chica heard boards being shifted. She talked to Abuelita as the old woman worked. Alice felt something drip on her neck, looked up overhead and peered into the dead eyes of the ugly man she'd only recently spoken to on the train. His mouth was agape, the incomplete tobacco-stained teeth showing through his slack-jawed gaze.

Only his head and neck remained, stuffed through the shattered splinters of the wooden wall of the train. She could not determine where the rest of his body had gotten to. She caught her breath, pushed back the urge to wretch, wiped her neck quickly and continued to work.

"Where is Rebecca?"

"I don't know, child, I don't know. Hold on, I nearly have you free."

It was going to be dark soon. Chica had been unconscious for some time and had missed the attack. By the sound, or lack thereof, she figured there were few if any survivors. The last boards were removed and she pulled herself free.

The old woman looked terrible, but there was light, and fight, in her eyes. Chica patted her hand as she pulled herself up onto her feet.

"Maria, look." She pointed up at the remains of the corpse hanging above them. "I just spoke to him a little while ago." She looked ashamed of herself. "I wasn't very kind to him, Maria."

Chica looked at the man's head. "He is beyond our help, Abuelita. He is either with God or the devil now."

"I looked everywhere for Rebecca but could not find her, Maria. I fear the worst. I came back in here to try to find you when I heard you call out. Where could she be, child, where could she be?"

"Come, Abuelita, we will find her." Chica

took her mother-in-law by the hand and led her outside. Here and there a few survivors stirred, wandered about, dazed, not knowing what to do next or where to go, or even if the attackers were finished with them. The bandits had left little of value and few victims alive.

Only old people seemed left, all the young ones who'd survived the wreck had been taken captive. Some, unrealistically, looked for a porter, expected it, demanded it, looking for some kind of aid, some manner of authority to tell them where to go, what would happen next, when help would arrive. But there was no help: no porters or conductor or engineer. They were all, every one of them, dead. The two women were lucky to be alive.

Chica looked down at the ground and saw the rubber ball she'd recently given the little boy. It stood out bright amongst the starkness of the desert floor like a solitary wild flower. She reached down and picked it up and put it in her pocket.

She surveyed the area, her mind racing to formulate a plan. A sudden storm came in, as if God was in congress with the black hearts who'd destroyed their train, disrupted the lives of the fortunate and destroyed the lives of the less so. The air was ionized, metallic, cool and it made the women cold.

And then, just as oddly, as incongruous as the entire surreal experience laid out before them, a middle-aged man, a retired soldier, a veteran of the Indian wars, appeared before them, seemingly unscathed. He was a fit-looking and handsome man with a tiny beard and thin mustache, salt and pepper hair with more white than grey in the sideburns and throughout the facial hair. He was dressed smartly in a grey pinstriped ditto suit and had a large six shooter stuck in his tailored trousers.

"Ladies." He bowed to them and tipped his Homburg and then was distracted by something he saw off in the distance, farther down the track. He looked on.

One bandit remained, too greedy to give up on the site and too bent on squeezing out the last bit of booty. Chica saw him from a distance, recognized him as the bandit she had seen on the horse just before the explosion. She squeezed Abuelita's hand, pulled her close and whispered in her ear without taking her eyes off the bad man. She told her to stay still and to listen to her every command.

They waited for what was to come next.

The gallant soldier took charge. He was performing for the ladies now. He'd do something brave to impress the beautiful one. He marched up to the bandit and pointed at him, as he'd likely done a thousand times before as a leader of men, ordering a private or scout or Indian brave or squaw around.

The bandit looked down upon him from his horse. He raised his pistol and shot the soldier through the head. All the energy left the gentleman's body and he immediately dropped to the ground as if his legs had magically been turned to jelly.

Alice Walsh was immediately ill. The world spun all around her, out of control. She'd never seen a man murdered and she was certain she would vomit or faint or both. Chica sensed it through the loosening grip of her hand and she shook the woman, bringing her back from her loss of equilibrium.

The bandit rode past the corpse as he casually holstered his six shooter and stopped next to the women. He smiled at them and did not speak as he dismounted. He walked up to Chica and grabbed her by her pretty neck and pushed his ugly lips against her mouth, as if he were planning to devour her.

He stood back and looked her up and down. She stood still, emotionless, waiting.

He ran his hands along her body and made a cursory inspection of her nether regions. Abuelita stood, shocked and mortified, first the poor soldier and now her daughter-in-law, it was nearly too much to bear. She could not understand her companion's complacency.

He held out his dirty hand and the two women handed over their valuables. First the watches pinned to their blouses, then the rings, then the necklaces and earrings.

Chica looked the man in the eye. She waited for him to put his booty in a pocket, then gave him the look she had not had to use for many years. He was pleased. With great deliberation, as if performing a special seductive show that promised to ultimately end in pleasure, she put her left foot high up on one of the broken wheels of the train. Slowly, steadily, Chica raised her long skirt, all the while looking the bandit in the eye. The hem of her gown slowly revealed her ankle, then shin, then knee, then thigh.

Abuelita could not comprehend what was happening.

The bandit swallowed hard, felt a stirring deep in his loins. He was pleased that he had not ridden off with the others. He was missing out on the abuse of the big red-haired one, but this one was superior. He could not believe his good luck; such a beauty, so willing to succumb to his power.

Chica finally stopped with her skirt at mid-thigh, holding off revealing her pelvis, pudenda. But that was okay, it was fine to let the seduction last a little, let the moment and the promise of what lay ahead titillate a while longer. They were such beautiful thighs and he could barely contain himself, could not wait for what was coming.

Chica had reached the object tightly secured under the garter at the top of her stocking but he paid no attention as to why she was acting in such a way. He was mesmerized and, seemingly, as if by magic, the gaping holes of the Remington's barrels stared like a death's head into the bandit's eyes.

He dared not move; he waited.

Chica lowered the muzzle and pressed the trigger; once, then twice, and two forty-one bullets crashed into the man, first through the left lung, then through the right. He crumpled and Chica was on him. She pulled the big knife from his belt and grabbed his greasy hair. He looked at her, fearful and bewildered.

She spit into his eyes and spoke close to his ear. "Culero, I am going to kill you, but not yet. Do you understand?"

"Sí, sí." The bandit nodded his head slightly.

"Culero, how did you like to kiss me? You din' know you were kissing the one sent by God to kill you, did you? That kiss was nothing compared to what the devil have in store for you, cagada. I hope you enjoyed it."

She tested the edge of the knife with her index finger. "Ah, nice an' sharp. I think you could shave with this, mierda." She dragged the blade across his cheek, changing its angle and fileting a bit of skin away.

"No, I guess not. You keep a pretty good edge on your blade, though, mierda." She got closer to him, speaking into his ear.

"I will kill you fast if you tell me what I want. If you do not tell me what I want, I will cut your cojones off and shove them up your ass. Do you understand?" Abuelita gasped behind her, Chica ignored her.

"Sí, sí."

"Tell me, culero, what happened to a pretty little black-haired girl with blue eyes?"

"No sé, Señora, no sé."

"Come now, excremento, you mus' remember."

Chica took the point of the big knife and

pressed it into the corner of his mouth; she pulled sideways and slit the man's cheek halfway to his ear. He winced but did not cry out.

Chica continued, matter-of-factly. "She had a pretty blue dress on and a blue ribbon in her hair. You must remember her. There was no one else like her."

She stuck the knife's tip up the man's nose and pulled outward, separating his left naris in two. He once again remained silent, his face now freely draining blood. "I will ask one more time, cagada, and then I start cutting down there."

She grabbed the man's trousers and ripped them downward, exposing his midsection. "Don' make me grab your greasy member, Pendejo. I will not like it, and you will hate it."

"No, no Señora, por favor." The man spoke with difficulty; the open wound on his face flapped and gaped, exposing partially toothed gums.

"Maria, please, no." The old woman could just begin to comprehend. Her daughter-in-law had become a wild beast, transformed before her eyes. Chica looked back at the old woman. She looked unnatural, as if she were in a kind of trance. The old woman was suddenly terrified of the young beauty she'd known so well and had loved for so many years.

Chica pointed the bloody knife at Alice Walsh. "Shush, Abuelita."

She went back to work on the bandit. "What do you say, shit? Shall I start cutting?"

"No, no, Señora. The girl was taken. She was taken with the other survivors, to San Sebastian."

"By who?"

"Que?" The bandit's lungs were filling with blood and it now ran out his nose and from the corner of the gaping wound of his mouth, a frothy pink mass of lung blood. He would soon be no use to Chica.

She pressed the knife against the corner of his eye, her rage quickly growing almost uncontrollable. "Goddamn you, I am going to pop your eyes from your estupido head! Who is your leader, you stupid shit."

"Sombrero del Oro."

"Good, good, mierda. I will not cut off your balls and I will not remove your goddamned eyes. I will let you die in peace. Where is your horse?"

She didn't wait for a reply and began pulling the bandoliers from the dying man, causing him to wince and make gurgling sounds of pain as he choked on his blood.

She pulled his gun belt off and checked his six shooter. She strapped the rig around her waist. She emptied his pockets and retrieved the jewelry he had stolen from them, handing the old woman the items she had just surrendered, without looking at her. She found some cigars and matches in his vest pocket and lit one. She smoked while the man breathed his last.

She finally seemed to remember her mother-in-law and looked back at her. The woman stood, jaw hanging, staring at the transformed mistress of her son's ranch. Chica looked wicked and wild and barely recognizable.

Chica touched the old woman's face. "Abuelita, I am sorry you must see such things. But it cannot be helped. The worst is yet to come."

"What . . . what do you mean, child?"

"I have to go get my girl back, Abuelita, and I will have to kill many of these bad men."

"But this is for the law, child. Let the law handle it."

Chica ignored her and began walking in the direction of the bandit's horse. She looked about for other guns. Nothing of any value seemed to be left anywhere.

"Maria, stop. Maria." Alice Walsh jogged

to catch up.

Chica turned and faced the old woman. "You stay here, Abuelita. Soon there will be help. Go to Arvel and tell him what has happened. Tell him I am getting Rebecca. He will know what to do. There is no law to help us, Abuelita. Sombrero del Oro has done what he has wanted for many years and he will not be stopped by any law."

"Then I will go with you, child. I must go with you." Chica stopped at the wreckage of the baggage car. Boxes were strewn everywhere and she began breaking them open. She found one box buried deep in the rubble, overlooked by the bandits. She was lucky and retrieved two shotguns and boxes of shells. She grabbed them and put them in a sack. She found a Winchester.

"You can ride, I know this, Abuelita, but you know nothing of what must be done. You are a pacifista and you will not like the things that must be done. That back there," she pointed to the dead man, "was nothing compared to what I will be doing to these bandits."

"Then I will just have to learn, my dear, I will just have to learn." The old woman grabbed Chica's arm, stopping her from her tasks. "I am going with you, Maria."

"Okay, well, go an' find a horse then,

Abuelita." She held the woman's hands and gripped them tightly and looked her in the eyes. "But you jus' remember, Abuelita. You do everything I say, and you never, ever tell me no, Maria, don' do that . . . whatever I do, you understan'? No matter what I do or say, no matter how terrible. You promise?"

"Ye . . . yes, Maria. I understand." Her mind reeled and wondered at what she was committing herself to.

"You promise! You tell me you promise, right now, or you may not go."

"I promise, I promise!"

"Okay, then. Go get your horse and come back here."

They were soon riding after the bandits. Alice Walsh was exhausted. She was seventy-nine years old. She was fit and a good rider. She could ride to the hounds with the best of them, all afternoon through the Maryland countryside in mid-winter, but she was exhausted now. The big roan stallion she had found hurt her legs; he was too wide and the great Mexican saddle was huge compared to the nice sleek jumping saddles she rode on all her life. She was sore all over and it was beginning to get very hot.

She watched Chica's back as they rode along the narrow trail. She didn't look like the beautiful wife of her only son. She now looked like a man, a terrible, terrifyingly cruel man.

Chica had found a couple of sombreros in the wreckage and put one on the old woman's head. She cut a slit up the center of their dresses and tied the bottoms to their ankles to protect them from the sun and allow them to ride more comfortably. Chica's new gun belt and bandoliers were sickeningly deadly and the old woman felt that she must be living a nightmare.

Perhaps she would awaken soon. She thought about Chica. She thought about how she handled the bandit. She did not know that Chica carried a gun. They'd traveled together, all over California for the better part of a month and she never knew that Chica was armed. No one she'd ever known carried a gun. No one in Maryland had to carry a gun. It just wasn't done.

She knew Chica was tough. She'd heard bits and pieces about the big fight and how Chica saved Arvel's life, but it never had much of an impact on her. It was so long ago and the girl had become so used to living on the ranch, so used to dressing like a lady. The only time she'd ever known Chica to touch a gun was when they were bird hunting. That was nothing like what she'd just witnessed.

She shook inside when she thought about this. She should have been revolted, but something about it made her, well, proud of the girl. She was so worried for her little granddaughter, she knew why Chica was acting this way and she secretly approved of it.

She thought back to the poor soldier. He seemed a nice man. He seemed a capable and tough man and he was snuffed out so casually, so unceremoniously. This is what these bandits were like, they not only cared nothing for the law, but they cared nothing for humanity. They were the worst kind of brutes and now they had her precious, sweet little granddaughter. She reproached herself for trying to stop her daughter-in-law and she resolved to keep quiet the next time. As they rode, the path widened and she came up next to her companion.

"What will they do to her if we don't rescue Rebecca?"

"Our little girl dying is not the worst thing that can happen to her, Abuelita." She did not look at the old woman as she spoke. She looked far up the trail.

"Could we pay a ransom, Maria? I have a big fortune. I will pay it all to get her back."

"Sí, I know you would, Abuelita. I know

very well that you would do this. And we will see if this thing can be done."

She rode on and looked down, studying the ground from the back of her horse. She stopped and put her hand up for Abuelita to stop. "I know where these bastards are going, Abuelita. I know where they will camp."

She stopped and they rested for the remainder of the day. The old woman slept soundly and Chica checked the guns and made her plan. She remembered her little Remington and reloaded it, replaced it in her garter holster. She killed a couple of chickens with one of the shotguns from the train and cooked them while her mother-in-law slept. When the old woman awakened it was going on dusk.

"I am sorry to sleep so much, Maria."

"It is okay, Abuelita." She ate her chicken. "You are old and I hope that I am so fit when I am as old as you."

She looked over at Alice Walsh and smiled. "Are you sad to see me act this way, Abuelita?"

"No. I am not sad, Maria. I am shocked. But I am not sad. And I must tell you, I am not sorry you did what you did to the bandit. I am not sorry at all, Maria."

"This is good, Abuelita." She took a long

drink from her canteen and handed it to Alice who drank deeply. "You must understand these people, these excremento we are after. They are no like human beings and they cannot be treated like they are. They understand one thing and that is more brutality than they can give out. Do you understand?"

"I do, Maria. I do." Alice wiped her forehead and replaced her sombrero. "Have you known much of this, Maria?"

Chica stiffened. She would not share with anyone, not Arvel, not the old priest she'd known, not Abuelita, what she had known. Her past was her own and she shared it with no one.

She snapped, "That does not matter."

She caught herself and softened. She looked the old woman in the eye and managed a weak smile.

"Did Arvel never tell you about me, Abuelita?" She looked down and adjusted the gunbelt.

"He told me that you were courageous, Maria. He said you were Artemis in the flesh."

"You two are very funny, Abuelita. You talk of things I know nothing about. What is this Artemis, Abuelita?"

"She was a Greek goddess, a huntress, a

protector of children and of women. Arvel says you are a hunter of bad men and that you are fearless and good and never use your powers for evil."

"My Arvel. He is a good boy, eh, Abuelita?"

"Yes, Maria. He is a good boy."

"It will break his heart if we do not get our Rebecca back right away. So we will do this thing, Abuelita, you know this, right?" She did not wait for an answer but began preparing to move out. They'd ride again and catch the bandits camping.

The old woman waited in a washout in the dark, all alone, next to the horses. Chica was suddenly next to her. She was preparing her guns. "Abuelita, they are all getting drunk. I could not see Rebecca. She is probably not with them."

"Should we just go around them, child?" Alice Walsh was suddenly terrified. She did not want to fight the gang of men. Her legs and arms felt leaden, as if she would not be able to get them to work when it was time. She began shaking again. "If Rebecca's not with them, why fight them, Maria?"

"The more we kill now, the less of them we will have to worry about later, Abuelita. They must all die."

She worked the action of the shotgun. "Do you know this gun, Abuelita?" The old woman did not. "No matter, this is what we will do."

The bandits sat smoking and staring into the fire. They felt good. They made a generous haul at the train and had some quality captives to trade further south. They had plenty of excellent whiskey and mescal and had not been followed. Soon they'd be in Mexico and into the wild where no one wanted to follow.

This was the best of times for them. They were slovenly, worthless beasts. They did not like to work or be productive or have a family or make something of themselves. They lived for slothful pleasure; they lived for malice and depravity. They could neither give nor receive love.

Other than fornicating, sitting on their asses around a fire with full bellies and plenty of spirits was their greatest pleasure. They sat and drank and got drunk and spoke their stupid, simple-minded conversations with their stupid simple-minded companions. There was no boss around and none of them had the discipline to work collectively or post a guard or take turns being sober in order to keep a watch out. They were like little spoilt children whose parents were not around. It was going to be a good night.

The two women appeared next to them as if by magic, as if they were two ghosts. Perhaps they were the ghosts of some of the victims of the train robbery. None of the bandits stood up or even addressed the two. They just sat there, around the fire, smoking and passing the jug. The women just stood there, saying nothing. A good breeze was blowing and the women's hair and clothing blew about in the wind, making them look even more ghostly. The fire reflected on their faces and dresses turning them red, as if they'd returned from some otherworldly place, hell perhaps. Certainly real women would not act in such a way, they must be ghosts; they must not be real.

The men became quiet and looked at each other and then at the two ghosts. None of them knew what to make of them. They didn't notice the shotguns in the women's hands. Finally, as the younger one began firing into them close up, so close that there was not even enough distance for the buckshot to open up, they comprehended.

The first bandit took the fist-sized wad of pellets to the head. Most of his brain blew into the fire causing it to hiss and smoke. The fire let off a puff of steam and the acrid odor of burning meat or flesh or grease.

The next one's breastbone was destroyed, driven to the back of his spine. This went on and on until the sixth shot had been fired. The old woman did nothing. She did not fire at them and she did not run or help or hurt the bandits. She just stood there, watching the carnage, expressionless, until the young one dropped the shotgun she'd been firing. The old one then handed her shotgun over, in a casual, matter-of-fact way, like she'd hand over a bauble or a bouquet of flowers. The young one took it and fired another six shots, just as quickly, into the backs of the now fleeing survivors of the first barrage. She dropped the second shotgun when it was empty, pulled the six shooter from her belt and emptied it. When she stopped firing, they were all either dead or dying, with one exception. Chica had carefully avoided a lethal shot at this one so that he could be interrogated.

Chica approached this man directly, moving through the air thick with gun smoke and the stench of death; the stink of gut and offal, torn flesh and flowing blood. He was wheezing and blowing bloody bubbles out his nose.

Chica shot him low; aimed at his gut and then went a little higher, destroying most of his left lung. He wasn't more than seventeen and was as pale as Abuelita.

Chica did not have to threaten him, instead giving him some water to drink. She brushed the hair from his eyes and propped him up to ease the last of his breathing. She held him gently, like a mother with a suckling babe. "Tell me, muchacho. Where are the rest and where are the hostages?"

"With the gold hat, señora, they are all with the gold hat." His eyes were wild with fear and he looked into Chica's beautiful brown eyes. He wanted her to hold him and make his pain go away. He didn't yet realize he was dying. He gagged and spoke with difficulty. "He told us to stay behind and stop any posses." He breathed hard again. Chica looked up at Abuelita.

"This is what Sombrero del Oro do all the time, Abuelita. This is what he did to Arvel the day I met him. He keeps part of his gang back and he always get away."

She turned back to the boy. "How many are in the gang, muchacho?"

"Many, many, Señora. At leas' fifty." He gagged and choked up a rope of clotted blood.

"How many hostages?"

"Que?"

"How many captives from the train?"

"Cincuenta, Señora."

"Did you see a girl with a blue dress?"

"Sí, she was one."

"Is she unharmed, muchacho?"

"Sí, she is. Sombrero del Oro said she was a special prize. She was okay, Señora."

She looked back at Abuelita and nodded. There was hope.

"You are going to die now, muchacho. Do you wanta pray or say something?"

"Sí, Señora, lo siento mucho, lo siento mucho."

Chica shot him through the head.

Alice Walsh jumped at the shot. She looked at Chica, shocked. "Why'd you have to shoot him, child?"

Chica turned and looked her in the eye then pushed past her. "Shush, Abuelita! No questions, you promised."

They rested by the fire, upwind of the corpses until morning. Chica did not sleep and watched the old woman as she rested. Arvel was his mother's son, there was no mistaking. They were good, kind people.

She found some cigars amongst the bodies and picked the ones not wet with blood for smoking now, the rest she saved for later. She smoked one after another through the night.

It would be difficult to kill fifty men. She thought and thought. She considered everything she'd ever been told about Sombrero del Oro. She considered his strengths and limitations, his proclivities and weaknesses, what motivated and what made him fearful.

It was perfect timing for the new millennium, the year of nineteen hundred, and all the talk about the things that the new century would bring, the various theories that the world would come to an end and, perhaps, the second coming of Christ.

These things would help to prey on Sombrero del Oro's diseased mind. This would be her advantage. This would be her ace in the hole. Every man had an Achilles' heel, and Chica was certain of Sombrero del Oro's, certain he could be defeated if she played off this weakness. She knew she could beat him and ultimately get her little girl back.

Finally, after three cigars, she came up with a plan. She'd let the old woman sleep until sunrise and would then get her to Bisbee. Bisbee held the key to Chica's plan.

She picked through the corpses for better guns and more ammunition and rode out after eating the bandits' breakfast. Abuelita looked spent, utterly played out. She was much older than she appeared and Chica realized this as they rode.

She finally spoke. "Abuelita, I killed that boy back there because he was gonna die in a few minute anyway. I decided to end his suffering. I am sorry, Abuelita, I do not like to make you sad."

"No, I'm the one who should be sorry, child. I promised no questions and I failed you. I am not used to these things. I have never killed a human being and even shooting birds or hunting foxes has always upset me. The suffering of any creature is appalling to me."

"Understood, Abuelita."

She looked back at the trail. The old woman could see they were no longer traveling south and asked why.

"We are going to Bisbee, Abuelita. You must go get Arvel and get help and I will go on after the bandits and get Rebecca."

"But I want to go with you, child. You promised!"

The old woman suddenly sounded childlike herself and this amused Chica.

"Ay, no questions! We are all of the same purpose, Abuelita, and you must do what I say. Arvel will know what to do, we need many good men to get these bandits. I am counting on you, Abuelita, to do this thing.

Arvel will know what to do when you tell him."

The old woman became quiet.

As they entered Bisbee, Alice Walsh dozed in the saddle until the crack of a shot and the whir of a bullet past her ear brought her out of her trance. She looked over at Chica who sat her horse, unfazed. She looked down the street at the two lawmen pointing their rifles menacingly at the women.

"Go on out of here, you Mexican scum."

Alice was incensed and galloped her horse up to the men, nearly running them over.

"Stop that this instant, you fools! We are not bandits!" She pulled the big sombrero off her head and placed it over the horn of her saddle. "I am Mrs. Walsh and this is Señora Arvel Walsh, wife of the Captain of Arizona Rangers."

"Beg your pardon, Ma'am." The older one tipped his hat and the other followed. "From a distance you didn't appear as yourselves."

"Well, we've been after the ruffians, doing your jobs."

Chica lit one of the blood-tinged cigars she'd taken from the bandit gang. She looked at the two lawmen, amused at the lambasting her mother-in-law was giving them.

"We were sure you all were dead, ladies. Captain Walsh, poor fellow, will be relieved. He's had quite a bad turn of health."

"Que?" Chica looked down at the man, the first time Abuelita had seen any real emotion in the young woman's eyes. "What is wrong with my husband?"

"Well, ma'am, not sure I'm the right person to tell you all this, but it seems he had a sort of fit . . ."

"A stroke."

"Yes, an apoplectic fit is what they called it; at the train station when he learned about the attack and the report that you all were not found in the wreckage."

"Where is he? Where is my boy?"

"He's home, ma'am. His Uncle Bob got him home. Last we heard he's better, resting comfortable."

Chica looked at Abuelita. "I must go now." She looked at the youngest deputy. "You take Abuelita to a hotel and get her cleaned up and get a telegraph to my Arvel and tell him that we are okay."

"Yes Ma'am."

"Abuelita. Go an' tell Arvel to get as many men as he can and go to San Sebastian. Tell him that I am going to get Rebecca and I will meet him in Mexico. Go on, Abuelita."

She rode quickly into town and the old woman watched her, tried to understand what just happened, tried to make sense of Chica's cryptic instructions. She looked down at the two deputies who seemed just as confused.

Chica knocked on the door of the Convent of the Sisters of the Poor Clares. A diminutive nun let her in and led her to the mother superior. They offered her food and Chica ate ravenously. She did not speak.

Chica knew the place, but none of the nuns recognized her. Dressed as she was, her beautiful dress now in rags, wearing the bits and pieces of the garments of the disgusting bandits she had killed, she did not look like the wife of a wealthy rancher and captain of Arizona Rangers.

She felt calmer now, calm in the austere environment of the nunnery with its plain adobe walls and tile floors. Here and there were simple paintings of religious images. The windows were bare. It reminded her of the trip she and Arvel had taken to Italy; the lovely monasteries and the friendly Italian people who understood Chica so well.

"How may we help you, child?"

"I needa become a nun, sister."

She drank so quickly that water poured down her chin and onto her front. She wiped her mouth with the back of her hand. "Not to join your order, Sister. I needa get my little girl, she has been captured by Sombrero del Oro and taken to Mexico.

The diminutive nun gasped and crossed herself at hearing the name of the terrible man. Everyone, especially the nuns, knew of the terrifying bandit boss. They'd spent enough time helping the poor creatures who'd survived and, ultimately, escaped his barbarity.

"I am the wife of Capitan Arvel Walsh of the Arizona Rangers, and have much money. I will give you much money if you will help me."

"What do you have in mind, child?"

"This man, you know, is a man of the devil. He trades in people and he will take my little girl and sell her and I will never see her again. I have been a bad woman, Sister, and I know how to fight and kill many bad men. Sombrero del Oro have over fifty men and I cannot do this thing alone, they are too many to kill. I plan to sneak into their camp and I needa be a nun to do this."

The nun sat and watched Chica as she spoke. She now made the connection. She knew of the young woman, knew of Chica, everyone in the territory had heard of the courageous young Mexican woman. She knew that Chica had killed many men and knew by the stories that she had a good heart, that she was no wanton murderer.

"When will you be embarking on this journey, Señora Walsh?"

"Tomorrow. I ask you to let me clean up and sleep here tonight. Please teach me to dress and be like a nun, to trick the bandits."

They showed her to a cell and gave her hot water and soap and a towel. One of the nuns had gone to the dry goods store to get Chica a riding outfit. After she bathed and was dressed, Chica headed to the gun shop she had visited many times over the past years with her husband. The proprietor welcomed her. The news had already spread.

"Miss Chica, I am so sorry to hear of your troubles." He shook her gently by the hand.

"Gracias, Señor." She placed the shotguns she had used in the earlier slaughter of the rear guard on the counter.

"I need these barrels cut down, Señor Wallace. I want the stock cut like a pistol on this one. An' I need swivels put on and a leather sling. Okay?" He nodded.

"I need a rifle and two six shooters of the same size bullets and I need a powerful rifle to shoot from far away. I need belts for the bullets for all these. I need five hundred bullets for the six shooters and rifle, one hundred bullets for the powerful rifle and one hundred bullets for the shotguns, and I need all of these things sent to the convent. I need them by sunrise tomorrow."

"It shall be done, madam. Think nothing more of it. It shall be done."

Later, the nun escorted her to Mother Superior. They put Chica near the fire and began dressing her. The transformation was quick and Chica soon looked like the others. The nun whispered into Mother Superior's ear and the old woman smiled.

"Sister Margaret says you are too pretty and your feet and hands are too appealing to be those of a nun."

Chica examined her hands and feet. They'd become soft since her long trip through the civilized places of California with her mother-in-law and little girl. The last two days on the trail had not roughened them sufficiently.

She began biting the nails on her fingers and tore them down to the quick. She licked her ring finger and pulled the diamond encrusted wedding ring that Arvel had ordered from Tiffany's in New York for their engagement. She handed it to the young nun. "This is my firs' donation to your order, Sister. You sell this and use the money any way you like. I wan' you to make many prayers for my baby and make sure I get her."

She reached into the hearth and grabbed a handful of ashes and broken mortar. She rubbed them across her nails, dulling their luster.

She looked at the old nun. "What can we do about my face, sister? I will let you make me ugly if you need to. I will let you do anything you need; you may destroy my face if it is required." She caught herself and looked at both women. "I am sorry, sin ofender."

Mother Superior smiled. "I have an idea, Señora."

She called the young one over to her and whispered in her ear. The nun smiled and left the room.

Mother Superior looked at Chica. "I have an idea that will help you move about amongst the bandits and assure that they will not detect or molest you. Sombrero del Oro has no respect for any women, even ones who have taken vows."

That night, the young nun held the diamond

ring up to the light as she reclined on her cot in the cell next to the one housing their special guest. It was the most beautiful object she had ever seen in her life and as she moved it one way and then the other the candlelight's reflection became all the colors of the rainbow. Mother Superior had charged her with the safekeeping of the ring and she was pleased. Though she had no desire to own such a worldly object, it was lovely to behold. She put it on the finger that fit best and held it up to the light, then across her knee, across the covers of her bed, everywhere she placed it, it seemed to change. She moved the ring in one direction and it made a little rainbow across the bed sheet. It reminded her of the sacristy of the lovely big church up in Tucson where she worked for a little while, when she first arrived in Arizona. The two objects were equally beautiful.

She began to think about all the pretty lights on her first Christmas in the order, how happy she was to be warm and safe among good people who regarded her well, how the church and the convent kept out the New Hampshire cold and how happy she was to be a nun.

She was brought back from her musing by the sound of crying in the cell next door.

She couldn't believe it was the Mexican lady, but it was. She wanted to comfort her but was too afraid and she listened intently to the crying. It was the sorrowful expression of a mother with a broken heart. It was sadder, more desperate than any other crying because it came from a woman who, at least from what she had in a short time learned about her, never cried and she prayed to God that this woman's suffering would soon end.

She knew that the woman would likely kill many men and she regretted this. She was a nun, a woman of God who did not condone violence or killing. But she also knew how terrible Sombrero del Oro was and that perhaps, like the Archangels and the soldiers who fought in righteous wars, the Mexican lady was sent by God to smite this foe and bring some calm and peace and justice to the land.

She'd once helped care for a child who'd escaped Del Oro's clutches and the scars, both physical and emotional, were nearly too much for the nun to bear. The poor child was so badly abused that, despite their best efforts at nursing, she soon died, a pathetic broken shell of a human being. The young nun could only imagine what lay in store for this poor woman's daughter.

She felt like she too would cry, but instead said a rosary and prayed harder than she usually prayed. She heard the woman move in the bed, heard the old ropes creak. Apparently Chica turned on her side, away from their common wall. The nun heard Chica talking to someone. It didn't sound like a prayer, more a conversation.

The Mexican woman sounded like she was talking to a child. She guessed Chica was having an imaginary conversation with her little girl. She was going through what sounded like a nightly ritual, probably what they had done since the child could speak and walk.

Chica was repeating a childlike prayer and then said her father would be in shortly to kiss her goodnight. She spoke lovingly to her little girl and kissed her goodnight. The young nun started to cry because her heart was breaking at the muffled sound of a heartbroken woman talking to her child who was likely in the most hellish place on earth. She finally put her veil tightly over her ears and tried her best to stop listening. Eventually, she fell asleep.

Ben Wallace worked through the night in the back room of his shop. He tore the shotguns down and stoned the working parts until they were glass-smooth. He fixed the barrels and stocks according to the señora's requirements. He next worked on the rifle, stoning its working parts and then made sure the trigger broke crisp and clean, neither too heavy nor too light. He checked the screws on the telescopic sight assuring it would keep its zero, be dead-on.

As he worked, he thought about the first time he'd met the Mexican beauty. Arvel Walsh and his Uncle Bob had been good customers for many years and the day Arvel brought his new wife in he recalled how proud the rancher was to show off his bride. He grinned a little at remembering his own silliness, how he wanted to impress the pretty young woman, showing her in the most rudimentary terms, the mechanics and methods of guns and shooting.

Oh, he felt such the fool when he realized how expert his new patron was in these martial arts. She took the guns from his hands and he knew immediately that she knew what she was doing. She'd ask questions of him about the various guns that soon proved this without question. He remembered that he was smitten. She was beautiful, alluring, smart, worldly, fearless, and a crack shot. He remembered that he was glad his wife was not in the shop helping him that day. She'd surely notice his enchantment and would tease him about it for the next year.

He also remembered the pretty Greener, the day it had finally arrived from England; how pleased he had been to present it to her and so proud when she put it up to her cheek. He recognized how nicely it fit her, as if she'd personally stood for a fitting in Birmingham. He'd done a good job measuring her.

He remembered her broken English, how she looked at him and gave him a little smile, I feel like it is a part of my arm, Señor. He was so pleased to please her.

As he worked, he also thought about the last time he'd seen her, last winter, just before she went on her trip through California with her little girl and mother-in-law. She was looking for a new hideout gun and selected a nice two-barreled Remington that he always kept in good supply. The men who liked to hang out at the shop all stood up from their places around the stove and bowed to Chica. They watched her handle the little silver derringer, feel the weight of it in her hand, try the trigger.

He remembered the collective gasp that went up as, without warning, she put her foot up on one of the powder kegs next to the counter, hiked up the skirt of her long dress exposing her lovely leg and thigh, to check how the gun would ride there, secreted away under her frilly black garter until needed.

He remembered grinning when Arvel blurted out, Je-sus, Chica, you're going to give these boys a heart attack. He was genuinely embarrassed. He remembered Chica's reply, Don' say Dios name in vain, Pendejo. These men are all married; they've seen a lady leg. And then old Mose Harper, a man who was likely the oldest resident of Bisbee, leaning forward and, in his frail, laconic voice commented, Young lady, in all my ninety-three years on this earth, I've never seen such a leg.

He fixed that gun up for her as well, went to the harness maker and had a little holster made for it. He ordered it to be kid-lined, with loops sewn around it to hold extra cartridges. He remembered Chica telling him she did not want the holster to chafe her down there and she gave him that look that excited and melted his heart simultaneously. She was a beauty. It was likely the most provocative thing he'd ever experienced in dealing with any woman, even his wife, and the best part of it was that the lady was neither intending nor expecting to titillate him. That was Chica.

He worked through the night thinking about the guns and how the lady would use them. He looked through the telescopic sight and imagined, wished it could be he who got the bandit in its sights and sent him to the next world. He thought it strange that he wasn't worried in the slightest for her safety. Somehow, he knew in his bones, that she'd be fine. She'd be fine and her little girl would be fine and the son-of-a-bitch Sombrero del Oro would not live another week.

By four, he'd finished up, wiping down the oil he'd put on the wood of the pistol grip he'd carved for the shotgun, as ordered. He built a fresh pot of coffee and twisted a cigarette and sat on the front porch of his shop and waited.

Chapter II:
Getting Ready

Dan George would wake Ging Wa before sunrise. He'd been up all night, thinking, scheming, preparing. He checked on his baby, little Bob, who was sleeping peacefully, looking like an angel. He liked to walk around his house in the middle of the night, watching, listening to his wife and baby sleep. He liked to listen to the house, it would make little insignificant noises as it would either heat up or cool down, depending on the time of year. He liked to hear the metal from the lamps contract and cool off and make little sounds and enjoyed the tic of the stove cooling down.

He liked the soft caress of the wind blowing through the cracks around the windows. It was the feel of the outdoors, of Mother Nature. His substantial house kept them safe, secure, happy. They were all safe. He had provided a good home, a safe haven for them, and it made him feel good and useful and happy when he could know these things. He had spent his entire life, from the time that he was deposited at the Indian School, working toward this goal.

The Indian School was initially a terrifying place for a boy of eight. It was in a foreign land and the people there were so severe. They weren't mean to him. They provided all the things required for a child to live; food, clothing, shelter, but the place was without love, without nurture.

Dan soon learned that he could read fast and well. He loved reading and quickly realized he could escape his austere life in the world of books. He learned about others in his situation, characters like David Copperfield, Oliver Twist and Pip. He pretended to be Pip and decided when he was nine that he would make something of himself.

He thought about a young teacher named Hobbs who one day, as the children were leaving the classroom, stopped him, looked him in the eye and, in a matter of fact tone, told him that he had it in him to be something great, something special. Dan never forgot that.

He also remembered the warnings from another teacher, an old schoolmarm named Miss Sullivan, who constantly warned the children of the dangers of predators; monsters who would touch them in their private parts. She taught them that most people where wicked and, essentially, that all men were wicked. They should always be on their guard for bad men.

  She told them they should never interfere with themselves and that any intimate relations should only be between married people and that only for procreation. She told Dan that he had a fine fist which had inspired him to become a law clerk at seventeen.

Dan George was patient with Miss Sullivan but he never paid her any mind. He was a big fellow, nearly six feet tall by his twelfth birthday and in possession of a certain innate confidence — a presence — so he never had to worry much about men who might want to do him harm or abuse him in any way.

  His first foray into the carnal world was when he was sixteen. A merchant's wife, who had business with the school, seduced him. She was a tall woman with blonde hair and dark blue eyes and a magnificent bosom. She ground herself against the young man and made animal sounds that he had never heard before. It was very amusing to him at the time and he didn't mind it at all.

He learned that he was especially attractive to the opposite sex and, while brief liaisons never did compare with what he eventually had with Ging Wa, they at least made a less-than-perfect substitution for real love and compassion.

He was known in the region as quite the lady's man and many were shocked at his choice of the little plain-looking Chinese woman with bad skin. She was not beautiful to anyone but Dan George. The first time he met her at Arvel Walsh's ranch he could think of no one else. He was smitten.

Dan fiddled with the stove and washed a cup. He thought about little Rebecca Walsh and suddenly felt a despondency that he had not known in many years. He pushed back the urge to cry and considered what his friend, Arvel Walsh, might be going through at the moment. He hoped that poor Arvel was sleeping now, dreaming good dreams of his little girl.

He suddenly felt energized and looked at the clock in the hall. He was anxious to do something for the Walsh family.

Arvel had assured Dan's place at the bar and that was just one of many kindnesses he bestowed on the Indian. He could still remember Arvel coming to see him at the Ranger's office where he worked as Dick

Welles' secretary. Dan was the glue that held the Rangers together and kept the enterprise humming.

Arvel had suddenly had a wonderful scheme and could not wait to tell him. It was illegal as all hell, and unethical from a lawyerly point of view; completely outside the realm of what Dan would ever imagine doing. But Arvel just went ahead and pulled it off.

Arvel Walsh never minded skirting around or outright breaking the law when he thought the law was stupid, or if his motivations were pure. He called in some favors from some lawyer friends back in Baltimore and created a bogus pedigree for Dan. The result was to declare Dan, a Sioux Indian, as white as Arvel Walsh.

When Dan balked, Arvel put up a hand. "Now, Dan, just let it go. Let it go. Stupid laws need to be skirted around and we are just righting a wrong, so there's an end to it."

So Dan George became a white man and a lawyer, and everyone pretty much knew it was all bogus but at the same time, no one ever questioned it or cared. Dan was one of the most competent lawyers in the territory and it was ridiculous to not allow him to practice law. Besides, there now would be a place for all the Indians and Chinese and Mexicans and all the other undesirables to go for legal help. It would keep them out of the hair of the sophisticated white attorneys in the region. There was no money in helping them anyway, and that was the thing that motivated the majority of them. Everyone benefited when Dan was admitted to the bar.

That was the way with Arvel Walsh. No one ever questioned his integrity. When it came to significant things, he was always given whatever he wanted. He had the reputation of taking the law into his own hands, and no one ever questioned it. He was a man with a conscience and never took his actions lightly as it was always for the greater good.

Dan crawled into bed and gently pressed himself against his wife. He held her tightly in his arms and watched her wake up. She turned onto her back and pulled him over so that he was facing her. She smiled at him and rubbed his back, pushing his head against her breast. She wondered how long he'd be gone.

"All ready?"

"Yes, just leaving."

"Take care of her, Dan. Take care of her, and get everyone back safe."

"I'll do my best, but we are talking about Chica. I don't know that anyone takes care of Chica."

"You do. She's a sweet soul, and she's vulnerable now. Watch her, Dan, watch over her and don't let any harm come to her."

"I will, darling." He pulled himself reluctantly out of bed and headed for the gun shop.

It was a pleasant morning and Bisbee was not yet awake in his part of town. He and Ging Wa lived and worked out of a fine brick home down the street from the Opera House on a steep hill overlooking the town. They had become a fixture in the community. Ging Wa, the only female Chinese physician in the territory, and Dan George the only Indian attorney.

They had done well despite spending half their time providing service to people who could not pay them. They were always well stocked with fresh meat, chickens, cheese, bacon and homemade wine and Ging Wa used to laugh about being paid in livestock for every baby she'd brought into the world. She'd never anticipated that she would need a slaughterhouse next to her examination room.

Uncle Bob had put them together, and Dan was immediately in love with the kind little Chinese girl saved from the clutches of Madam Lee by the Walsh family and the Arizona Rangers.

It was Uncle Bob who took her in and treated her like a daughter, who immediately appreciated and helped to cultivate her sharp mind, assuring that she was received into The St. Louis Women's Medical College where she became a physician. So competent was the couple that no one ever kept them from commerce. Often, people would seek them out over the older more settled white practices. They worked hard and were both proud of their success.

When Ging Wa and Dan heard the news about what had happened to Rebecca, and that Chica was going after her, they knew they had to help. They knew Chica well enough to know that she would not allow anyone other than Dan to accompany her and, at that, it would take some convincing to get her to accept even his help. Dan was a good negotiator, and they thought that somehow, if he accompanied Chica, perhaps he could negotiate Rebecca's freedom. They simply had to try something to help the Walsh family.

Dan collected the guns and supplies, showing up at the convent just after sunrise. He had hired three horses for the journey in addition to his own favorite mount. He waited in the courtyard while a young nun fetched Chica and the Mother Superior.

He'd never visited this place before, though he'd passed it hundreds of times over the years. Dan had little use for organized religion. Now that he was inside the place, it — as it had Chica — reminded him of the convents and monasteries he'd visited on his grand tour through Europe many years ago. For a moment, he didn't feel like he was in Arizona, preparing to go after slave traders.

He was brought out of his reverie by a diminutive nun who shuffled past him peering out through a habit that was much larger and more confining than what was worn by the others.

Her face was covered except for her eyes which revealed the horrible disfigurement of a person who'd once been afflicted with leprosy. The veil hid most of the evidence of her affliction and he pitied the wretched creature standing before him.

He'd heard stories and seen photos of the poor unfortunate victims in places like Calcutta and various parts of Africa and China. They were appalling and showed poor creatures who had literally lost a nose or ears, developed huge growths, had terrible scarring with monstrous disfigurement and were left to live out their lives alone or among others similarly afflicted.

The little nun held out a basket, offering him bread. He wanted to recoil, put distance between himself and the poor woman. He checked himself and nodded, bowing to her he took a piece of bread. It was his attempt to hide his initial shock and revulsion.

"Buenos días, Señor George." He was startled that she knew his name and immediately recognized her voice.

"Chica?"

"Sí." She laughed for the first time since the attack, pulling the veil down to reveal her face. "I tricked you, no?"

"You did, indeed."

"Mother Superior made me look like a leper with some bumpy wax."

She proudly revealed the makeup job to Dan George. "You see, it is stuck on with honey-and-hide glue. She said Sombrero del Oro would probably not molest me."

She looked at the horses and traps. Dan had everything in order. "Why are you delivering these things?"

"Because I'm going with you."

Chica smiled and suddenly Dan didn't need the half dozen arguments he'd been preparing for when Chica would invariably refuse him. "This is good, Dan. This is good and I thank you for your help. I can think of no better man for it."

She looked through the guns and found the shotgun she'd ordered modified. She hiked up her habit and tucked the gun underneath, slipping the sling over her right shoulder. Once everything was back in place it was impossible to detect that she was armed. "Now, Dan, here is what we will do."

Chapter III:
Resolution

Alice Walsh gently woke her son. He was dreaming and roused slowly. Awakening to the reality of his predicament made him dread opening his eyes and when he did, the sight of his mother made him cry.

She was played out: sunburned, thin, exhausted, spent. He reached out with his good arm and tried to pull himself up in bed. She reached over and wiped his face, he could not stop drooling. He did not know why he was so emotional all the time. He seemed to drool and cry constantly.

"My boy." She helped him up in bed, wrung out a washcloth and wiped his face.

He worked hard to speak clearly. "Where are they, Mother? What's going on?"

"Maria has gone after them, Arvel. She told me to come home to get you and tell you to get to San Sebastian."

She watched him take in the news. He looked panicked, desperate, helpless.

"Rebecca is alive, Arvel. We have to remember that at least she's alive."

He cried harder at the thought, the realization of what it was that his little girl must be going through. He looked at his mother and smiled weakly, trying ineffectively to hide his dejection.

"I'm sorry, Mother. I don't know why, but since the train, and the news, and my fit, I can't stop crying."

He reached out and cried into her breast. He emitted a lament, a wail that sounded otherworldly, a cry of terror and hopelessness that she had never known, would have never, in a thousand years, thought her son capable of uttering. The old woman patted him and rocked him and did her best not to fall apart. She shushed him and eventually quieted him down.

"Arvel," she tried to cheer him, "what sort of creature did you marry?" She got him to smile. "She was like a . . . like a wild animal, Arvel. Like a wild, wonderful, unearthly creature. She scared me so."

He stopped smiling and began to think of things to say to defend his wife and his mother cut him off. "I was appalled and awestruck and proud, simultaneously, Arvel. She was ruthless. She killed many . . . men.

It was like being with an unnatural creature, Arvel."

"Where is she now, Mother?"

"I don't know. She left me in Bisbee. Dan George went with her and an old nun. They all went into the desert. She told me to get you and to tell you to get to San Sebastian."

Uncle Bob leaned in the door. He suddenly spoke up. "My God, that's two hundred miles into the Chihuahuan desert."

Arvel looked up at him and then at his mother. He began to move, to try to get out of bed. He fell onto the floor. Pilar and Umberto were there instantly and got him back into bed. Pilar gave him more of the elixir ordered by the doctor and Arvel soon fell back into a deep sleep.

Alice watched Uncle Bob over her cup of coffee. She was always fond of the old fellow and never had any animosity for him, as did her husband, for taking their boy to the Wild West.

He knew what she was thinking and began, "There's no question that he can go." Bob was not an emotional man and held back his tears as he thought of his favorite nephew, his friend and partner, lying in the bed in the next room as helpless as a newborn babe. He looked up at Alice and had to look away.

"No, no doubt, Robert. But what do we do?"

"I got the word out to Dick Welles as soon as the men delivered the news to us that you and Chica were alive. He's working up a plan and he'll be here with a posse tomorrow. We . . . I'll ride with them."

"What will I need for the journey?" Alice stared into the man's eyes.

Bob nearly choked on his coffee and stopped from blurting out an answer. He knew that you did not tell Alice Walsh that she could not do something. "I'd, I would rather you stay here, Alice. Stay with Arvel and help him. It is terrible country down there . . . and, frankly, Alice, I'm too old for it, and . . ."

"So am I." She finished for him.

"Yes, so are you."

He pulled a cigarette from its packet and struck a match, offering her one. They smoked together. She would only smoke with Uncle Bob and thought that her secret was safe, as upper-class ladies from Maryland did not take tobacco.

"Robert, Arvel is in the best hands possible with Pilar and Umberto. He is either going to stay the way he is or he is going to get better, with or without me. But little

Rebecca can benefit from my being there when we find her. I'm going. I will not hold you up and, if it kills me, then I will be out of my misery, Robert."

She stood up, and suddenly did not seem so frail and worn out. She had renewed purpose. "I'd rather be dead than continue on without my little granddaughter. The sooner we are on this expedition, the better."

Alice slept late and was awakened by the sound of a troop of men. She peered through her window at the source of the commotion. They had come from every part of the territory when they found out her boy's family was in danger. Dick Welles was there, speaking with Uncle Bob. An old priggish man stood between them. She dressed quickly.

Uncle Bob looked up from his conversation. "Alice, you remember Dick?"

"Of course." She shook his hand.

"This is Mr. Hennessy." The Irishman bowed and removed his hat. Uncle Bob gestured with a sweep of his hand. "These men have all come to help, Alice. They are here to do whatever needs to be done to get Rebecca back."

This was an overwhelming gesture, as there were more than fifty men: white,

Mexican, Indian, Negro, people from all walks of life, all levels of education and income. It was Alice's turn to fight back her tears. She suddenly felt heartened at the notion that they would soon have her little granddaughter back, safe and on her way to Maryland.

"Mr. Hennessy here is offering a large remuda for us, Alice."

"I am sorry, Mrs. Walsh, but that is the extent of what I will be able to do. Me heart is failin' me," he coughed deep from the base of his chest, the rattle of a man not long for this world. "I am afraid I would be little use to your party."

"Your help is greatly appreciated, sir." She smiled at him and he averted his eyes.

She looked on at the others. They were good men, tough men. They were all well-armed. This was not a well-meaning bunch of amateurs. This was a force that would make Sombrero del Oro pay. He would pay by turning over little Rebecca or pay with his life. She suddenly felt queer. These were not the thoughts of an old-line blueblood abolitionist. These were the thoughts of someone who had everything at stake and who would do whatever she needed to get her little girl back. She suddenly felt invigorated, eager to get on the trail.

"When do we begin, Robert?"

He looked a little nervously at Dick. "Dick's running this show, Alice."

He waited for the inevitable and Dick suddenly looked up from his conversation with one of the men. He smiled broadly at Alice Walsh.

"I've been told that you'll be coming along, Mrs. Walsh." He smiled at Uncle Bob. "We sure aren't the youngest chickens in the pen, but we'll give'm hell, won't we, folks." He touched Uncle Bob's elbow and dusted off his chaps. "I believe we should get this show on the road right off, so as soon as you're ready, ma'am, we'll ride."

Pilar and two hands carried Arvel out into the mid-morning sun. He was dressed and looked pleased at the little army that had come to show their support, to show that they were ready to make the ultimate sacrifice for him and his family. He started crying and Pilar held his hand, stroked his back and held up a handkerchief to wipe his eyes.

He was broken-hearted. He was useless to his family, his wife, his little girl, his mother and his uncle. He was like a weak child and at that moment felt deep in his very being that it would have been better if he died on the train platform that horrible day. He wished he were dead. He wanted to thank the men, thank Hennessy, whom he'd known for many years. He used to make fun of the man and now, Hennessy, king of the skinflints, and himself dying of a bad heart, was there, to render aid. Arvel could not form the words to adequately thank him. He patted Pilar's hand and beckoned her, pleaded with her, to get him back to his bedroom.

Hennessy spoke to him before he could leave. He patted Arvel on the shoulder. "My old friend, don't give it another thought. Your wife and babby will be back in your arms before you know it, I feel it in me bones."

Others approached and repeated Hennessy's prediction. They patted him and squeezed his good hand. He broke down and the tears ran freely down his face. The men had to turn away, get to their horses and get mounted or risk doing the same. They'd rather ride into the hale of Sombrero del Oro's bullets than see Arvel Walsh reduced to such a state.

Dick hung back. He'd catch up to the men quickly enough. When Arvel was finally alone in his room, Dick sauntered in. He sat down next to his partner and waited for him to calm down. Arvel had worked himself into quite a state and Dick poured him some bourbon and lit a cigarette for him. Arvel drank it down and breathed deeply. Dick looked at him, seriously.

"You all right?"

"No, I'm not goddamned all right, Dick!"

"No, I mean, you're not going to go do anything stupid, are you?"

"What, like drool all over my pillow or shit myself?" He was actually amused at himself for saying that.

"No, I mean eat a bullet or hang yourself, jump out a window."

Arvel looked out his first floor window several feet away. "Dick, you're a real dope. How the hell am I going to do that? Unless you can figure out a way to commit suicide by defecation, I think I'll be pretty safe."

Dick smiled at him. He felt uncomfortable asking, but he had to.

Arvel saw what he was thinking and spoke up. "Don't worry about me, Dick. I'm not that far gone. I'll be all right. I'm miserable and, frankly, I wish I'd a outright died on that train platform, but I didn't die and I still want to play the game a bit longer."

Dick brightened. "I'm glad to hear that, Arvel. I think we both gotta lot to do yet."

"Right and you remember that, Dick."

He worked hard to get the words out and Dick could see him struggling. "You are an old fart, you remember that. Let the men do the work, you be the brains of this operation, okay?"

"Understood." He leaned over and wiped Arvel's chin, then his forehead. He looked funny, out of place being the nursemaid.

"What's going on with Michael? How is he?"

Dick became guarded. "Oh, okay." He abruptly looked away, out the window.

"You've seen him?"

"No. No, I haven't. But I heard he's okay."

Arvel fell back into his pillow. He wanted to fight Dick a little about Michael, then thought better of it. He watched Dick smoke. He was glad his partner'd hung back. Nothing more needed to be said and Dick sat back and smoked some more.

Even though he had nothing more to say the old partner and ranger captain didn't want to leave yet. He squirmed a little in his chair and Arvel reached over, grabbed him by the hand.

"How 'bout one more smoke before you leave."

"Good idea."

CHAPTER IV:
CAPTIVE

She awoke to darkness, all alone in the dirt. No one was around her, none of the other captives or the boy, no one. She slowly sat up, aching all over. She'd never known anything like this, never dreamed anything, anyone, any man could engage in such brutality. She'd been bleeding in many places and the blood had dried, sticking her petticoat and hair to her skin.

She thought about what had happened to her. At one point during the worst of it, when many men and many hands were upon her, she'd drifted off into a dreamlike state. She dreamed that she was floating above them all. She looked down and saw a form, like a poor animal that many other animals were savaging, and she wondered what the poor creature had ever done to deserve such cruel treatment.

She saw her boy sitting on a rock, holding the red ball. He was watching the attack.

He was much younger, a toddler. He sat and watched while the animals savaged the poor helpless animal. The whole time he was sucking his thumb and pressing the rubber ball to his ear. She thought back to the day when she rubbed a habanero on his thumb and let the child stick it in his mouth and it made him cry. She laughed at him, telling him that it would cure him from sucking his thumb.

She gagged as she remembered the attack. She could smell the stench of the animals who'd attacked her: rotten breath, horrible body odor, greasy hair, filthy fingers with even filthier nails, digging and probing every part, every opening of her body. Now she had the odor up her nose, like the time her husband had them living next to the tannery in one of the hell-holes — one of many. The stench of tanning got up her nose and everything smelled of it: the bed linens, the boy's hair, her own clothes.

Now she smelled of the stench of her attackers, it oozed from her pores, oozed from her very being. She could taste the remnants of her attackers, like a thick coating on her tongue and teeth and she wretched and vomited until she had nothing more to give up.

She drifted off to sleep for a while. She

awoke, aware there was someone nearby and was able to roll her eyes far enough to see her new tormentor without moving her head.

This one was diminutive. She tensed her body, waiting for another attack, but none came. The small figure reacted when she moved. She was still alive, but just barely. The little figure leaned down and pulled her up to a sitting position. She poured water from a canteen into a cup and gave it to her to drink. She poured the remainder of the canteen all over the woman and it felt better than anything she'd ever felt in her life. She finished drinking and no longer needed to wretch. She looked up at her savior and comprehended that it was a child.

The small figure looked down at her and breathed smoke through her teeth. Why was a little child smoking?

The child bandit reached out and touched the woman's once pretty red hair. "I knew you were in for it."

She looked around and found the woman's dress, picked it up and beat the dust off it with her tiny fist. She handed it to the woman who put it on. The woman looked at the girl and wanted to ask her what she meant, but could not speak. She tried to speak and her throat burned and no words would come. The girl sensed what the woman was wondering and went on.

"Anything different makes them more animal-like. You are different. You're so big and pale and have spots all over your skin and your hair is all red. That is very big to them . . . and you are well made up there."

She pointed at the woman's big breasts, casually, clinically, as if they were not private, not personal parts of her body; no more personal or private than a milk cow's udders.

She thought about that, too. She was proud of her lovely, big breasts. She didn't have to do a thing to make them happen, just God's gift. Men were always looking at them. They were magnificent and now she understood that they were part of the reason for her being savaged the way she was. They were objects of deranged desire.

The child gave her another drink. "You are very strong to go through all that and not be dead."

The thought of the girl witnessing the attack made her feel ill again. Another person had watched her in the most vulnerable state of her life, saw every part of her body, saw her placed in horrific and mortifying and humiliating postures, and she'd done nothing to stop it.

She looked at the child smoking her cigarette, casually, as if nothing was out of place. She didn't seem bothered by bearing witness to the attack at all. She thought again. What could a little child do to stop a dozen big men, even if she were part of their band?

She couldn't help feeling some animosity toward her, even if the child was helping her now. She was so confused. Another Mexican, but this one showed some kindness. She was so queer, dressed like a cowboy; a girl, a child, dressed like a man, smoking cigarettes, wearing a gun. It made no sense.

And she was part of them. She was part of the bandit gang. Even though she was a child, the woman couldn't help thinking that she was one of them, part of the gang who'd done this to her. Now one of the gang was helping her, giving her some water, ensuring that she would not die.

Fully dressed now except for her shoes, which she couldn't find, she motioned to the girl. The child looked at her and shrugged. She walked away from the woman and came back with some men's boots, at least a third larger in size than what she needed.

"Come on, we'll be moving out soon. You

can't be left here, you'll surely die."

Rebecca rode behind an ugly fat bandit on a horse that was not gaited. It walked as if its feet hurt and jostled her constantly. She had to press up against the cantle, her bony behind riding directly on the skirt's edge. The animal's rump was so wide that the tendons of her legs pained her terribly. Her feet dangled, unsupported, and they soon fell asleep, tingling and aching.

She did her best to not touch the bandit. He smelled awful and when they took breaks and she was allowed to stand on her own, the stench permeated her nose. She was convinced that the stench had gotten into her dress. She did not want to smell like the bandit. But despite her best efforts, she would doze and find herself resting against his back. When she awoke, she'd pull back hard, straighten her spine and put as much distance as possible between herself and her captive.

She drank from a gourd canteen often. Her father had taught her to eat and drink as much as possible when on the trail and despite not being hungry or thirsty, she complied. She shook constantly.

She felt like she did when she'd seen one of the hands on the ranch get killed. He was a good man, a good friend and when he died it made her so sad and she shook and shook inside. She told her mother about the shaking and her mother held her tightly and told her that it was natural and it meant that she was a good girl with a good heart. It meant that she loved the poor dead man and it was normal to feel this way. Her mother kissed her all over her forehead and told her that she was kind, just like her father. She thought about this now, and wished her mother was there to hold her and make the shaking stop.

She rode on and thought of her mother and father. She occupied her mind with what her father had taught her when they went on their adventures in the desert. He told her to always think about where she was in the world. Always look at the terrain, look at the sun, look at the moon and the stars, to remember the way any water flowed. Always know where you were.

He taught her to think about the gait of the horse, consider how far a horse would take you every hour. So she counted the gait of the horse and it helped to take her mind off the terrible situation she was in and the stench coming from the fat bandit's backside. She knew she was heading south and decided that she was probably in Mexico by now.

At one point, she saw a mountaintop and thought it looked familiar. She remembered seeing it when she had visited her Uncle Alejandro's ranch. It was in the east, so it was to her left. She reckoned she was somewhere between her uncle's ranch and the sea. They were going deep into Mexico.

In the evenings she was allowed to bed down on her own. She was isolated from the other captives. She was lucky in this, as they were treated horribly and given little food and water.

She watched throughout the day as one woman in particular, a big red-haired lady, was especially ill-treated by the bad men. She thought about the hands at the ranch who had female dogs. Every time they went into heat, the male dogs would constantly follow them, bother and pick at them; constantly pestering them.

The bandits were the same way; they would not leave the big woman alone and as she walked along, limping considerably from poorly fitting boots, they'd come upon her, throw a riata around her and drag her off. A little later she'd show up again, filthier than she had been before, as if she'd been rolled thoroughly about the desert floor.

Rebecca realized she was special for some

reason and took advantage of this as much as she could. She was sorry for the others, but depriving herself of things that would help her survive would not help them in any way. She found a sombrero and gourd canteen which she filled every time they stopped. She found a rebozo and put it around her shoulders, despite the heat. Her father taught her to do that. She was half Mexican and had her mother's features and raven hair, but she had her father's skin color and bright blue eyes. She had to be careful in the sun.

In the evenings she sat near the fire and stole glances at her captives. They were a festive bunch, always laughing and usually drunk. They were crude and dirty and vulgar. They spoke ugly swear words, even in front of the women and children. Rebecca knew all the swear words the men said, both in English and Spanish, and didn't mind hearing them. Living on the ranch it wasn't possible to avoid hearing cursing, but the men on the ranch only spoke the bad words when they didn't think women and children could hear.

These bandits didn't act like the men on her or Uncle Alejandro's ranch. They didn't care how they looked and didn't shave or comb their hair or clean their teeth or wash their clothes. She didn't like any of them and they left her alone only because their boss had told them to and not because they were gentlemen or nice or kind. They were not vaqueros; they were ugly bully bad men.

After two days she met the boss. He was called Sombrero del Oro and he looked very old to Rebecca. He was also fat and wore his hair long. He had long mustaches that made his face look as if it could only frown. Despite his age, his hair was raven black, like her mother's, yet it did not look right. It was the color of the hair of a man they once saw in California. Her mother chuckled at the man and when Rebecca asked why, her mother told her that the man dyed his hair because he was afraid of looking old. This is how the old bandit looked and it made Rebecca feel better. Sombrero del Oro could not be so strong and ruthless and unbeatable because he worried about looking old and his hair looked like someone dumped black ink on it. When he was very hot he would sweat and black streaks would run down his face and his gold sombrero bore black stains from the silly hair dye.

He walked up to Rebecca and stroked her hair gently, lovingly. Rebecca knew there was no love in his actions. Another man was with him all the time. This one was fatter still and had bushy eyebrows, like two fat caterpillars had been pasted to his forehead. The hair on his eyebrows was so long and wild that he looked like an evil genie. Just like the genie on the cover of the book about Arabia that her father used to read to her at bedtime.

Rebecca could not be certain, but the second man seemed to wear ladies makeup. He looked like the ladies she'd glimpsed at the bad saloons in Tombstone when she went with her father to get supplies.

Rebecca looked at him a little too long. He was fascinating in his ugliness. She'd never seen a man wear makeup. He had two red splotches on his cheeks and dark paint or something around his eyes. His eyelashes were black with some sort of coating, charcoal mixed with beeswax maybe. He looked like a clown she'd seen at one of the traveling shows up in Tucson. He looked at her and leered.

Almost automatically he approached her and began running his hands all over her body and she stood, frozen, not knowing what to do. His great fat fingers rubbed her neck and hair and across her chest and down into her private parts and just as quickly as he started, the boss looked at him and made a quick hissing noise and the man stopped. He grinned at her and his eyes were wild, like an animal sick with hydrophobia or a creature who'd been mesmerized like what her father said about the cobras in India, that they would put their prey under a spell and that's how they would capture them.

She looked at the clown man and the boss and became angry. She decided that she would be ready for them next time and they'd not touch her like that again. She began shaking again, this time so hard that her knees knocked and she thought she might fall over. She wanted to stop shaking but could not and it made her angrier and she hoped that the two would not see her shake. She didn't want to give them the satisfaction of making her upset and scared.

Later that night she was summoned to the bandit boss's tent. He was a vain man, and every time he camped, for no matter what duration, he made his men erect a giant marquee tent that he'd stolen from some Mexican soldiers. It was well furnished with cots, a writing desk, although Sombrero del Oro was illiterate and had no use for such a piece of furniture, a dinner table, chairs, and canvas partitions, so that the tent could be divided into several little rooms. Each little room had its own coal oil lantern to light it.

She walked in, head high. She decided that cowering would not help, and it was not in her nature. She was too much like her mother. She'd be polite and to the point, but she would not cower. This made the shaking stop, and she decided to pretend to be her mother, to act like a little version of her mother, and in this way, she made herself kind of go to sleep or disappear from the madness. She was now little Maria, not Rebecca any more.

The boss looked at her and grinned. The clown man sat next to the boss, on a low chair, like a court jester or trained monkey, waiting for his master's commands. She did not like them looking at her, but would not look down. She decided to focus on an object, a little hole in the tent wall, just above the boss's head. She stared at it and waited.

"So, you are the daughter of the famous Capitan Welles?"

"Walsh," she found it comforting that he did not know her father's name. His English was bad, too, not like Uncle Alejandro's. This made her feel better. "My father is Arvel Walsh. You are confused, or ignorant. Welles is my daddy's partner. He is a

Captain of Rangers as well." The clown man spoke in a hushed tone into the boss's ear. The boss nodded.

"Sí, sí. Yes, that is what I meant. Walsh."

"It would be a good idea if you would let me go. My daddy and mother will be very cross with you if you don't. I think it would be better if you gave me a horse and some provisions and let me go on my way. I can find my uncle's ranch from here well enough."

"Ah, yes, I know your mother. She is the whore who married Walsh."

"My mother is not that. You are a very bad man, Señor. You should not speak of her that way. She is a good lady and she will come to get me and you will be sorry if you don't let me go."

"So, you don't know that your mother es muerto?" He looked at the clown and laughed. "I blew her up, on the train."

Rebecca took a deep breath. The news was a hammer blow and she suddenly felt weak, like she might fall over. She breathed deeply again. The man was a liar. He was a bad man and he should not be trusted. Her mother was not dead. She knew it. Nor was Abuelita. She decided to not tell him he was a liar.

"Well, even if she is dead, my father is not,

and he'll be after you."

The boss was impressed with this one. She did not scare easily. He grinned at her and then picked up a little bell on the desk, summoning a servant. He spoke quickly to the man who, in short order, brought a chest full of women's clothing into the tent, depositing it at Rebecca's feet. The clown man jumped up from his little perch next to the boss and looked into the opened container, perhaps for something in his size. He found something, balled it up and put it next to his chair. He was pleased with his prize and once it was securely in his possession went back to leering at the little captive. He was a disgusting man who constantly handled himself as he watched her. She was becoming angry again and remembered his insult, his groping her earlier in the day. She spoke automatically.

"That will make you blind." She nodded and looked down at his hand, manipulating and pulling at his crotch. She remembered hearing the hands at the ranch say that one day, when one of the men was caught absent-mindedly scratching his privates. She did not know what it meant, but it seemed funny and teasing at the same time when the hand had said it, and she hoped it would offend the clown man.

The boss laughed out loud. "Hah, you are a funny little girl." He slapped the clown man on the back and looked over at Rebecca. "I make him wash his hands all the time, little girl, before he can touch any of my food." He looked back at her as if he suddenly remembered the task at hand. "You find some nice clothes in there, little girl, and you go get cleaned. You will stay in here with me from now on." He motioned for her to go into the little room next to his quarters.

She peered around the canvas wall. There was a comfortable cot, washbasin and clean water. There was a fine linen towel and washcloth and a new bar of soap. She quickly grabbed a dress from the chest and left the room.

She was alone at last and began searching the tent walls for an opening, some way out. The boss seemed to read her mind and called out. "If you try to run away, little girl, I will cut your legs off with a dull knife." She swallowed hard and took off her old dress.

She looked at the dress from the chest. It was way too big. It stunk, too. Musty and the armpits smelled like sweat. It was once the dress of a prostitute and now she had to wear it. She made lather with the bar of soap and scrubbed it carefully, periodically smelling it to measure her progress. In short order, the stains were gone and it no longer stunk so badly. She began to bathe and listened to what the two were saying.

The clown man was hissing something into his boss's ear. She could just make out that he was bargaining. For what, she did not know, but it scared her and she felt that she wanted to cry. She knew that the boss was the only thing between her and the clown man and that the clown man wanted her for something. Her prepubescent brain could not fathom what horrors he could have in mind, but she knew it was not good and she became terrified. She suddenly regretted making the remark about the man going blind. She was afraid that she'd gone too far and that it would not bode well for her.

Rebecca was suddenly exhausted. She lay back on the cot in her petticoat. It was the closest she had experienced to a real bed in many days and she fell into a deep sleep. She dreamed of her mamma and daddy and the ranch. She dreamed that Pilar had made her some pan de muertos, her and her daddy's favorite and she was permitted to eat as many as she wanted. She ate the little sugar covered bones until she was full and they made her thirsty.

She suddenly awakened and sat up on the cot. She thought she'd get a drink of water when she heard a curious sound on the other side of the canvas wall. It was the muffled sound of a child crying and the hissing clown man and the rhythmic slapping sound that she'd never heard before and suddenly she was terrified again. She grabbed up the pillow on her bed and placed it over her head. She blocked out the sounds and the world of the clown man and fell back to sleep.

Chapter V: Hunting

Mother Superior was second in the line of unlikely avengers on the road to Uncle Alejandro's ranch. She was followed by Dan George, three horses and a burro. She would be seventy on her next birthday and this was the millennium. There was talk of the return of Jesus Christ or, perhaps, the unleashing of Satan on earth. There was much talk of what would transpire in the year nineteen-hundred and she thought that perhaps Chica's coming to her was a sign or adventure that she should not fail to pursue.

She was a pious but practical nun. She did not really expect that anything would happen in the first year of the new era. She held out little hope for mankind and did not really expect the end of the world or a new era. But something in Chica promised something important in her life. Some destiny lay ahead for her and she was glad when the pretty Mexican woman came to her convent.

They connected immediately and Chica knew that she could trust the old nun. She did not hesitate a moment when the old woman suggested going with her to free Rebecca. The old burro was slowing their travel a little but the old woman was not. She would not impede their progress.

The old nun watched the back of Chica's head as they rode. Chica was a diminutive woman and looked even smaller on the big horse Dan had gotten for her. She'd shed her nun costume for the journey in hopes of perhaps meeting some of the bandit gang sooner, in hopes that she could perhaps kill them in ones and twos.

Right now, she was dressed like a man with crossed bandoliers of cartridges and her big sombrero. She looked like a child dressed in men's clothing. Mother Superior had heard the legend of Chica over the years. She secretly admired the young woman, despite having taken vows that rejected violence. She knew that Chica never killed without cause and she'd heard about her many kindnesses to the poor over the years, especially now that she had become Mrs. Arvel Walsh.

Mother Superior was kind and caring but

world-weary. She'd had her fill of the evils of the world. She was tired and no longer averse to the idea of letting someone like Chica take out a few of the worst examples of the human condition. She was not afraid to be one of the players in Chica's scheme.

She was glad for Dan George as well. He was a kind and intelligent man and was well known in Bisbee for helping the poor of the community. The old nun was completely unafraid and knew in her heart that their task would be completed, the little girl would be rescued, and Sombrero del Oro would be brought to justice. It was just a matter of time and luck and God, she was certain, was with them. She prayed for this as she rode.

They got to Uncle Alejandro's ranch by late afternoon. He was waiting for them. He grabbed Chica as she got down from her horse and squeezed her as he had never done before. His eyes were wet. She'd seen him just six months before, but now he looked as if he'd aged a decade. He loved Rebecca and the strain of her abduction was showing. He helped the nun down and held her hand gently. He welcomed her to his ranch.

He nodded to Dan George, "Consejero, I

am glad you are here." He waited for Dan to dismount and without thinking, grabbed the Indian, hugged him and held onto him for several moments. He patted Dan on the back and held his hand as they walked to the veranda.

"What do you know of Sombrero del Oro, Uncle?"

"My boys have been following him, Maria. As soon as Capitan Welles got word to us we began to track him. He is not far, not more than eighty miles southeast."

"How many men do he have, Uncle?"

"About fifty, Maria."

She nodded as she walked up onto the veranda. "Tomorrow we will go."

Chapter VI: Healer

Arvel had been dreaming of the old days, when he had first met Chica and all the strange things that had happened to him during that time. He dreamed of the strange aborigine man who'd saved his life. Thought about the gold coin the healer had placed in his skull after boring a hole through his head.

Chica often joked that no matter how bad things got, Arvel would never be without money. He had not thought of Billy Livingston in a while and was suddenly roused from his sleep by a presence in his bedroom. He looked over at the figure working at something on the table by his bed and smiled.

"Dr. Livingston, I presume."

Billy looked up from his work. "Mornin', Captain."

"Arvel."

Billy Livingston could not stop calling the

man Captain, despite Arvel's constant admonitions. He started looking Arvel over carefully. He looked into his eyes, opened his mouth and peered about, then grabbed Arvel's clenched right fist and gently pried it open. He placed the palm of his hand into the crippled hand and looked Arvel in the eye. "Give me a squeeze, Captain." Billy grunted and turned away, began looking at the items on the table again.

"I'm glad you're here, Billy."

"Came as soon as I heard, Captain. I'm mighty sorry all this happened, Captain. Mighty sorry."

The tears flowed again and Arvel choked on his words. He cleared his throat hard. "I'm always cryin' Billy. I'm sorry, I'm sorry."

"That's part of your condition." Billy surveyed him, clinically, calculating, he was formulating his treatment plan as his eyes passed over his old friend. "That'll pass with time, Captain."

He managed a weak smile as he brushed his cheeks dry with his good hand. "That's good to know, I thought I was losing my mind."

Arvel was seized with cramps. "Please get Pilar, Billy." He was losing control of his bowels again. Billy grabbed the bedpan and put it under his behind. "Where's your commode chair, captain?"

"Don't have one. Doctor said to keep me in bed." Billy looked on, disgusted by his friend's condition.

"Oh, Jesus, Billy, feels like I'm crappin' out my guts.

He cleaned Arvel up as Pilar came into the room. He smiled at her.

"Billy!" She was happy. She, as everyone else who knew him, loved the aborigine. "I did not know you were here." She took over the task and afterward pulled Arvel up in the bed.

She prepared his next dose of medicine and Billy stopped her. "First thing, Miss Pilar." He took the bottle from her hand. "We throw all this shit in the garbage." Arvel looked over at him, confused. Pilar smiled. "Who prescribed all this anyway?"

"Doc Hanson, from Tombstone."

"Quacksalver!" Billy began tossing the various ointments and pills and elixirs in a nearby trashcan. He read one of the labels. "Croton oil. No wonder your shittin' yourself, Captain." He looked at another, "Black Drawing Salve. Nonsense!" Arvel managed a weak smile. "You leave it to me, Captain. You gotta lotta years left in you. What do you say we start getting you back in shape?"

Pilar was pleased. She did not like the doctor. He treated Arvel as if he were dying and she knew that he wasn't. He wanted Arvel to be treated like an invalid, a baby, and Pilar knew in her bones that that wasn't right. He encouraged her to keep him in his bed and told her not to even bother with the chamber pot, to let Arvel soil himself, that the extra movement would be too much for him.

"Miss Pilar, get one of the lads to make up a nice commode chair for the captain, and we need a good padded chair for him to sit in. Get the lads to bring it in." He pulled a bottle of powder from his bag and a pill mold. "Make up a slurry of this and fill this mold for me. When they dry, pop 'em out and bring me two." He began forming a ball from some window putty he kept in the bag. He dropped this into a leather bag and once again pried Arvel's hand open, placing the bag of putty inside. "That feel better?"

In short order Arvel was in the chair next to the bed. He was already feeling better and he did not feel so much like crying now.

He watched the man work. Billy was constantly working, just like back at his camp, the day they'd met when he was traveling to meet Uncle Alejandro for the first time. It felt good to be sitting and his bowels were already calming down. There were a few hours left until dinner and Billy set up a basin of hot water. He asked for Arvel's left hand. "Steady as a rock, strong as ever. You ever shave left-handed, Captain?"

Arvel nodded no.

"Well, it's time to learn." He put up Arvel's shaving cup and brush on a table before him. He set up a shaving mirror. "Go ahead, Captain. You're a grown man, and we'll start treatin' you as such." He patted Arvel on the shoulder.

Arvel made it through his shave without spilling any blood and lay back, exhausted. Billy Livingston was not finished with him. "No sleepin', Captain, 'til bedtime." He began messaging his weak limbs, starting at the shoulder and working down to his hand. "That's good. You ain't contracted yet." He went to work on his leg.

Arvel winced, then smiled at Billy. "You might not get control back of your limbs, Captain, but, then again, you might." Arvel began to cry. He could not help himself, and he was too grateful for Billy's help.

"Thank you, Billy. Sure am glad you're here, thank you."

■ ■ ■ ■

At supper time, Pilar did not think to check with Billy and brought the dinner prescribed by the doctor. "What the hell is that shit?" Billy picked up some of the gruel on a spoon and let it pour off, back onto the plate. He caught himself as he didn't want to offend Pilar. "Sorry, Miss Pilar, but that will not do. And we'll be dining at the dinner table anyway."

"The doctor says that normal food will kill him, Billy."

"Malarkey! Miss Pilar, you go on and make up your normal supper, what the Captain's been used to all these years. Just cut it up good and small. We'll be fine."

He patted Arvel on the back again. He helped Arvel transfer to the wheelchair and they were soon dining with the hands, outside in the cool breeze of the early spring evening. The men jumped to attention and all smiled when Arvel raised his hand to them. He beckoned them to sit down. Pilar reached over to spoon some food off the plate and into Arvel's mouth. Billy stopped her. "Miss Pilar, Arvel's practicin' usin' his left hand." Arvel nodded and picked up a fork. He began to feed himself.

■ ■ ■ ■

That evening Billy Livingston had a smoke on the porch outside of Arvel's room. Pilar was there. She leaned over and kissed the Aborigine on the forehead. "God bless you, Billy Livingston." Her eyes were wet but she was smiling.

"Aw, think nothin' of it, Miss Pilar. He's my mate, and I'd do anything for 'im." He felt a little embarrassed speaking so freely to the housekeeper. He watched her through the smoke of his cigarette. Pilar was not an attractive woman, but her strength of resolve and character made her beautiful. Everyone knew that it was Pilar who ran this ranch. Billy knew something else about Pilar as well. "Uncle Bob went off after 'em."

Pilar stiffened, caught herself and nodded emotionlessly. "He did."

"Well, you don't give that another thought." He patted her hand. "He'll be back to you sooner than you think."

Pilar looked him in the eye and gave a weak smile. It was the first time anyone had ever let on that she was the old rancher's woman.

"I am glad you have come, Billy Livingston." She headed off to bed.

■ ■ ■ ■

Over the next days, Billy worked Arvel hard. Arvel never complained, refused, or cried out in pain, though he wanted to do so at least a hundred times. He slowly began gaining strength and could squeeze Billy's hand with regularity. Billy had him standing and shuffling across the room. By the end of the second day, Billy came in to find Arvel working on dressing himself. He looked up at Billy and smiled crookedly. "I want to go get Rebecca, Billy."

The aborigine didn't blink. He didn't tell Arvel that it was a ridiculous notion. He sat down, pulled out two smokes and lit one for Arvel. He grunted and stared at the floor. "We'll have to tie you to Tammy."

Arvel looked up at him. "Are you serious?" He was working on the next sentence. He had difficulty at times, with many of his words. His mind knew them, but his tongue didn't want to utter them. He thought hard again. "I didn't think you'd ent..ent..consider it, Billy. Is it a fool errand?"

Billy left the room, came back with one of Chica's pistols. "Here, mate. See what you can do with it."

Arvel turned the gun round in his left

hand. He held it out straight and aimed at a spot on the wall. He cocked the piece and squeezed the trigger. He reached up, pushed the latch, the gun breaking open at the hinge. Billy handed him a box of cartridges. He moved his right hand slowly, but it still would not work. He thought for a moment, placed the gun between his knees and picked the cartridges from the box, placing them one by one in the cylinder. He closed the gun, looked up at Billy Livingston and smiled.

"Good, Captain. Very good. We'll work on a rifle after lunch. When shall we leave?"

Chapter VII: Down Mexico Way

Dick Welles missed Chica at Uncle Alejandro's ranch by six hours. The Jefe was given strict instructions to pass on to Dick Welles. He was not to follow her under any circumstances. Instead, he was to find Colonel Kosterlitzky and join forces with him directly at San Sebastian. The old Jefe smiled and simply shrugged when Dick balked at this plan.

"You know my niece, Capitan. I do not know what she has in mind, but she does not want you going after her or Gold Hat. She was mismo específico."

Dick nodded respectfully. "I understand, Jefe." He knocked the dust from his chaps as he climbed up to the veranda, disappointment in his eyes. Del Toro gave orders, then grabbed Alice Walsh by one arm and Uncle Bob by the other, escorting his American family to the table.

"I am pleased you are here, Alice." She

smiled at him, putting the best face on despite the weight of anxiety hanging over them all. She gave his arm a squeeze.

"And Maria, she is okay?"

"Fine, she has Dan George and the Mother Superior of the convent in Bisbee. What she has planned, I do not know, but you know Chica." He suddenly grinned widely. "You don't really know my niece so well, I think, Alice."

She thought back to the wild creature she witnessed carrying out the carnage only days ago. She smiled back. "I thought I did, but I apparently do not, Alejandro. I apparently do not."

"Well, she will get our Rebecca back." He suddenly welled up and let out a little cry, he bit the back of his hand, stopping the outpour of emotion.

"Now, now, Alejandro." She choked back her own tears. "You are going to get me crying again and I only just stopped." She placed her hand on his cheek, brushing a tear away.

"I know. I am sorry, Alice. I cannot bear to think of our little girl with that demon. He was retired, you know. We did not let him run about like this down here in Mexico, you know that. He stopped all his murdering ways and lived out his time in an old fort in the desert. We forgot about him. Many thought he was dead, and now this." He smiled weakly. "I wanted to send men to help Chica but she wanted nothing." He laughed again, "Except for three old feed bags. That is all she wanted, Alice. Of all my riches, all the things I could give her on this ranch, she wanted three old feed bags."

The table was soon laid and talk turned to Kosterlitzky, the Mexican Cossack. Del Toro loved him. He came from Russia and soon became more Mexican than the Mexicans according to Uncle Alejandro. He was a warrior and a just and decent leader, though often his rurales were used for less than honorable deeds. He wanted to go after Gold Hat years ago but other priorities kept him from it and, as Gold Hat had been behaving, there did not seem much need to follow up.

Kosterlitzky was now organizing a force in San Sebastian between the Del Toro ranch and Gold Hat's stronghold in the Chihuahuan desert outside of the settlement known as San Joachim. Kosterlitzky knew better than to chase after the bandit. It was a waste of resources. He knew that the scoundrel would be heading back to his base soon enough.

Chica knew this too, and she did not want

Dick Welles missing the opportunity by chasing after her. With the combined force of Mexicans and Americans, they would be able to wipe out Gold Hat's operation forever. And besides, Chica did not want an all-out battle with the bandits while they were on the move, as Rebecca and the other captives would be in particular danger. Gold Hat was a wily and calculating slave trader. When his back was against the wall, he never hesitated to kill his hostages so that there would be no witnesses to attest to his barbarity.

Uncle Bob was cheered by the news. He wasn't certain what good he'd be on this expedition other than to try and keep a protective eye on Alice, who now seemed more capable than he of handling the adventure.

He watched Dick take in the information. He was pleased to have the man running the show. But now he began to have second thoughts. What were they doing if they weren't going after Rebecca? Was it really their business to go halfway into Mexico to destroy a Mexican bandit's camp and operations? It suddenly became a bit preposterous to him.

He decided to speak up; after all, this wasn't really their fight. It wasn't even the fight of the Arizona Territory or their Rangers, and what if Alice got hurt in all this?

He leaned forward. "Folks, I don't like to quibble over details, but is it really appropriate for us to be involved in all this?" They all looked at him as if he'd been speaking in tongues.

Dick replied, grinning a little sheepishly. "Uncle Bob, you're right, always the voice of reason." He glanced at Del Toro. "I was getting a bit caught up in the moment. I . . ."

Alice cut him off. "It is what Chica . . . Maria asked you to do." She looked at the men as if they'd suddenly lost their minds. "Of course it's what must be done, and it shall be done."

"But Alice," Del Toro covered her hand with his own, "these men are correct. This is Mexico's battle, and you all are a long way from home. Perhaps it is best to leave it to Kosterlitzky. He has a good force and he is a good man. He will bring them to justice."

"But that's not the point." She sat up a bit straighter in her chair and covered part of Del Toro's great hand with her own. "Until three days ago, I had no idea that people like Gold Hat existed. I didn't know that humans were still traded like livestock. I didn't know the heartache and pain suffered by so many at the hands of this brute and now you tell me he's out of retirement. That he could do more of these things to others. I don't care about him being brought to justice, or punished for what he's done. I want . . . I want . . ." She looked at Uncle Bob and smiled. "Robert, you know how remarkable what I am about to say is, but this man, he needs to be snuffed out. He needs to no longer exist, and all who follow him need to die."

Uncle Bob grinned. "Then there is nothing more to discuss." He looked at Dick Welles. "Are you in?"

Dick Welles smiled broadly and took a sip of his wine. "Uncle Bob, I was never really out."

They stayed with Del Toro until the next day and the Americans enjoyed the hospitality of the old bandit, who'd opened his hacienda to every one of them. The cowboys and vaqueros sized each other up. Most of the Americanos had little knowledge of the considerable skill of the vaquero, did not know that their very craft had originated with the Mexicans. Despite the gravity of the business at hand, Alejandro Del Toro had his men put together a fine Charreria.

The men demonstrated the purpose of the big Mexican saddle horn as they roped running steers, stopping them in their tracks as smoke poured from the reata's friction on the burning wooden horn.

One vaquero showed his prowess at roping from the ground and stopped a running mustang without the aid of a mount. Del Toro proudly told his guests that this came in handy if one ever found himself in the desert without an animal to ride. Then he shrugged, ironically, "I don't know what a man would be doing on foot in the desert with his reata, but . . ." he grinned sheepishly.

They watched the coleadero, an accomplished rider, grab a bull by the tail under his right leg, make a sharp turn and flip the creature onto its back.

Another vaquero performed the paso de la muerte, where he jumped onto the back of a wild horse from his own mount. He rode the animal, without the aid of a saddle or bridle, until it stopped bucking and began to follow the rider's commands.

The women of the ranch gave a display of their riding prowess as well, each lovelier than the next; half wore long white dresses adorned with embroidery, rode sidesaddle, seemingly glued to their mujeriegas as the skirts of their lovely dresses decorated their mounts, while the other half wore tight fitting vaquero pants and jackets and rode like men. They all sported lovely sombreros. Many of the Americanos were smitten. Not only were the ladies beautiful, but they could ride with the best of them.

The men wandered about late into the evening. They'd refrained from imbibing too much as they were preparing for the long journey south and wanted to be sharp for battle. Despite this, they had a fine time touring and experiencing all the wonders of the Del Toro ranch. They were impressed with the old Jefe's harnessing of water power, the big ceiling fans that kept the inside of the home and bedrooms cool, even during the hottest parts of the day.

The next morning Dick Welles was shocked to see Del Toro and many of his men mounted, fully provisioned and armed to the teeth. The men each carried a big Winchester and at least one six shooter, and all had a deadly daga carried in a sheath in front of their guns. They wore cartridge belts around their waist or in bandoliers across their chest. He was glad that they were on his side.

Alice, too, was ready and rode to Del Toro's side. She reached over and kissed his cheek. "God help the old scoundrel now."

Chapter VIII: Marta

Rebecca sat quietly in her little room in the tent. They were apparently camping at this place and she was not made to do anything. She found some leftover food and ate and had some time alone, out of the sun, away from the ugly dirty men.

She fell asleep and had good dreams and was happy until she awoke and realized that she wasn't home. She began shaking inside and thought of her daddy and mamma and Pilar and all the good men at the ranch, especially Uncle Bob. She thought about crying and decided it wouldn't help and thought that forcing some food into her body would help. It did.

She was going through her little bag, the one Abuelita bought her in California, when a diminutive form pushed back the flap of the tent and strode, with great purpose, into the room. She was a miniature adult, not much older than Rebecca. She looked officious and scary and silly all at once. She smoked a little cigarette and was wearing a miniature vaquero outfit; she even had a small six shooter and fighting knife.

She looked at Rebecca holding her bag. For a split second she became a little girl herself, looking at the captive girl's treasure. Then, just as suddenly, she reverted to her persona as a junior brigand.

She put her cigarette between her teeth and grabbed the bag from Rebecca's hand. She began pulling out the contents and placing the items on the cot. She picked up the rosary given to her by Pilar on her last birthday. "Hmm, you better not let the Maestro see this."

"Who is the Maestro?"

"Sombrero del Oro."

"Did he capture you, too?"

The miniature brigand looked with severity at the remaining contents. "He's my father." She picked up a pile of lacework. "What's this?"

"Tatting. Where is your mother?"

The child shrugged.

"How old are you?"

The girl shrugged again. She was never told her age, never had a birthday party and didn't know even what day or month she was born.

"What is this . . . tatting?"

"Just a way of making lace. Sailors used to do it. I'm making this for my Mamma."

The girl found no value in it and let Rebecca keep it. She looked about officiously again.

Rebecca watched the girl move with authority around the room. She was not afraid of the girl and wanted to talk to someone close to her own age. "Were you the one crying last night, in the next room, where the man with your father sleeps?"

"Hah! I don' cry, and I don't let that pig have nothin' to do with me." She seemed pleased with her response and looked at Rebecca.

The captive was pretty and a cultured girl; she looked refined now, despite what she'd been through. She touched Rebecca's earrings and saw a little string around her neck. She pulled on it.

"What's this?"

"It's called a Scapular. It's meant to protect me."

Marta looked it over and handed it back to Rebecca, who returned it to its place.

"That was one of the captives you heard crying. A boy."

"What is your father doing with us? What did that man do to make that child cry last night?" She was not really certain she wanted to know.

The child brigand dropped her cigarette on the floor and crushed it out with the toe of her boot. "You do not know?" She grinned knowingly, actually, more a leer, that a child of her age — whatever that might be — should not be capable of.

"You are going back to our land to live out your days as one of my father's wives. The child was crying because the old man was doing what you've seen horses and cats and dogs do to each other." She looked at Rebecca to see if she comprehended and added, "What a bull does to a cow." She smiled a crooked, cruel smile. Rebecca was once again shaky inside.

"I don't understand. I am eight years old, well, almost eight, and I am not to be a wife to any man, not an old man like your father."

"Well, that is what will happen. My father has many, many wives and more than one hundred children, but he says his wives are no good now, most of the babies come out sick or dead, or don't live very long, or have to be put down, like a bad horse. So he says he needs more wives, and that is why we went to your country and robbed the train and the settlements."

Rebecca could not understand all this. She looked at the little thug. She was so queer, like looking at a miniature version of a woman. She could not understand her attitude about all this. "But that's not right. Do you think it's right? Do you think your father should have me as a wife?"

The child shrugged. "I don't much care. By the time you are old enough to breed, he'll probably be dead and I will take over." She was suddenly distracted, as if she'd remembered some important task. "We will stay here the rest of the day, then we will move on tomorrow. I'll be back later and you will teach me this tatting."

The little vaquero didn't come back all day. Rebecca stayed on her cot and tried to do her tatting, but her insides and her hands were shaking so badly that she couldn't hold the shuttle properly. She looked toward the flap whenever she heard a sound. Eventually, it grew dark and she got sleepy. She wasn't hungry and didn't look for food. No one brought her any.

The anxiety invoked by the little brigand had exhausted her. She was more afraid than she had ever been in her life. She kept thinking about the horses and mules bred on the ranch. She couldn't imagine herself like that with the ugly, mean old man and it made her shake so badly that her teeth clicked together. She pulled her knees up to her chest to try to stop the shaking. She didn't want to cry but the thoughts and her fear of what was to come were too much and she did cry, very hard. She shook and cried into her pillow and tried so hard to think about her mamma and how much she wanted to hold her and be held by her. Finally, mercifully, her brain stopped torturing her and she drifted off to sleep.

She slept for a short while. Suddenly, she was startled out of a light slumber by the mean, fat assistant to the maestro. She peeked around the tent flap and watched him. He was changing clothes and, despite her anxiety, Rebecca had to suppress a laugh because, when he pulled his shirt off she could see that he was wearing a chemise under his clothes. He looked ridiculous with his bloated brown skin pressing tightly against the white satin garment, great tufts of black hair protruding from his armpits. His breasts were as big as Pilar's and he wiggled a little to get the garment to fall back down around his bulbous buttocks after it had ridden up while removing his shirt. He pulled a bit of the material out of the crack of his behind.

He looked through the chest the maestro brought in the first day, when the bandit boss made her go through it and put on one of the dresses. The ugly assistant now searched through them with great care and smelled the armpits of each. He decided on a red satin dress and pulled it over his head. He looked in a mirror, turning one way and then the other, and finally sauntered out of the tent.

He was feeling good tonight. The maestro was in a good mood and the little half-breed girl was now just inches from him. He could smell her. He wanted her and he knew, if he played his cards right, he'd have her. The maestro could be persuaded.

He wandered about the camp and made his way down a little hill to the place where the captives were held. The men had tethered them to each other by the neck with hemp rope. They were all nearly starved and were kept from drinking enough water. This was always the best way to keep them from running. It was also a good way to entice the ones he selected. A little water and meat would always get them. Once he had them lured away, he could control them easily.

He became distracted by one of the bandit groups. They were especially drunk now and were firing their six shooters at empty bottles. Some bullets whizzed past him and he yelled at them to stop. They laughed at him and cursed him. He walked in their direction; he was going to give them hell.

He was distracted by another group playing a guitar — badly.

He thought about the old days. He and the maestro had been together many years. They were children together in the same village and they were not always the way they were now.

In the old days, the maestro was scrawny and weak. He was four years younger than the clown man who was the biggest of the children. The kids used to tease the maestro and beat him and the clown man was usually the one to instigate the humiliation.

One day, everything changed when the maestro lured the clown man into the fortress ruins. He awoke in one of the dungeons to find the maestro had trussed him up with some old chains that had been left behind.

He was hanging, naked and bleeding, with the maestro watching him. He writhed in pain, pleading for water. The maestro began beating him with a quirt until the blood ran freely from everywhere on his body. The maestro abused him many times over the course of as many days and something strange, something completely unexpected happened to the clown man.

He learned that he enjoyed the terrible humiliation. From then on, he was the devoted servant of the maestro. For fifty years he served the man and was well rewarded. He was given money and power and able to satisfy all the vices an earthly being could imagine. He could abuse children as often as he liked and, even when the other bandits objected, the maestro stood between them and the clown man. He was impervious to any of their insults or attacks.

The maestro learned from this experience as well. His control over the clown man gave him confidence and he learned that, if he was cruel enough, he could control others. Soon, he had an army of misfits following him like he was a great military leader, which he was not. He was neither clever nor wise. He was just more malicious than the rest.

The men eventually quieted down and he remembered the task at hand. He changed directions and moved back down the hill to the captives.

The red-headed woman saw him and called out to him, "Where is my boy? What have you done with my boy?"

The boy had been taken from them a day ago and never returned. She thought a lot more about him than she ever thought she would. She'd been abused so many times by now, she was numb to it. The poor little fellow always stood by her, though, and always just kept his mouth shut. He kept his eyes to the ground. He felt so sorry for her and didn't dare look in her direction for fear of upsetting or embarrassing her. Even though she was never very nice to him, she was still his mother and he loved her very much. He'd never actually seen her abused but knew, nonetheless, that the bandits were very bad to her when they took her away. She could tell he wanted to help her, but there was nothing he could do.

She knew, instinctively, what he was thinking and now that he was gone, she felt despondent and sorry that she hadn't treated him better. She could only imagine what the fat man had done to him. This made her ill again but she was so dehydrated and starved for food that she couldn't even vomit.

She looked at the powdered buffoon and thought that if she ever had the chance, she'd cut his throat and be happy about it.

He ignored her, pushed past her, untied

another child who had just fallen asleep. He looked the child over, grunted, disappointed. This one would have to do.

Rebecca woke some time later. It was fully dark and there was no sound outside. All the bandits and captives were apparently asleep. She listened intently for the noise that woke her. It was coming from inside the tent. It was Gold Hat. He was having a violent nightmare. He spoke terrified gibberish.

At first, it scared Rebecca but she soon calmed down and listened. She sat up on her cot and pressed her ear against the flap closest to the man. She remembered the clown man and looked in the direction of his little room. She could tell he wasn't there and suspected he was on some terrible adventure. She turned back and listened to the old bandit. He was hissing and babbling.

Rebecca stood up, ready to go to his aid, to wake and comfort him. Then something brought her to her senses. She became aware of a sensation she'd never experienced before. It slowly dawned on her, for the first time in her young life, that she was actually glad for the pain and suffering of another human being, she was glad for the suffering of Sombrero del Oro. It was a strange sensation. She wasn't certain she liked it, but somehow it seemed right. This man needed to be punished, and punished he was in his fitful night terrors.

She thought of Mamma who said one time that a bad dream was normal, and that everyone had them from time to time, but to have terrors meant that you were not right with God and you weren't right in your own mind, that you had done some bad thing in life and it was torturing you. Mamma told her that people who were evil never slept well and it was one way that God punished them for their wickedness.

Rebecca listened again. It made her feel glad and sad at the same time. She thought about the old maestro. Maybe he really would die before he made her his wife. Maybe she would escape, or Mamma would find her, or Daddy. She knew they were okay. She knew Mamma was fine and didn't believe the old men when they said she was dead.

She thought about the little girl. She felt sorry for her. The little brigand didn't scare her and, despite the fact that she smoked a cigarette and dressed like a man, Rebecca could tell that she was just a girl, like her, and that she apparently didn't have a good mamma; that she was not nearly so tough and wily as she acted.

She thought about all her wonderful birthdays, as far back as she could remember, every birthday even better than the last, and this girl never had a birthday, not one. She didn't even know how old she was. That made Rebecca feel very sad and she wondered at how completely evil the place was where she was headed.

She wondered where the girl slept and how she spent her day, wondered with whom she kept company. She tried to imagine the girl as the leader of the bandits. It didn't make any sense.

Finally, Gold Hat became quiet. His terror had burned itself out, either that or his mind became exhausted enough to stop terrifying him. He became quiet, so quiet that Rebecca thought that he might be dead and for the first time in her young life, she was glad at the thought of the death of another human being.

She finally drifted off to sleep and dreamed of helping Pilar bake her favorite, pan de muertos.

She was up early and found the camp active. They were about ready to move out when an excited guard rushed into the tent.

Gold Hat and the clown man were sitting at a desk when he interrupted them. "A man, Maestro." He pointed excitedly toward the south.

"What man?"

"He looks to be an Americano. He is sitting on a rock with a white flag. He wants to parley."

Gold Hat grunted. "Go out and see what he wants. Then kill him and tell me what he said."

Two riders approached the man, who was wearing a fine ditto suit and sitting at a small table. The men rode up quickly and looked down at him from atop their horses.

Dan George stated his business. He motioned to a small chest beside him and told them he'd speak only to Gold Hat. The first bandit pulled his six shooter but before he could point it at Dan, the man's head came apart, splattering brain onto his colleague's lap. The other bandit looked on, dumbfounded.

"You tell Gold Hat I have enough money to make him richer than he's ever been in his life, but I'll only talk to him. If anyone tries to do me any injury," he looked down at the corpse, "that'll happen to them."

The bandit wheeled his horse and galloped back to camp. In short order, Sombero del Oro and the clown man slowly rode up.

Gold Hat dismounted casually. He looked down at the corpse and stepped over it. He didn't bother looking out at the mesa for the shooter. He looked at Dan George indifferently.

"What's your business, Indian?"

"Rebecca Walsh."

"Don't know such a thing as this."

"The pretty girl with black hair and blue eyes. She was wearing a blue dress when you took her."

"So, what's your business, Indian?"

"In this chest is thirty thousand dollars." He gestured for the clown man to look. He did and pulled out several stacks of notes, held together with paper bands.

"Paper money means nothing to me, Indian. Words mean nothing to me. Gold coins and good human flesh mean something to me."

"This is good US currency and it is only one quarter of what we will pay for the child."

"And where is the rest of this great fortune?"

"In notes. I have the power to release the balance to you, to be redeemed at the nearest bank of your choosing."

"What is this, redeemed?"

"Made good." Dan George was surprised at the man's ignorance. He thought that at least Gold Hat had to be an intelligent man to evade the law for so many years. He was just another stupid bandit.

"So, what am I to do with these notes, eh?"

"I don't give a good goddamn what you do with them. Turn them into quarters and jam every one of 'em up your ass for all I care."

Gold Hat did not understand and turned to the clown man. "Que?"

The clown man shrugged. Dan George was growing impatient. "Let me tell you something, old simpleton. When you attacked that train, you unleashed the Leviathan, and if you don't take heed of my warning, it will be very bad for you."

The two old men cackled back and forth to each other and the clown man spoke up, "What's this Leviathan?"

"One of the monsters of hell, its gatekeeper, and I warn you it will be coming for you. You should take my offer now, Gold Hat. Because if you do not, I can guarantee you that a rain of shit will fall on you like you have never known."

This the old bandit understood and he became angry at the Indian's impudence. "Tell me, swine, why did this Walsh family send a red-dog savage to make a trade?"

He reached for his pistol and the ground kicked up near his left foot. The report of a shot could be heard off in the distance. He stopped.

Dan George stood up from the table. He whistled for his horse and mounted up. He grabbed the chest of money and began to slowly ride away. Suddenly he stopped and looked down at the two men and then stared at Gold Hat. "You are doomed." He rode away.

The two old men stood, staring stupidly for a moment, then suddenly pulled their pieces. They pointed them at Dan George's back but before either could pull the trigger another bullet found its mark, striking Gold Hat in the left buttock. He spun about, as if he'd suddenly been nipped in the backside by a mean dog. He limped to his horse and both men rode back to safety.

Chica smoked a cigar as Dan rode up, disappointment in his eyes. "Well, that didn't pan out."

Chica helped him with the chest and gave him a little smile. She never expected it to work, but had to give Dan his chance.

"Don' worry, Dan. He have a sore ass now, and we've killed one bandit. Only forty-eight-and-a-half to go."

They rode off quickly, going south. Dan was livid. "There's no reasoning with that son of a bitch, Chica." He remembered Mother Superior and nodded, "Beg your pardon, ma'am."

When they were a safe distance away and certain they'd not been followed; Chica stopped their little party. "You go find my Arvel and Dick Welles, Dan."

He suddenly looked hurt. "I want to stay with you, Chica."

She lit another cigar off the butt of the one she'd been smoking. "We," she looked at the old nun, "have to go in the camp and get Rebecca. You go an' get the rest of the boys and wait at Sombrero del Oro's fort. Mos' of his band will be heading there, you can get them then."

Dan was confused, as usual. Chica did not let him in on her plan, but he could not argue with her. He shrugged and quickly got his bearings. "I hope you have a good plan, Chica. I'm not going to tell you to be careful. I can see in your eyes you don't plan to be careful at all, but I'm not afraid for you. God help those poor bastards now."

"Adios, Dan." She grabbed him and kissed his cheek. She sent him on his way.

Chapter IX:
Arvel

Arvel and Billy rode most of that morning without incident. Arvel's right leg was tethered to his stirrup which was in turn tied to Tammy's front cinch and he was able to keep upright on his favorite mule well enough. He'd been working on controlling his right thigh muscles, then calf, then ankle. He was convinced he could move his ankle by late morning and that pleased him very much.

They rode into a little settlement, pretty well a ghost-settlement by now and Billy grunted at the dilapidated sign with its words barely discernible. It read The Hump. Arvel looked over Billy's shoulder.

"They ought to change that sign."

"Don't think anyone cares much, mate."

"No, not to make it clearer. They need to change the name of this God forsaken place."

He pulled a cartridge from his pocket and

handed it to Billy, pointing crookedly at the sign. "Billy, make that H a D."

Billy complied and scraped at the sign, using the bullet point like it was a pencil.

"There, that's more like it." He looked on at Billy's change approvingly. The H was now a D.

Billy wanted to top off their canteens and check on Arvel's skin. He didn't want the man getting saddle sores as Arvel still had little sensation in many parts of his body. The one and only good thing The Hump offered was decent water.

Two ruffians stood outside the only building. They eyed the two riders suspiciously, with obvious contempt. They would have been more dangerous had they not been so drunk. It appeared that getting inebriated was the only pastime at The Hump.

Arvel dismounted with Billy's help and shuffled past them into the establishment. It was filthy dirty. There was a broken down piano in a corner and a disused faro table with no chairs anywhere. The saloon once sported a big mirror behind the bar, but that had been shot to pieces a few years ago when a horrendous battle had taken place.

Arvel knew of the battle. It helped to relieve him and Dick of eight bad hombres who had given them trouble in the southernmost part of the territory. It was a mismatched battle between two rival gangs; six on one side and two on the other. The only difference was that the two had repeating shotguns and the others only six shooters. They all killed each other, the first justice any one of them had ever done in their miserable lives. Arvel managed to hobble over to a table and sat down on an empty beer keg. He leaned back against the wall.

The proprietor brought him a bottle of whiskey, there had been no beer for many years. It wouldn't keep and no one cared much anyway.

Arvel asked for mescal instead and the barkeep brought that over along with the requested two glasses.

When Billy walked in the man put his hand up. "No niggers."

Arvel called out. "Bullshit!" He laid the Greener on the table, muzzle pointed at the proprietor's middle. The man ignored him and let Billy pass.

Arvel grinned sideways at his companion and spoke loud enough for everyone to hear. "Right friendly around here, aren't they, Billy?"

"Yeah. But the name shouldn't be Dump, it should be Shithole." Billy drank the mescal down quickly and removed the rawhide loop from the hammer of his six shooter. Arvel sat back and looked at the ruffians, who'd by now taken up positions on either end of the bar.

Arvel watched them. "What do you boys do for fun around here?"

"Drink," one called out and the others snickered.

"And hang niggers," said the other.

"Hah!" Arvel laughed out loud. "Good thing there aren't many of them around."

The bigger and bolder of the two walked over to Arvel. "Why don't you buy us a drink, Mister?"

"Now, why the hell would I do that?"

He grinned his crooked grin at the man. Billy sat, staring at the bottle in front of him.

The man moved quickly for a drunkard, covering the distance between them and casually picked up the cut-down shotgun. He looked it over carefully. "Why would anyone bugger up a nice shotgun like this?"

Arvel grinned.

"What the hell happened to your face, Mister?" He stood back, out of reach of the two seated travelers. He held the shotgun casually.

"Had a fit. Made my body go all catawampus. Weak as a newborn baby."

"Awe, that's mighty sad, Mister."

The other one was emboldened now, as was the bartender. They were pleased at their luck, a dude and his servant, wandering into their little lair with expensive traps, nice mounts, a nice healthy mule . . . It had to be worth at least several hundred dollars when you added it all up and that didn't count whatever cash they had on them. The dude evidently had money, he was dressed well enough.

"Well, son, I thank you for your concern and kind words. It isn't everywhere you'd hear that sort of compassion for one's fellow man. God bless you."

"So, how about that drink?"

Arvel leaned forward a little and shifted his weight. "Well, boys, get the bartender to bring you glasses. Hell, you can have a drink."

They drank in silence and they poured greedily, knocking down three apiece before getting back to the business at hand.

"Why's it you're traveling with a nigger?" The man grinned at the others. He was pleased with himself. "You own him?"

"No, no. Technically, the term is used to describe the peoples who originate in sub-Saharan Africa. This gentleman is actually from Australia."

"Subsa what?" The man laughed again, but he wasn't smiling, "Gentleman? Mister, you sure use some fancy goddamned words."

"Yes, well, lads." Arvel brushed the dirt from the palm of his hand as he'd been resting it on the dusty table. "This has all been very stimulating." Arvel pulled a twenty-dollar gold piece from his vest pocket. He dropped it on the table. "Can you make change for that, barman? It's time my friend and I went on our way."

The bold man guffawed. "You ain't goin' nowhere, Mister."

Arvel grinned again, "Well, that's true. I am not going no-where, it's actually quite impossible to go no-where, but I am going somewhere, and that is on with my journey down to old Mexico. You boys wouldn't want to impede me and my companion."

He looked at Billy and nodded his head solemnly, "I believe that would be against the law."

"You sonofabitch. Ye'r playin' with the wrong hombres."

The bold man was livid now. He'd grown sick of the dude's stupid grin and lack of concern for the danger he was in. He should be shitting his pants and he just sat there with a stupid, sideways grin, just as casual as you please.

"Mister, let me tell you what we're goin' to do." He pointed the Greener at Billy's head. "First, we're goin' to shoot this one in the head, and then you."

With that he pulled the trigger and the Greener's left barrel emitted nothing more than a crisp click. He tried the other barrel, with the same result.

Everyone stood still, waiting for what was going to happen next.

Arvel spoke up, "Now you see, boys, that's the first lesson in the safe handling of a shootin' iron. Whenever you pick up another man's gun, always check to see if it's loaded."

"Sonofabitch!" The drunk dropped the shotgun and went for his six shooter as Billy squeezed off a shot that removed the back of his head. Arvel fired next, from under the table, shooting the other man in the lower gut, the bullet tearing an oblong trench in the battered tabletop. The proprietor stood behind the bar. He was shaking and suddenly cried out.

"No, no, no!"

Arvel prepared to shoot him but changed his mind. He turned his pistol and pointed to Billy's left. "Cover your ears, mate." Billy complied and Arvel shot the glass out of the only intact window. A strong breeze began clearing the smoke from the room.

Arvel suddenly had a thought. "Damn it, Billy." He looked on at his friend now casually pouring another mescal. "I never got to tell 'em you were half Dutch."

Billy grunted, then drank his mescal. "A little too much with the twenty-dollar gold piece, mate. I think you had 'em pretty well hooked without that."

"Sorry." Arvel looked down at the man with half a head. "That's some brain surgery, doctor."

"Never had any complaints after performing that procedure." Billy looked on at the man behind the bar. "What do we do with him, mate?"

Arvel looked at the man. "You have a horse?" The man did. "You've got five minutes to get your shit and get out of this place."

"Yessir."

Arvel drained the bottle equally between himself and Billy while the man knocked around in a little room in the back of the bar. Eventually he had his gear together. He looked at the two.

"You ain't just some dude, are you?"

Arvel pulled back the lapel of his coat,

revealing his star. "No, son, I'm not."

After the man rode away, Arvel limped up to the bar. The Dump was now officially a ghost town. He lit a smoke and, with the match still burning, set fire to the contents of the bottles of mescal he'd upended on the floor of the old saloon. The whiskey was too watered down to catch fire.

Making their way outside, Arvel and Billy watched it burn. "I should've done this years ago, Billy."

They rode out and Arvel looked over at his companion. "Did you see how that fellow dropped? I never killed a man so quickly without shooting him in the head."

Billy thought on that for a moment. "Probably got the superior mesenteric artery. That's a big one. One thing's for sure, mate."

"What's that?"

"You can shoot with your left hand."

Will Panks waited on the trail. The two riders were a quarter mile away, but he could see them and they him. When they finally arrived, he pulled off his hat and wiped sweat from his forehead. "Welcome to Mexico."

Arvel grinned crookedly. "Will!"

"Jesus, Arvel, you're bent over worse than

me." He patted his old friend on the back.

"What have you been up to, old fellow?"

"Back to prospecting again; can't shake it. When I heard of your troubles I came as quick as I could, Arvel. Sorry about your little girl."

Arvel choked back his tears. He looked at Will's traps and then remembered Billy. "Will, you know my doctor, Billy?"

The old prospector shook the aborigine by the hand. "Everyone knows Billy Livingston." He nodded respectfully at the healer. "You boys keep away from old Pop," he nodded to his mule, a nice big black that he'd gotten from Arvel many years ago, "he's full up of dynamite."

"Jesus, Will, you got enough here to take down a mountain."

"Or enough to kill old Gold Hat and a bunch of his minions."

They rode on together until just before dusk and set up camp near some good water. Arvel limped around and handled his own traps. Will watched him as he fought his debility, remembering his own battle many years ago when he'd shattered his spine all alone in the desert. "How's it coming along, Arvel?"

Arvel grinned his crooked smile. "Oh, thanks to Billy, coming along pretty good. I was droolin' like an infant, now I can control my spit." He smiled. "I can hobble along and I am moving my right hand a bit. And most important, I don't shit myself anymore."

He reached over and massaged his right hand with his left.

"Keep fightin' old friend, keep fightin'."

It was a clear night and the men passed a bottle and smoked and stared into the fire. Arvel felt like talking. He felt good to be with a man who had overcome a trial similar to that which he was now living through.

"So, back to prospecting." Will grinned and looked into the fire. "You ever find anything out there, Will?"

"Oh sure. Millions." He looked over at Billy who was looking a bit confused. "Problem is, every time I find a million dollar claim I soon figure out it would cost a million and one dollars to get it out of the Godforsaken land I find it in." They all nodded, knowingly.

Arvel looked up at the canopy of stars overhead. "The Old Man is playing with us, sure enough." He blew smoke at the moon. Billy Livingston grunted and Arvel grinned. "What?"

Billy poked at the fire and kept his eyes

fixed on an ember. "Nothing."

"You think there's a grand plan, gents?"

Will Panks spoke up first, "Naw, Arvel, you don't want me to give you advice about the Great Beyond or God or heaven or hell." He'd been playing at an anthill next to his saddle.

Billy nodded at Will. He scratched under his arm and echoed Will's sentiments about his own agnosticism. "Yep, don't look at me for any idea about some great spirit sittin' on some clouds, dispensin' justice to mankind either, mate."

"My God, in the company of a couple of atheists." Arvel smiled and passed the bottle to Will. "You boys just don't think there is any Great Creator who made all this?"

Will picked an especially feisty ant up on a stick. "How's it that we're any different than this ant?" He crushed his cigarette out. "Maybe we come up with the idea of God to make us feel better about our situation. Maybe we're no different than any other creature on earth, that the life of this ant colony's no more or less important than the lives we lead." Billy grunted out a plume of smoke.

Arvel sunk down into his blanket. He worked at the exercises Billy had taught him. "Well, I'll be damned."

It wasn't a new thought for Arvel, he'd struggled with his own mortality and faith for years. He decided to pry into the minds of his companions a bit more. "So, what's the point of going on, boys? Why do we do it, why do we fight the Gold Hats of the world, or work hard, or constantly look for gold in the hills of Arizona, kill wolves for the government, heal gimps and apoplectics?"

"Don' know about that, mate," Billy watched Arvel working and reached over, grabbed his right arm and shoulder and began stretching it for Arvel, "but some idea of a God floatin' around up on a cloud never did it for me. Like that bloke — what's his name — Marx, said 'Religion is the opiate of the masses,' or some such nonsense."

Will grinned and looked up from his ants. Arvel smiled through his pain at Billy pulling on his arm. "Son of a bitch, you're a regular philosopher, Billy. Never took you for a utopian socialist."

The aborigine sat back down and lit another smoke. "Not one, not at all, mate. Just always struck me, the idea that people made God, not the other way 'round. But I don't have anything against it. Whatever gets you through the day."

"Amen!" said Will. "Whatever keeps you from findin' a stout rope and a stout beam to throw it over. Religion's as good as any other crutch, better'n booze or the pipe or whorin' around. My religion's hard work." He took a sip from the communal bottle and pointed it at Arvel, "Yours is breeding mules." He pointed to Billy, "Yours is readin' tripe in the Bisbee library." Billy grinned.

Arvel finished the bottle and thought of starting another but he was growing drowsy and decided to call it a night. "Billy, remember that shit you fed me in the clay jug, the first time we met?" Billy grunted and Arvel looked over at Will, "That was the craziest potion I ever had."

Billy sat up and arranged his blanket and spoke into it. "Never did figure out what was in it."

"I had the oddest dream I ever dreamed after drinking it. My God, that was a long time ago." He yawned and began to drift. "You boys ever hear the story of Kit Carson?" He fell asleep.

Arvel was up before the others. He suddenly thought of Rebecca and Chica and wanted to cry. His gut contracted and the pain ran through him, into his back. He sat up and took a deep breath and lit a smoke. The fire was out but Billy had put plenty of kindling and makings together and he soon had it going again. He felt better doing tasks and was certain — no, convinced — he'd gained more strength and control over his right side. He was not shuffling as much and could move his arm about, helping his left side do the work at hand.

Soon he had coffee going and the men awoke to the aroma of pork frying. They ate silently and by sunrise were all mounted up with the old dynamite pack mule, Donny, and Alanza in tow.

They were getting well into Mexico now. Will led the party because he knew the location of Gold Hat's fort and the fastest route to San Sebastian. By early noon they arrived at a dirt crossroads where a small boy, no older than five, sat, waiting.

It was as if he was waiting for them. He looked as if he had been in some great distress recently. His eyes were puffy and his nose ran. He was hungry, thirsty and exhausted. He barely had the energy to address them.

Billy and Will looked at him indifferently as they passed. There was much heartache, pain and suffering in this land. The men had learned to disregard it and ignored the boy the same as they would if he were a deer or horse carcass, or any other poor creature who'd met its doom. They moved on past; moved on with their lives. It wasn't that they were cruel or uncaring, both Billy and Will were the opposite, but they had a greater mission on their minds. They couldn't save every creature they ran across out here from pain. They'd never get anything done.

Arvel stopped next to the boy and lowered his canteen by its strap. The boy drank, guzzling the water down. Arvel handed him a hunk of jerked beef and the boy hardly tasted it, gulping it the way a dog eats steak gristle if given the opportunity.

"What is the matter, muchacho?" Arvel looked at Will and Billy as they stopped and turned back in their saddles.

Billy got down from his horse; he knew they'd be there a while. He gathered the makings for a small fire as Arvel comforted the child.

"My mamma." The child began to cry again and Arvel had difficulty understanding him.

"Slow down, muchacho." He dismounted and sat on a rock next to the boy. He patted him softly on the shoulder.

"My mamma. A big man with a hairy face,

he took my burro and he said he would go back to my home and get my mamma."

"For what, to come and help you, are you hurt?" He began looking the child over for an injury.

"No, no, no! He is a bad man. He hurt me, he pulled me from my burro and he beat me. He said he would go to my home and do the same to my mamma." The child began to cry harder. Will Panks walked up on him.

"What does the man look like, muchacho?"

"He is big. He have a big beard. His face is funny, all crooked. His mouth is crooked, like this." The child lifted his upper lip, pushing it upward, as if to stick it up his nose.

"Son of a bitch." Will Panks slapped dust from his chaps. Arvel looked at him.

"You know him?"

"Yeah, I know him, all right. Should've killed that bastard a long time ago, when I had the chance."

"Mexicano?"

"Naw, Goddamned Dutchman. Features himself a prospector, the son of a bitch couldn't pour piss from a boot if the directions were written on the heel. Always shadowin' folks who know what they're doing and try to claim jump when he can. Likes the whores. He cut one real bad up in Jerome two winters ago. He's been wandering down here ever since. No goddamned beard'll ever hide that harelip, though. It's a dandy."

Arvel looked on at the child who did not seem to have any English. He didn't seem to understand Will at all. "When did the man leave to go to your home, muchacho?"

"Esta mañana."

Will motioned Arvel to the fire Billy had been working on. "Arvel," he looked at the boy for any comprehension. "That woman's probably dead by now. That crazy Dutchman likely had his way with her and cut her throat." Arvel looked at the child.

"What'll we do with the boy?"

"Let's give him some provisions and a few pesos, tell him to go to his family. He's gotta have family somewhere around here. We give him two dollars in pesos and he'll be the richest peon for miles."

Arvel considered it. He looked at his watch; it was nearly two in the afternoon. He looked up at the sun as if to verify the watch's time. He looked on at the men. Billy spoke up.

"Arvel, it's the only thing we can do, mate." He'd seen that look in Arvel's eyes before and he knew what it meant. "We gotta get moving, mate. We can't drag a child with us."

Arvel grinned his crooked grin.

"Jesus, Billy." Will Panks looked at Arvel, then at the child. "He's not thinkin' of taking the boy."

"No, boys, I'm not." He threw the dregs of his coffee on the fire and kicked the flame dead with his good foot. "Come on, we're wasting time gabbin' about it."

They rode fast. Arvel put the child between himself and the saddle horn. Tammy moved out ahead of the others. The mule was moving at a good pace, as if she'd understood the importance of the task. The boy was too small and too weak to ride Alanza and Arvel feared he'd fall off. He felt the boy shivering as they rode.

Off in the distance, Arvel spotted a rabbit feeding on some grass under a little washout. He pointed it out to the boy. "That rabbit there reminds me of a story, an old Yaqui legend. You want to hear it?" The child nodded his head. His back pressed against Arvel's chest and every now and again, Arvel would put his hand gently on the boy's shoulder. He forgot himself for a moment and thought he was holding his little girl. He kissed the boy on the top of his head. It made the boy feel good and happy and calm.

"Well, one day there was this rabbit and this bear, and they were squattin' in the desert, takin' a crap." The boy suddenly sat up straight in the saddle and looked back at the man, not certain what he had heard.

"True; true story. They were squattin' down, takin' a crap, and guess what?"

"Que?"

"The bear says to the rabbit, "Mister rabbit, do you ever have trouble with shit stickin' to your fur?" The child giggled. "And the rabbit says, well, no, I don't, mister bear. So, the bear reaches over and picks that little rabbit up and wipes his ass with him." The child sat silently for a while. He suddenly laughed out loud.

"Now, you tell me when we get close, but not too close to your home, okay?"

"Sí, Señor." He tensed up and once again began to shake.

They hit a rocky patch and slowed. The little boy told him it would be another mile.

Arvel felt good. For the first time since Gold Hat's attack on his family, he felt good. "You know, I'm very popular with animals and old people and children." He waited to see if the boy comprehended. He was listening to Arvel and he was calming down. He did not shake as badly.

"Everybody else thinks I'm a pendejo." The little fellow turned to look up at the strange gringo again.

"That is a very bad thing to say, Señor. And you are not a pendejo."

They hid in an arroyo while Billy and Will completed their reconnaissance. They were back in short order.

"He's there, and I think the woman's still alive. Looks like he's settin' up house, just sitting outside, smoking a cigar. Don't see the burro. She probably thinks the boy's okay."

"So, he's a bad hombre, Will?" Arvel looked on, as if he were a judge at the bar.

"Bad as they come, Arvel."

Arvel limped over to Donny and pulled out his Greener. He tucked the barrels under his right arm and opened the gun with his left hand. He reached into his pocket and loaded it just like he'd been practicing. He was ready. He looked down at the child.

"Muchacho, you need to take care of our horses and mules. Can you do that for me?" The child nodded energetically. "We'll be back in no time, and your mamma will be good."

The Dutchman had sensed an impending change, like the smell of a rainstorm coming in the late afternoon and decided to have a little fun while the opportunity was upon him. He'd suddenly turned severe and the young woman sensed it. He was an ugly gringo but, initially, seemed fit and pleasant enough. She thought that he would stay and help her and her son. She would welcome company, and an able-bodied man would be good for a change. She had heard nothing from her husband for nearly two years and she feared the worst. She and her boy were just surviving. Perhaps their luck was going to change for the better with this new man to help them.

He was upon her before she could react and, as he was twice her size, there was little she could do. He worked quickly and it was over and done before she could really comprehend the malice and cruelty of the act. For good measure, he belted her soundly across the face two or three times. She lost consciousness and lay on her bed while he ambled out to the little broken-down porch at the front of the hovel. He found a bottle of mescal and had a proper celebratory drink.

This is how Billy and Will found him. They weren't aware they'd missed foiling the heinous crime by mere minutes.

Arvel worked his way slowly forward and peered through an opening between the rough boards of the shack's north wall. He could see the woman lying on her bed, unnaturally, not in the way a woman would normally lay. Something wasn't right. She was nude from the waist down, too exhausted and sore from the rough handling to even cover her body, more in shock than in pain. This wouldn't do.

Arvel had an intense dislike for all bad men, but he particularly hated rapists. Murderers generally just took a life, which was bad enough, but a rapist was the lowest of the low, to his mind. They took something from a woman and then left her to think about it, be tortured about it and have to live with the horror of it for the rest of her life. In a way, it was worse than death.

He naturally loved women, women of every shape and size and age; ladies, whores, Mexicans, Whites, Orientals, Negroes, all women. He honestly felt that women were the best of humankind. They were better than men, smarter and kinder and the most splendid creatures. They made men civilized, made lands civilized, made everything that was good about the human race. He loved women and he knew they were, physically — only physically — the weaker sex. The fact that a man would force himself on a woman was loathsome to him. He often killed bad men on the spot, he pretty much always killed rapists.

Billy and Will approached from the back of the shack. Arvel insisted and, since it was his idea, refused to let the men lead the assault on the bad man. Arvel shuffled slowly to the front of the hovel. The Dutchman was relaxing with a cigar. He didn't know he was under attack and only wanted to savor the moment, think on what fun he would have with this little Mexicana over the next several days. She was good. She was appealing to him and she served his appetite and depravity well. He'd have to be careful. He wanted to stretch this out. The last time he'd gotten overzealous and killed the last one way too soon.

Arvel was upon him, just inches away, when the man understood what was happening. He turned his head slowly and stared into the Greener's barrels. His harelip quivered and he slowly lowered the cigar. He looked at Arvel and smiled.

"Howdy," the man spoke with a thick accent. He looked at Arvel, looked him in the eye and kept smiling. He adjusted himself a little in his chair but dared not move quickly.

"Howdy." Arvel smiled his crooked smile.

"What do we do now?" The man was bold. Arvel grinned again.

"I shoot you and you die."

Both barrels rocked the afternoon's silence and the harelip disintegrated into a soup of blood and flesh and brain and bone. The body sat upright for a moment, the hand grasped the cigar, casually, as if nothing had changed. Then the massive frame toppled over onto the dusty floor. Chickens ran about cackling at the sudden noise and gore.

Will and Billy raced to the front of the little building, guns drawn. Will was surprised, Billy not so much. Arvel broke the Greener open and replaced the spent shells.

"Jesus Christ, mate!" Billy looked up at Arvel, terror in his eyes. "You've shot the gardener!"

Will ran to the corpse, looking on in a panic.

"Nice try, Billy." Arvel grinned. "I saw the harelip." He looked down at what was left of the man's head. "Think you can patch him up, doctor?"

Billy grunted, lit a smoke and handed one to Will who took it from him with shaky hands, "I'm a healer, mate, not a bleedin' magician."

Will eventually found his voice, "My God, Arvel, I didn't think you'd just execute him!"

He stared at Arvel, as if he was looking at a new man, as if he'd seen Arvel for the first time in his life. "I've heard stories, Arvel, but my God, man."

Arvel felt a little foolish. "I'm sorry, Will. Didn't mean to get you rattled. I say, good riddance to bad rubbish. You told me the fellow was bad, and," he tipped his head in the direction of the poor señora in the shack, "I saw what he did to her." He took one of Billy's cigarettes and lit it, then limped through the doorway, just far enough to address the lady. "Señora, it's okay. The bad man es acabado. He will not harm you again."

She slowly emerged from the darkened room, a blanket wrapped around her body. Her face had ballooned up on the one side, eye swollen shut where the Dutchman had beaten her. She looked bad but would survive. They'd already dragged the Dutchman's corpse away from the porch. She looked each man in the eye through the one that wasn't swollen shut, and then down at the ground. "Gracias, Caballeros, muchas gracias."

Will jogged back to retrieve the boy and the animals while Billy worked on the lady. There wasn't much he could do for her. She'd just have to wait for the swelling to go down. He made her some coffee while Arvel rested. The little fight had exhausted him, but he felt good. He was certain he could move more of his right side.

He watched the señora sit quietly, suffering. It made him so sad and he wanted to cry again. He swallowed hard and tried to comfort her.

"You have a good boy, señora."

She managed a weak smile and a quiet gracias. He decided that she probably didn't want to talk and sat silently as they waited.

In short order, Will was back. He was riding with the boy in front of him, just as he'd ridden with Arvel at the beginning of their little adventure. The lad hopped from the horse before Will had even slowed down. He ran to his mother, then stopped short when he saw her face. He did not want to hurt her further by hugging and kissing her.

"Ay chingao, Mamma!" He walked up on her slowly. "You are hurt, Mamma."

She reached out and wiped the dirt from his face. She checked his bruises. The nice gringos didn't tell her that her boy had been abused. It would have only added to her anxiety.

They watched the reunion. Will had not seen anything like this before. Arvel had, many times. In all his years Rangering, it was the best experience he'd ever known, bringing poor victims back together with their families. He looked at Will with wet eyes but he was smiling. "Worth the detour, boys?"

Billy grinned. "Sure, mate. It was worth it."

The señora insisted, despite her injuries, on making them supper. Arvel was sorry to eat her meager offerings but the men dined heartily and appreciated her hospitality. She made good chicken and after a while was even getting a little talkative, especially with Will. Arvel smiled at the old prospector who was enjoying the attention of the plain, but wholly feminine, young woman.

As they mounted up, they each shook hands with the boy and then his mother. The señora disappeared into the shack and quickly returned. She had a gift for each of them. She'd passed many lonely nights weaving horse and goat hair trinkets. She gave each man a cross on a neatly woven hair chain. They were very plain, she didn't have the means to dye the hair, but they were beautifully made. One could see the care and reverence and love that went into each of them.

The three saviors removed their hats and leaned low from their saddles. They bent their heads so she could place one around each of their necks. She kissed Will, the last in line, on the cheek. They were strange gifts for the three of them, a confirmed agnostic and two atheists, but they all wore them proudly.

Chapter X:
The Mexican Cossack

They arrived at San Sebastian with their numbers swelled to one hundred. They were a strange army, led by old people and counseled by an Indian. Dick Welles was at the front, followed by Del Toro, Uncle Bob, and Alice Walsh. With the addition of Del Toro's vaqueros who'd joined the expedition and the volunteers from Arizona, they comprised a formidable force.

Dan George had found them in the night and reported on Chica and Rebecca. He was thoroughly dejected by his failure at buying the little girl's freedom but heartened by Alice Walsh's smile. She also had good news for him from her attorney in Baltimore. They now had easy access to a quarter of a million dollars. She gave Dan the particulars.

"It doesn't seem to be about money, Alice." He walked with her to Kosterlitzky's office. "Maria was amazing, of course." He grinned and looked into Alice's eyes. "She shot the bastard in the rump."

Colonel Emilio Kosterlitzky graciously welcomed them. He was particularly attentive to Alice Walsh. He recognized her as a lady and treated her accordingly. He knew Alejandro del Toro and Dick Welles very well and greeted them as old friends. "And Captain Walsh?" He looked at the group enthusiastically.

Alice Walsh spoke up, "He's ill at present, Colonel. He's back at his ranch."

"Well, please tell him I asked about him and tell him to get well soon."

He turned his attention to Dick Welles. "What do you propose, Captain Welles?"

"Colonel, we know Gold Hat's between here and his fort. Mrs. Walsh . . ."

"Miss Chica?" Kosterlitzky knew of Chica long before she had become Mrs. Arvel Walsh. He and his men even chased her once, after she'd stolen a wealthy American colonel's fancy hunting rifle on the Mexican side of the Sonoran border. He'd only ever caught a glimpse of her then and didn't actually meet her until she'd been married to Arvel for more than two years.

Dick smiled briefly. He was very serious these days.

"Yes, Miss Chica. She's shadowing him and fifty of his men. They've got the Walshes' eight year old daughter as captive. Mr. George here," he nodded toward Dan who extended his hand to the Colonel, "tried to pay a ransom to no avail. Miss Chica shot Gold Hat in the ass for his trouble, though."

"And killed one of his men." Dan interjected then grinned sheepishly. "She told me she only had forty eight and a half to go."

"So," continued Dick, "we know Gold Hat won't negotiate, for whatever reason, we don't know. But we know his propensity for killing hostages when under attack. Because of this, we don't want to attack him. We're going to destroy his fort, his base of operations. Miss Chica will get her girl back on her own." He looked a little doubtful.

Dan George cleared his throat. "No disrespect intended, Colonel, but Gold Hat didn't seem the cleverest fellow, intellectually speaking. How is it that he's been free to roam for so long?"

Kosterlitzky smiled. He waved his hand, as to reassure that the comment wasn't considered a threat. "Two reasons, Mr. George. One, tertiary syphilis has dulled his brain, and two, he's been inactive for quite a number of years.

"We don't know why, but he hasn't been a great threat until this raid into your country. We've just had more pressing issues here and he became unimportant to us." He lit a cigarette and smiled, "And, frankly, we've never had the resources to attack his stronghold." He blew a plume of smoke into the air over his head, "Which is substantial."

"Will you go with us to attack it, Colonel?" Alice Walsh looked the man in the eye.

"I will, Mrs. Walsh. I certainly will."

Dick began to calculate. "How substantial, sir?"

"Five hundred bandits. A fort that is three hundred years old but still fairly secure, the walls not all together rotten. And some old Napoleons, but few men in his outfit capable of putting them to good use."

Dick Welles stroked his chin. "And we, a hundred good men with Winchesters and six shooters."

"And I with another hundred men, rurales, well trained with Mausers."

Alice Walsh sat up straighter in her chair. "Two hundred against five hundred."

"Ah, my lady," the colonel smiled, "but we have three French seventy-fives."

"And a mule full of dynamite." Will Panks

stepped into the colonel's office, "And Arvel Walsh and Billy Livingston." He grinned as the two men followed him into the room, "So God help 'em."

Chapter XI:
Subterfugio

Gold Hat was deposited onto his cot in his marquee tent. He was bleeding badly. He was furious. He'd lost the money in the box the Indian presented to him, one of his bandits was dead, and he now had a gaping wound through his left buttock. He looked at Rebecca Walsh and sneered.

"Come over here!" he shouted and pointed to the ground next to him.

Rebecca stood, frozen, not knowing what to do until the old bandit screamed again. She reluctantly complied. He grabbed her by the hair and pulled her down to his level. "You little bitch." He softened momentarily when he looked into the pretty blue eyes. "You offspring to a bitch whore."

Marta suddenly glided into the room, ubiquitous cigarette between her lips. She'd heard that the old man was shot and hoped to find him dead. She spoke firmly to the old man and the clown man standing beside him.

"It isn't her fault."

She helped Rebecca up and sent her to her room.

"Leave her alone."

She began looking over Gold Hat's wound. "It's not so bad. The wound is clean and the bullet came out. You now have two extra holes in your ass, that's all."

The clown man chuckled. Marta looked at him with disdain. "Counting him," she pointed her cigarette at the clown man, "you now have four assholes."

Rebecca suppressed a laugh. Despite the rough handling and the shaking inside, she could not help finding Marta's remark very funny. She was glad the girl had shown up when she had. She quickly obeyed when Marta ordered her back into her room. She thought certain she was in for a beating and the little bandit had come to her rescue.

Once Rebecca was safely out of reach, Marta inquired about the meeting with the American. The clown man spoke as he watched his maestro bleed.

"You missed getting thirty thousand American dollars?" She blew smoke at her father's fat face.

The clown man spoke up, "plus ninety

thousand."

"One hundred and twenty thousand American dollars?"

Gold Hat refused to look at the girl. He harrumphed and looked at the canvas ceiling of the tent. "It was just paper, and no more than an empty promise for the rest."

"You stupid son of a bitch." She looked at him with contempt. "Paper money, how many times must I say it, is just the same as gold. Especially American dollars."

She tipped her head toward Rebecca's room. "That girl is not worth so much and now you have nothing but extra assholes. You are muy estupido. And for what? So you can breed her? You don't even know if you will be alive so long, she will not be ready for four or five years."

She was growing tired of lambasting the two old men. They stared stupidly, vacantly, as she berated them, as if she were the parent and they the two spoilt children. She began to walk out, then remembered her date with Rebecca. She threw the flap back and called for the young girl.

"You come with me." She looked over her shoulder at Gold Hat. "The problem is not with the women, you know. The problem is with you."

■ ■ ■ ■

Marta marched, she never walked, and Rebecca had trouble keeping up with her despite the fact that she was not much bigger. Rebecca jogged a little to get beside her. "What are we doing?"

"Going to see the big red-haired woman." She stopped by the cook's camp and picked up some food and water gourds, handing several items to Rebecca.

"Who is she?"

"One of the captives. The animals are especially bad to her."

"Why?"

"You'll see."

They moved on to the corral where the captives were kept. Rebecca immediately felt ill. She felt guilty when she saw the way the poor people were mistreated while she lived in relative opulence. Many of them were so sunburned that they looked as if they'd been in a fire: faces red, lips cracked and bleeding at the corners of their mouths. They were gaunt and dehydrated and slowly starving to death.

She saw the big woman Marta was talking about.

Marta handed the woman water and she

drank a little. She picked at the food they'd brought her. Marta reached out and touched the woman's hair. She was a pretty woman and Rebecca could see that she was a special treat for Marta who'd never seen a woman with such features and hair.

"What of the rest?"

Marta looked away from the red hair and around at the others, as if she hadn't noticed them before.

"Oh." She shrugged and looked back at the woman.

"Marta, the rest need help too."

Marta ignored Rebecca and turned away. She said nothing as they walked through the camp. Rebecca could not understand the girl. She looked so mean, like the rest, she seemed to care for some and then not at all for others. She was such a queer little girl. Now she was walking about the camp as if she owned it. Rebecca considered her predicament. Now that she understood the true condition of the captives, she felt compelled to do something to help them.

"Marta, we need to help the others."

Striking a match, Marta lit the end of her cigarette, inhaled deeply and pulled it out of her mouth. Staring into the glowing tip, she spoke at it.

"Okay, but later. We can't let too many

see or there'll be trouble."

She looked at Rebecca like she was looking at a special mirror reflecting her own conscientious self. It wasn't that Marta didn't care for the others, she actually did, deep-down, but niceness and decency were qualities that were neither taught to her nor encouraged. Rebecca was a sort of paradigm of goodness and Marta did not resent that quality in her at all.

She pointed in the direction of the tent. "Go back to your room. I'll get you later."

Rebecca waited. She rested on her cot and felt guilty again. A pleasant breeze blew through the tent and made it good for napping. She thought about the poor souls in the corral. Her daddy and Uncle Bob would not let even the livestock stay in such conditions. They always made certain they had shade and plenty of food and water. The people in the corral didn't even have a place to do their business and they had to stand among their urine and excrement. It was a thousand times worse than the life of a mule.

Good to her word, Marta came in at just around dusk. They quietly picked their way through the camp. The men had eaten and were settling in to their preferential groups to lay on a good drunk. They were preoccupied and the fading light helped hide the girls' activities.

Marta loaded Rebecca down with foodstuffs from the cook's camp. They had many water gourds, beans, chicken and dried beef. No one seemed to notice anything until they were picking their way through the barrier to the human corral.

"Alto!" The word seared through Rebecca's brain like a lightning bolt. She froze and looked over at Marta for her next move.

Marta turned and looked at Dark Jesus. She hated them all, but Dark Jesus really angered her. He was officious and smart and had designs on taking over one day. He did more to run the gang than the maestro. He seemed always to be awake, never drunk, always watching, particularly Marta. She knew he hated her just as much. He hated how smart and precocious and fearless she was. Despite being more than twenty years her senior, he considered her a serious threat to his accession to the throne of evil.

"What do you want, Jesus?"

"I want to know why you are taking food to them."

"Because I was told to."

"Who told you?"

Marta looked at him, hate in her eyes. "What is this? What gives you the idea that you should ask me anything, Jesus? Go away and bother some others."

"You will tell me, now!"

"Maestro."

"Well then, you two come with me and we'll ask him again, because he has told me to keep them weak. This is not the same thing as what he told me to do."

"No need. I have a note."

Jesus laughed. This was preposterous. The Maestro was illiterate and never wrote anything down for anyone. "Hah! I would like to see such a note." He was closing in on them and Marta waited.

"Then I will show you." She reached down and began fiddling with her belt. The man was towering over her now, just inches from them. He stood, resolute, arms crossed. He scared Rebecca. He was big and lean and very dark, with black eyes, not brown, black and deadly and hate-filled. The eyes of a giant shark, like the one she'd seen on the pier brought in by fishermen in San Francisco with her momma and Abuelita.

He tapped his foot, impatient with the girl. He looked over at Rebecca laden with all

183

the food and drink. He didn't see Marta pull the miniature six shooter from her holster, did not have time to unfold his sinewy arms and pull his own piece or wrestle the one from the girl. A tiny hole appeared, as if by magic, from between his mean black eyes. He stood for a moment as the lead slug worked its magic on his gray cells. His body reacted and shut down. Jesus fell forward, stone dead.

Marta looked down at him, pleased with what she'd done. The little lead ball exited the back of Dark Jesus' skull and left a large crater. She remembered her task and looked at Rebecca who'd gone totally white. "Come on." She moved through the thorn bush barricade and began handing the food to the people.

"You must eat and drink quickly." She spoke to them with authority and looked at Rebecca. "Get the gourds back and make certain they hide any remnants of the food. I'll be back."

The red-haired lady was not hungry. She drank some water and helped Rebecca distribute the food. She made certain the children ate and drank. She had more energy from the meal she'd been given earlier in the day. She looked at Rebecca and gave her a weak smile. She managed a feeble thank you and patted the girl on the cheek. Rebecca blushed and momentarily forgot about Jesus.

Marta worked quickly. She pulled Jesus' corpse into a shallow depression, not far from where he lay. He was heavy and she just managed to roll him out of view. She looked at his stupid face and gave it a quick squeeze. She whispered into his ear, "See you in hell, Jesus."

Mother Superior rode behind Chica. The cigar smoke reminded the old nun of her father as he used to smoke a cigar every night before bed. She hadn't thought of that for fifty years.

Every now and again the pretty Mexican woman would dismount and wander into some brush carrying one of the sacks she'd gotten from Uncle Alejandro. She'd return with the bag closed securely with a string. The nun didn't know what the young woman was up to or what she had in mind.

They finally stopped when they were about ten miles from the bandit camp. She realized that Chica planned to stay here through the night. She made a small fire and prepared a meal while Chica foraged with her little sacks. She returned with firewood, a rabbit and a prairie chicken.

They ate in silence for a while.

"What shall we do next, my child?"

Chica lit another cigar. "No questions, Madre." Chica looked at the old woman. She was very tough and Chica was pleased to have her. Chica decided to share some of her plan. "This bastard Sombrero del Oro, he is evil, you know."

"Yes."

"He is also very afraid of God and Jesus and all the saints. I know this, I have heard many times that he is very, how do you say . . . believe in magic things."

"Superstitious."

"Sí, supersticioso."

Chica poked a stick into their little fire. "And his men are the same. They have been with the old bastard too long. Their evil ways have made them scared of God and of going to hell."

"I see." The old woman was beginning to understand.

"It is a new century." Chica continued. "And there are many things going around about the end of the world. I have read in the papers. And this is going to be very much on the Gold Hat's mind. And, how do you say, the sun going dark today . . ."

"Eclipse."

"Sí, eclipse. This will scare all hell out of

the old man." Chica thought hard about the eclipse. "Do you think, Madre, that God is helping us?"

"I don't know, my child."

"It is very strange, no, that we need to scare hell out of Gold Hat, and at the same time we have this eclipse?" She smoked hard and shrugged her shoulders, as if to answer her own question. "No matter. Tomorrow, we will meet up with them and we must say many thing to scare Gold Hat. I need your help, Madre. You need to make a profit . . ."

"Prophecy?"

"Sí, sí. Every time something happen, you must say to the Gold Hat, see, that is a prophecy, the end of the world is near and all the bad people will go to hell."

She was pleased with herself and the old nun was pleased to see the pretty woman smile a little.

Chica built up the fire to afford some good light. She stripped the horses and sent them on their way. She told them to go home. They wandered off into the night. She hid her rifle and her cowboy outfit and feed sacks in a crevice in a rock wall and donned her nun's costume. She checked the cut down shotgun to make certain it would fit properly under her habit. She also had her big knife and a six shooter.

She got the old nun to apply the makeup around her eyes. When this was complete, she checked the rack on the burro, now heavily laden with benign traps, the traps of a couple of nuns on a pilgrimage. She was ready.

Sombrero del Oro got as drunk as he could, but the pain was still unbearable. He was completely miserable and the eclipse of the sun had put him into a state of extreme anxiety.

It was big news in the rest of the world; all the scientists were excited about it. It was in the newspapers and was going to be a big event throughout this part of the world, but Sombrero del Oro did not care to know of scientific things. He was so caught up in his evil little world that he knew only the barest bit about the eclipse; it was especially foreboding to him. He was a stupid and superstitious man.

He did not like this year of nineteen-hundred. It was a bad year, a new century, a new millennium, and he did not like it one bit. There had been talk of the coming of Christ, or the end of the world and it made him very afraid. His nightmares were worse than ever and he was perpetually exhausted. His head pounded all the time. Now he was wounded and in pain, and many of the men were jumpy. Half of his captives were dead and his prize was losing her luster very quickly. His mind wandered. He wondered why he was here. Why did he go to the US and rob the train? Everything was fine at his fort. He could have stayed there, comfortably, for the rest of his days.

He could not understand why so many of his offspring were sick, or why the women were not bearing children so well. He was fornicating nearly every day, yet there were no good offspring.

Something was amiss and he was sure that he needed more breeding stock. It was the way with horses and cattle and it must be the way with humans. The clown man was not helping matters, either.

He looked over at his assistant who was now occupied with freshening up the colors around his eyes. The bandit boss suddenly wanted to shoot the man through the head, but the pain in his leg kept him in check. He pressed himself against his cot and drifted into a light slumber.

The clown man finished and looked over at his boss, doubtfully. He didn't want the old man to die, not because he loved or cared for him, but because he would likely not live the day out once the maestro was gone.

He was pleased that the maestro had been shot, though. He saw that the girl was falling out of favor. He wanted her for himself so badly that the other children meant nothing to him.

Every chance he got, he asked Gold Hat for the girl. "Just a little taste, a little slice." He would not hurt her badly, she would still be good for breeding in a few years.

Finally, Gold Hat stopped saying no and this made the clown man very happy. He did not say yes, but at least he stopped saying no. He knew that was the first step. Now he only had to come up with something, some item to negotiate, and she would be his.

He was so excited at the prospect that he had to look in on the girl, now sleeping soundly in the room next to his, only a thin curtain of canvas between them. She was marvelous. She had not yet been spoilt by any vestiges of womanhood. She had no breasts and he imagined she had not gotten her feathers, yet. It was almost too much to bear.

He lay back on his cot and thought the thing through. He set the stage in his mind; what would he wear? What would she wear? How would he present himself to her?

They were always afraid at first, but then

they learned to love him, learned to enjoy his offerings. They always did this. Even when they cried and tried to get away, he knew that secretly they loved it, they loved him and he was glad to know this. Finally, his racing mind slowed and he drifted off to sleep.

Next day, Del Oro got a late start. He felt like hell. Now his head hurt with a hangover, as much as his buttocks. At least the bleeding had stopped but he could only lie on his right side. The entire left side of his body was dark purple and the pain ran all the way down to his toes. A cot had been fashioned on a wagon so that he could be transported without riding a horse. That wasn't an option now.

By midday, they stumbled upon an odd sight. Two nuns and a burro were heading south. He did not like this one bit. Nuns in the desert, another bad omen. How many more could there be?

"Whore of Jesus, what are you doing out here?"

The old nun looked up at him, her younger companion, face shrouded, kept her eyes to the ground. She could only be considered younger by her posture. She did not dare look at the bandits.

"We are going on to San Cristobal, to pay homage there."

"Homage to what, whore?"

"The miracle. The statue of the virgin cried tears of blood there, on the first day of the new millennium."

The young nun grinned behind her veil, the Madre's explanation was completely unexpected. "And the eclipse of the sun. We are going there to make an offering and to prepare."

"Prepare?" The old man looked at his men. "Prepare for what?"

The old nun shrugged. "No one knows. The end of time, the coming of Christ, the coming of Satan. The four riders of the apocalypse? We do not know."

The young one whispered something into the old nun's ear and the old one nodded.

"What, what did the bitch say?"

The old nun crossed herself and spoke to the ground, "The sun will be turned to darkness and the moon to blood before the coming of the great and dreadful day of the Lord."

The hair stood up on the old man's neck and he shivered. "You will pay homage to us, old whore. You and that scrawny thing you are with. Why is her face covered?"

"She is disfigured."

Several of the bandits surrounded them. They rifled through the burro's pack to look for anything of value. They grabbed the women by the hands to look for jewelry. The nuns wore pewter rings and, as these had no value, they were allowed to keep them. One of the bandits took the burro and trotted away.

They motioned for the nuns to climb on the maestro's wagon. One looked at the young nun and ran his hands across her breasts. He stopped abruptly when he saw the scars around her eyes and called out to his boss, "Es una leprosa."

A gasp went up in unison and she was suddenly ejected from the cart. The old nun held up a hand. "She is no longer a carrier. She's been cured. She is maimed, but cured. You will not catch anything from her."

The old man thought for a moment. He considered shooting the young one. He became distracted and after some conversation they could not hear, decided to let her back on the wagon. They rode like this all afternoon.

During a brief stop the old nun offered to look at the maestro's wounds. He allowed it. She applied a poultice from her pack which relieved the bandit's pain. They were going to be useful, these two.

As the nuns rode they listened to the clown man speak incessantly about the captive girl. He would plead, then bargain, then negotiate, then whine. Finally the maestro had had enough. The clown man had worn him down and he finally relented.

The fat bandit boss looked on at the clown man in disdain. He held up a chubby index finger and looked the man in the eye. "Just once, and there better be no permanent harm."

The clown man rejoiced, his face flushed red with excitement. "Not any harm, maestro, not any harm."

Rebecca was oblivious to this scheming. Ever since she'd taught Marta to tat, the two were inseparable. Marta selected a small pony from the remuda and found a saddle that fit properly. They rode together, back from the maestro's caravan. The transformation was remarkable. Marta acted like a little girl. She chatted with Rebecca about little girl things. She did not smoke. They played with their hair and Rebecca patiently pulled the knots out of Marta's tatting when she blundered. Rebecca was so distracted by all this that her mind momentarily let her forget about her predicament for a little while as they rode along.

When they finally stopped for the evening, the girls eventually caught up and they waited near a campfire for the marquee tent to be erected. The two nuns busily worked with the others. Rebecca looked at them and asked Marta about them, who they were and when had they arrived. Marta shrugged and worked at her tatting.

The nuns were a strange addition to the company of miscreants. The old one was stout and worked quickly and efficiently. The young one was more sullen. She looked about often and Rebecca would now and again catch her looking her way. Something about her eyes was familiar. Something about the way she moved reminded her of her mother, but that was preposterous as the nun was worn, haggard and she could see the ugly scarring around her eyes. There was nothing about her to suggest any relationship or connection to her mother.

The nuns served the maestro, the clown man and the little girls. A special drink was given to Rebecca. She did not like it as it burned her throat. She put it aside and the clown man ordered the scarred nun to make Rebecca drink it. She complied.

The little sandy-haired boy had been watching from a distance. He'd escaped and now he waited on the periphery of the camp. He didn't know what else to do. The desert was huge all around him. He had no provisions or good shoes or a hat to keep the sun off.

He found some water along the way and drank as much as his stomach would hold as he had no canteen or a way to save any. He was hungry and thought half a dozen times about surrendering, coming into the camp. At least maybe he'd get a little food and he'd be with his mother. The fat man wearing the dress was motivation enough for him to not do this, however. He'd rather lie out there all alone with the snakes than be near that man again.

He saw the nuns before they were captured. They were an odd sight, out there in their dark clothes, like two little bears in the bright red-brown of the desert. He thought about asking them for help, but he was afraid. After a while, he resolved to approach them just as they'd been captured by the bandits. He was sorry now; he could have, should have warned them. It was almost as if they'd wanted to be captured.

He remembered the small thin one. She changed the way she acted once she'd been caught. Up until then, she walked boldly, like his mother, head high. When she was captured, she sort of deflated, as if her neck became fused at a downward angle. He remembered glimpsing her terrible face, around the eyes. She was hideously disfigured and he could only image what the rest of her face looked like behind the veil.

Now they were captured and he was completely without hope.

He waited for nightfall and slipped in to eat the bits left in the tin plates of the many bandits. They ate sloppily and few ever finished their plates. Some even left meat on the bones that they'd discard onto the sandy desert floor. He chewed them clean. The sand ground against his teeth and made his gums bleed, but it was at least something and he was glad for it.

All the time he thought of his mother. She looked worse every day. She was cross with him almost all the time, but he still loved her and cared very much for her. He knew that the bad men did the things to her that the fat man in the dress did to him, except many times over. He wished he could go and find her, but the corral where the captives were kept was on the other side of the camp and the ground was uneven. It was very dark and he suddenly became afraid.

He finished his scavenging quickly and was suddenly overtaken with terrible cramps. He lay in a crouch for a while and they passed.

After his meal he crawled away; away from the light of the fires and outside the perimeter of the guards' posts. The bad men didn't wander after dark and he was safe, hunkered down among some brush. He'd sleep there until morning.

Chica was becoming nervous. She had so much to do and so little time left. Now she had to worry about getting back to Rebecca's little room before the clown man made his move. He would not touch her child. The traps she had buried were not far away, as the gang made little progress due to the maestro's wound and the uneven terrain, but it would be impossible to ride, find them, dig them up and be back in enough time. She disappeared as the old bandits returned to the campfire.

The night was cooling off and it felt good for the old man to sit by the fire for a while. The maestro did not want to be in the tent when the clown man had his way with the girl. He still expected to breed her in a few years and the thought of the old fool with her made him feel bad.

The nuns didn't help either. This was all too much for his addled brain to bear. The eclipse and now the story by the old nun about the statue crying blood made the hair stand up on his neck again. He hated the hold his old faith had on him. He'd done his best to blot it out. He knew he was evil and didn't much care but the idea of the second coming of Christ gave him significant anxiety. He feared going to sleep, feared the kind of nightmares he was sure to have, and now his leg and buttocks were hurting badly. He swilled down great gulps of mescal. Soon he would have to sleep but the mescal would hopefully blot out the dreams.

Chica wandered about the camp, oblivious to the gang. They were settling in for the night and most of them were already drunk. She found all the items that she needed, along with a couple of feed bags and headed into the desert.

Chapter XII:
Gentle Will Panks

Will Panks crushed out a cigarette and moved from the veranda to the bedroom of the hotel he and the other Americans were occupying. The town was abuzz, excited about the gallant Americanos and the rurales and the Mexican Cossack preparing to finally put an end to the infamous Sombrero del Oro.

There was a certain promise now that the gringos were there, as if someone was finally going to actually do something. Kosterlitzky was an effective enforcer, but oftentimes uneven: Uneven in the consistency of his enforcement, uneven in meting out punishment, uneven in how and in whom he brought to justice. Everyone feared him, many liked him, many hated him, but now, with the Americanos and the refined white lady and the famous Arizona Rangers and Alejandro del Toro's fine vaqueros, it seemed that the end of the evil was near.

They prepared a feast, every person in town and from miles around would be there. It would likely be at least as grand as the Day of the Dead commemoration.

The Americanos accepted it, but were in no mood to celebrate. The anxiety over little Rebecca and Chica still out there in the unknown, still with the despicable Sombrero del Oro, kept them from partaking of the celebration.

Alice Walsh could not begrudge the town people the happiness they were sharing. They could not be concerned about one captive, they only knew that the beast was to be slain, soon, and it was cause for celebration.

She conferred with the mayor of the town and offered funds to cover the costs of the celebration. He and the elders would have none of it, so she offered the money to the town church, enough to pay for the bell they'd been saving to replace, they still did not have enough after more than twenty years. She'd given them sufficient funds to buy ten.

She also had taken it upon herself to hire men to prepare fireworks and she asked for five times the number used in the greatest celebration in the town's history.

Will Panks was just drifting off for a midday siesta when he heard the little war party in the next room. It renewed his anxiety and he could not sleep. He got up, didn't really know why, but he wanted to be with the men.

Kosterlitzky, Dick, and Arvel where planning their strategy. Billy stood over Arvel, pulling at his arms, continuing to help him along his road to recovery. Arvel had been gaining strength every day and could manage a pretty good shuffle. He would no longer need to be tied onto Tammy. He could now open and close his right fist. He felt good.

Dan George motioned for Will to join them in the smoky war room. They had a map laid out before them and had just finished up their plan of attack. They settled down and began to work on a bottle of cognac. Arvel smiled at the old prospector as he walked in and sat down.

"Will, you look like you've got the weight of the world on your shoulders." He poured a big glass for Will who upended it and finished it in one gulp. He'd been unnerved at the shooting of the Dutchman, and as they got closer to making their attack on the fort, his anxiety was beginning to overwhelm him.

"Just not used to all this, Arvel. I'm not a

warrior."

Arvel grinned, not so crookedly as when he'd first seen Will on the trail. Or was it just the way Will saw Arvel now, after what he'd done to the Dutchman? Will had heard all the stories about Arvel, but thought more than half fabricated, more myth than legend. No one so nice, and kind, and gentle could ever have done one fifth of what the stories claimed. He sat back in his chair and worked on another cognac. It seemed like being drunk was the only thing that helped him cope these past couple of days. He studied the men around the table and found himself suddenly talking without really thinking about what he was saying.

"What makes you fellows so sure we can do all this?"

Arvel sensed the tension in his old friend's voice. "What's eating you, Will?" He leaned forward, pressed his hand against Billy's chest as the aborigine leaned against Arvel's hand, stretching the tendons.

"Nothing, Arvel, . . . how do you fellows do it?" He looked at Arvel, then to Dick and Kosterlitzky.

"Do what, old friend, do what?"

"Kill."

Arvel smiled a sly smile. "Well, it ain't like we go around killing for the fun of it, Will."

"You do." Dick interjected as he blew smoke in Arvel's direction.

"Do not." His tone made him sound like a squabbling brother as he massaged his wrist after Billy had finished stretching him. "I never enjoyed killing anyone."

"Except the Dunstable brothers."

"Yeah, well, I really only, actually we, really only killed one of them, the other was killed by old Ben Johnson, remember, when the kid wouldn't surrender."

"You enjoyed killing that one."

"Okay, well, yes." Arvel grinned.

"And the killers of the Knudsens. You enjoyed shootin' all them."

"Yeah, well," Arvel looked for a cigarette and handed one to Billy, lit them both off of one match. "You've got to admit, they were some pretty bad hombres, and anyway, I didn't kill all of them. The boys in the posse got a least two of 'em."

"And that gimpy deputy."

Arvel sat up straight in the chair, "Now, I never did kill him, I just winged him in the toe. Chica was the one who killed him, Dick, don't be putting the blood of folks on my hands that weren't mine."

"And that rapist down in Bisbee and that fellow who'd shot all those Apaches on the reservation, and then there was that whole group . . ."

Arvel cut him off, "All right, all right, Dick. Jesus, you make me out a regular U.S. Grant, or old William Tecumseh Sherman. My God, never killed anyone who didn't need it. And," he waved his finger at Dick, "you can't count rapists, they don't count. They always get it, no matter what. That's a matter of principle. Whether I enjoy killing a rapist or not is inconsequential."

Dan George spoke through his teeth, automatically, "Neca eos omnes. Deus suos agnoscet."

Kosterlitzky laughed and Will looked on, not understanding what the Indian had said.

Arvel translated for him. "Kill them all. God will know His own." Dick and Dan got to him, and he grinned broadly. It wasn't easy to get Arvel, but they got him. Arvel smiled sheepishly.

Will was a little agitated. "How do you square it?"

"Square what?"

"Judge, jury, executioner, all rolled into one. And then you sit there and laugh about it."

"Well, Will, we all are out alone quite a bit," he nodded to Kosterlitzky who was thoroughly enjoying the conversation now. "The colonel will tell you, these are some pretty bad hombres, and we don't have the luxury of gallivanting all over hell's half acre, trying to get them to a proper jail."

"Anyway," Dick leaned forward and grabbed one of Arvel's cigarettes from its pack, "We aren't judges or juries or executioners. Those folks are looking to punish the guilty. We don't kill to punish."

"Oh, really?" Will was incredulous at the men's cavalier attitude for their actions. "Then why do you kill 'em?"

"We kill 'em so they can't do what they've done to poor folks ever again."

"Yep, Dick's right, absolutely right. Like that one, remember, that case in Texas? The rangers brought the bastard in and he ended up killing two of the deputies guarding him. They ended up shooting him anyway, before he could even be tried. So, why not just go ahead and shoot him or hang him on the spot, save everyone a lot of trouble, save the cost to the government, ensure that they don't kill or rape or torture or whatever black-hearted nonsense they've got on their minds."

Kosterlitzky added his two cents, "Mr. Panks, there is also the issue of a kind of sentinel effect." Will looked at the Russian, questioningly. The colonel continued. "It is a great demotivator, when you have people like us," he waved his hand across the room, "the bad men will think twice about moving around a land that is being watched by us."

"And, what of the mistakes?"

"What mistakes, Will?" Arvel looked at Dan George who'd dozed off. This philosophical discussion bored him. He knew what motivated Arvel and Dick, and just as likely Kosterlitzky.

"When you go on and shoot a fellow who's the wrong man."

"Never have done that," Arvel smiled at Will. "It doesn't exactly take a genius to identify a man who abused a woman, or killed or molested a child. I never killed anyone for stealin' a steer or robbing a bank."

"Except that fellow over in Yuma county, remember him?" Dick interjected again, "You put a ball right between his eyes," he pointed to, then tapped the bridge of his own nose.

"Goddamn it, Dick." Arvel glared at his ranger partner, "You know I killed him 'cause he shot the clerk, not because he robbed the damned bank, and he was fixing to shoot your scrawny ass." He looked back at the miner, "Will, tell me, tell us, what's eating at you?"

The old prospector stood up abruptly, "I'm sorry, gentlemen, it's been a long journey and I'm just tired, talking nonsense. I'm in way over my head here. I think I'll go have a lie down for a while."

He walked out and left a pregnant silence in the room, too quiet for Arvel to bear.

"Hey, you boys ever hear the story of Kit Carson?"

"Jesus, man!" Dick smiled at his friend. "Not the Kit Carson story." He stood up and excused himself as well, "Colonel, if I were you, I'd break up this party before he gets started on his old worn-out Kit Carson yarn."

Arvel watched the town prepare for the evening while having a beer and a smoke on the hotel's veranda. Will showed up and sat down next to him. He slept well but was no less distracted than before his conversation with the party of men.

Arvel offered him a smoke and poured him a beer from a bottle he'd just opened. "My friend, tell me, what's on your mind?"

Will knew Arvel well enough to speak freely. "I'm no killer, Arvel. And that son of a bitch Dutchman, he just, what you did back at that place, to him, that just," he looked into his glass, as if to find the words he could not conjure to express himself. He looked into Arvel's eyes, "God damn, Arvel, I don't know. I've heard stories about you, but back there, it was like you were another man, like you're two different people."

Arvel grinned, "Hah, just two. That's pretty good. Chica says I'm at least six different men." He crushed out a smoke and lit another. This was a two cigarette type of conversation. "I'm a killer, Will, you're not. It's like you being good at finding strikes; I'm good at killing men who need it." He looked at Will to get his reaction and laughed. "Good God, man, you think I'm something. Chica makes me look like a piker."

"Seriously?" Will was aghast. He'd heard stories of Chica, but thought most were exaggerated as well.

"It's why I've left her alone, to get our little girl." He suppressed an urge to cry, breathed in deeply and felt his throat quiver. "She'll get her, and leave a whole passel of dead men in her wake, I will bet my ranch on that."

Will sat silently for a few moments, gulped his beer and poured another. "I don't have any business in all this, Arvel. I thought I did. I'm no coward . . ."

"No, you're not, you are definitely not a

coward, old friend."

"I feel a fool, swaggering around toting that dynamite, like I'm some kind of Wild Bill Hickok. I just feel the fool. And I got no business questioning you or your methods. I know you and I know Dick, and the Colonel seems a moral fellow. I'm mighty sorry running off at the mouth like that. I'm just, I don't know . . ."

"Well, I tell you what. You stick with me and my uncles, Bob and del Toro, and my mother and Kosterlitzky. I have a feeling we'll be kind of directing the attack anyway, and I'll need your expert's eye, as a miner, to help direct the artillery, and when the time comes for your dynamite, and I'm certain it will, you help me with the strategy. Can you do that?"

"Sure, Arvel, sure."

"I know you can, Will. And you know, some killing's going to come of your work, but it won't be close in . . . it won't be."

"Shootin' a man through the head at two feet with a scattergun?"

"Right, right." Arvel shifted in his chair. "And Will, get the word out to the boys, tell 'em to enjoy themselves a little tonight. I'm not in any celebrating mood, with my girls still out there, but they should enjoy this a little." He cast his eyes over the street. You could feel the energy in the air, it was going to be a big time.

Some young boys were kicking a football around the street and it landed in Arvel's lap. He laughed and grabbed the ball. He hobbled over, down onto the street and dropped the ball, kicking it with his left leg, nearly tumbling over onto the dirt street. The boys ran after it and he followed, limping as fast as his broken body would allow. Will looked on. For a man of nearly sixty, a man who'd just had a stroke, and a man who just now sat before him and told him he was a killer, he certainly didn't look the part.

CHAPTER XIII:
NEMESIS

Rebecca was so sleepy she couldn't remember going to bed, but she was in her cot and someone had removed all her clothes. She lay on top of the blanket and was hot, despite the chilly evening. A single candle burned in her small room, offering an eerie yellow pallor to the canvas walls. She fell in and out of consciousness and felt dizzy, a little sick to her stomach.

The clown man was suddenly standing over her. His hair was wet with some sort of oil. She could smell lilacs coming from his hair. He wore a robe and began to untie the closure as he approached. He abruptly stopped and looked at the young nun as she opened the tent flap.

"What the hell are you doing here?" He was angry and excited and his voice quivered as he spoke; his hands trembled as he fumbled with the robe's belt. He was in no mood to be distracted by the nun.

"I am here to help."

The clown man grinned a greasy smirk. He had a weird notion all of a sudden. What could she mean? He watched her approach and looked on at the little girl, exposed, vulnerable, beckoning him to her bed. The candlelight danced across her face, he could swear she was smiling, certain she was happy to have him share her bed, she wanted him as much as he wanted her, he was sure of it.

He didn't see the branding iron in the little nun's hand. He didn't notice it flash across his periphery as it crashed down on the side of his head. He was down, on his back, on the floor of the tent and the lithe figure was upon him. He couldn't move. He could not defend himself. He looked into the eyes of a wild creature. This was no nun!

She hissed into his ear. "I am going to kill you now, mierda."

She turned and looked at the dreamy child. "Turn over, little one. I want you to look at the wall." Rebecca complied.

The little nun hissed again. "After I kill you, mierda, I will spread your guts across the desert and the wolves will feast on them. Do you understand?" The clown man nodded briefly. "I will cut your goddamned head off so that you will walk through hell and not be able to see nothing. Do you understand, mierda?"

The clown man nodded.

The little nun yanked the belt from around the fat man's waist. She slowly and steadily wrapped it around his thick neck and then twisted it round and round the blade of her big knife, every turn sliced into the side of his face until the blood flowed into the silk robe.

The clown man turned red, then purple, almost black. His eyes bulged from their sockets, as if the belt might exert enough force to pop them out of his head. He was finally dead.

The little nun covered the dead man. She reached over, covered Rebecca with a blanket and gently rubbed her back, just between the shoulder blades, as her mother had always done to wake her in the morning.

"Wake up, Cielito."

Rebecca sat up with a start. "Mamma?"

She was dizzy and thought she would be sick. Was this just a terrible dream after all?

"Sí, sí."

Chica was crying. She tore the shroud from her face and peeled the beeswax makeup from around her eyes.

"It is you, Mamma!" She looked around

the room, still too groggy to understand. She looked down at the form on the floor. "Is he . . . dead, Mamma?"

"Sí, he is dead, Cielito."

"Oh, Mamma, I missed you so. I have been so scared. My insides are shaking all the time. Can we go home now, Mamma? I miss Daddy. Is Abuelita okay, Mamma? I want to go home."

Chica grabbed her and squeezed her as she had never done before. She loved her so. She cried into her neck. "I missed you, too, my darling. Abuelita is okay, she is good and she is waiting for you." She hugged her again. "I am so, so sorry I did not save you sooner. I am so, so sorry. Please forgive me."

Rebecca had never seen her mother cry. She patted her on the back. "It's okay, Mamma. I never thought you didn't do your best. I always knew that you'd find me. Can we go now?"

Chica regained her composure. "Not yet, my darling. Not yet. But soon. I need you to make a little trick on the bandits. Can you do this for me?"

"Yes, Mamma." She was drifting. The drink was too much for her little body and the emotion of seeing her mother accelerated the effect it had on her small form. "What must I do?"

She began to shiver and Chica pulled an extra blanket over her. Rebecca looked down at the dead man. "He was going to breed me, like a bull does a cow, Mamma. The other one, the one called maestro, says I am to be his wife, Mamma. I don't want to do this."

"No, darling, no! This will never be done, you understand? This will never happen, but I cannot take you from here now, there are too many and we will be caught if we leave now." She pressed her cheek against Rebecca's forehead. "Here is what you must do."

The little nun approached Marta as the girl sat close to the dying fire, smoking the last of a cigarette and working on her tatting. She was alone. She'd gotten a bad knot and was trying to work it out. She looked absurd; the little girl bent over her lace with a cigarette dangling from her lips. This was a thoroughly corrupt place.

Marta liked the little nun. The men were afraid of her. They said she was a leper. She did not know what a leper was but was glad to see the men afraid. She liked it when the men looked stupid or foolish or afraid and this nun's making them this way pleased her. The little nun never looked up from the ground and spoke into her chest in a tiny, afraid voice. This amused Marta too.

"Where is the one named Jesus?" the little nun spoke into her chest.

"The fat one or the thin one or the tall one or the short one, or the very ugly one who stinks?"

The little nun was not certain which to choose. "The maestro said he was to guard the remuda."

Marta breathed her smoke and her answer at the little nun. "That's the thin one." She pointed with her cigarette butt, "He is over there, in the blue vest."

"Gracias."

Marta went back to working on her tatting as the nun approached the thin Jesus. The group of men saw her and gestured for her to stop. "What do you want, bitch?"

"The maestro said that I was to tell Jesus to guard the remuda tonight."

The men laughed at Jesus, who looked on forlornly. It would have been better for him to know this sooner, as he'd have gotten a little sleep and not had so much to drink. He looked at the nun and grunted, pulled himself up from his bed at the campfire, gathered up his saddle and blanket, and prepared for a long night.

■ ■ ■ ■

In another hour, all was quiet. The little nun surveyed the camp. She walked freely among the sleeping bandits and captives. She moved out to the perimeter and looked at Jesus and the remuda, then to the northern border, then to the south to check the men guarding those places.

She went back to the tent and moved Rebecca into the clown man's little room. She placed her on his cot and covered her. She kissed her a few times before she pulled herself away. Rebecca did not wake.

Chica went back to the room where the clown man lay. She needed to arrange his corpse. She removed the blanket she'd used to cover him and folded the collar and lapels of his robe up high on his neck to hide the marks left by her makeshift garrote. She didn't worry about the wound on his head and face, it would appear that he'd had a fit of some kind and fell over. It would look like he had died of natural causes, the excitement over his own depravity too much for him to withstand.

Just before two in the morning, she had everything prepared and moved on to her next chore.

■ ■ ■ ■

Jesus sat on his horse in front of the remuda. He dozed and woke, dozed and woke. To hell with the maestro. If he didn't give enough notice so that the guard could have gotten some rest then the old bastard bandit boss would just have to accept the fact that he'd have a sleeping guard.

He thought he heard something behind him and, half asleep, turned to see the figure of a woman in the shadows. He blinked to clear his vision and looked again. He never saw this one before. He blinked again. He couldn't believe his luck. She was wearing a blanket wrapped around her body, over her shoulders, and when she reached out to entice him, it fell to the ground, revealing a beautiful, ample form: unencumbered, natural, seductive, irresistible, naked as the day she was born. She had beautiful raven tresses and was so clean. She looked as though she'd just stepped out of an opulent California hotel.

He'd seen and abused all the attractive captives, so he was certain he'd not had this one before. He sat, dumfounded, and she held out a hand, beckoning him off his horse.

Quickly, he hobbled his mount. She turned and began walking into the desert, up a hill that overlooked the encampment. He had to jog to catch her. She had gone some distance and, like a dog after a bitch in heat, he could think of nothing else.

Marta sat and smoked close to the maestro as he slept, his mouth agape. She inhaled two long drags, filling her lungs to capacity and blew smoke directly into his mouth and up his nose. He woke gagging and sputtering. He sat up with a start.

"You might want to get up now." She looked at him with disdain and loathing in her eyes. "Your asshole is dead."

The maestro sat up straighter and looked around the room, as if he'd awakened in an alien place. "What are you on about, child?"

She hated it when he called her child. "The girl was too much for him last night. He's dead."

She motioned with her head toward the little room on the other side of the canvas wall. "In there, on the floor. Looks like his heart went bad."

He had started to comprehend what she said when a minion rushed in. "Maestro, up on the hill," the man was sheet white. He had difficulty forming his words. "Up, up on the hill," he pointed repeatedly.

The old man and Marta made it to the hilltop together. The maestro had to be carried on a litter because his leg had swelled, bloated like an eggplant that had lain too long in the sun. It was beginning to turn from purple to black. He could not bear to put any weight on it.

"Jesus!" Marta exclaimed through a cloud of smoke.

"I told you to never speak of Him!" The old man looked on at her and then at the horrible sight laid out before them.

"Idiot! It is Jesus. Look. The one in the middle."

Marta was correct. Jesus sat, arms outstretched in mock crucifixion. He'd been dead several hours and looked like a porcelain recreation of Jesus. He looked skyward and he was uninjured except for the stigmata. Someone, or something, had pierced his hands and feet. There was a spear wound under his right breast. He wore a crown of mesquite thorns and dried blood pasted his curly black hair tightly to his head. More blood had streamed over his forehead and into his eyes and onto his cheeks. He was naked except for a white cloth covering his loins, just as they'd all seen in the churches all their lives; hundreds, thousands of times, on the statues and various paintings of the crucified Christ.

These wounds were not fatal, yet Jesus was as dead as a clay pot.

On either side of Jesus lay two other guards, arranged so that their feet were touching, creating the shape of a cross, with Jesus at the top and his two companions forming each arm. They were dead, too, and were covered by blankets, up to their necks.

The Maestro began to call out in considerable anxiety, "Get the whore nuns, now!"

The nuns were summoned and soon stood beside Gold Hat. Both nuns dropped to their knees and crossed themselves and in unison spoke, "In nomine Patris, et Filii, et Spiritus Sancti." They prayed desperately in a tongue that the maestro didn't understand.

"Stop that!" The old man screamed. "Get up!" He pointed his finger at them. "You did this!"

Marta interrupted. "They did no such thing. I was with them all night. They didn't do anything, you fool."

He looked at her stupidly. "What does it mean?"

He noticed some movement under the blankets. The two corpses were moving. The maestro began shaking, his eyes darting around. He was fully terrified. "What does this mean?"

Marta approached the corpses and pulled back the blankets. The men's abdomens had been slit from sternum to pelvis, hollowed out and emptied of their contents. As she removed the covers, scorpions began to creep out of the abdomen of one and juvenile rattlers from the other, as if the two bandits were birthing the lowly creatures.

The old nun crossed herself again and began speaking as if she were reading, "Look! I have given you the authority to trample on snakes and scorpions and to destroy all the enemy's power, and nothing will ever hurt you." She began to pray.

Marta looked on at the two dead men. She stepped to the side so as to allow the scorpions and snakes to escape unencumbered. She pulled something from the mouth of the corpse closest to her. It was a piece of paper and on it was writing in a language she did not understand. She handed it to the old man. He looked at it and handed it to the nun. She read it aloud.

"The worst is yet to come."

An audible groan rose from amongst the group of bandits, who had by now come out in full force. The old nun looked at her companion and crossed herself again. "It has begun."

"What, what has begun, you whore of Jesus, you stupid bitch, what has begun?" The old man was completely beside himself, overcome with panic.

The old woman looked at him solemnly and waved her hands in the air. "The day of days, the end of time, the apocalypse."

She looked at the other nun who was praying and staring at the ground.

Little by little, the bandits began to leave. They were finished. The old maestro called for them to stop, to come back. He pulled his six shooter and tried to aim it at one of the nearest bandits. Two others came up behind him and grabbed the gun from his hand. Like a spoilt child, he was frustrated and furious at losing his power. There was nothing he could do.

The ones who'd carried him up the hill now grabbed him under his arms and unceremoniously dragged him back down to the camp, his putrefied leg bouncing over rocks and debris, leaving a little furrow in the patches of soft ground. He cursed them and cried out in agony and fury but no one paid him any attention. They plopped him down on his cot in the marquee tent and quickly walked out. He was all alone. There was no one to help him.

The bandits cleared out and now the nuns could attend to the captives. They were a pathetic bunch, the ones who'd survived. The gang had started out with thirty captives, including Rebecca, and now there were fewer than ten, a couple more children than women. Marta was animated and began to take over. She was a natural leader and had a good heart, in spite of being deprived of a proper upbringing.

Once the captives had been fed and given water to drink, they could understand that they were free and safe. They were elated. They hugged each other and asked the nuns to perform a prayer service to celebrate their freedom. Everyone was happy.

Rebecca stood by the young nun. She wasn't sure of her mamma's plan and didn't dare give her away. She asked Marta what happened on the hill and before the little bandit could open her mouth, she was firmly shushed by the diminutive nun.

Marta looked her in the eye and decided that the little nun had changed and that she was not so timid anymore. She deemed it better not to question or oppose her.

After the service, the little nun sauntered

away from the celebration and slipped between the canvas flaps of the tent. The old man was sleeping. She lit a candle and put it near the maestro's face. She sat close, staring at him until he awoke with a start.

He sat up quickly. "What's this?" He coughed and gagged and spit on the ground at the nun's feet, looking at her with hate in his eyes. "Ah, the younger one of Jesus' whores. What are you doing, bitch? Fetch me some water and something to eat."

"Go to hell."

The old man looked incredulous. "Such words from a nun?"

She began a transformation before his eyes. She pulled back the veil, then the garment covering her head. She grabbed at the damaged skin around her eyes and peeled it away. He gasped and could not understand.

She wrung out a wet rag and rubbed her face, then stood up and removed the rest of her habit, revealing a gunbelt with six shooter and a big vaquero knife. She shook her head until her beautiful black hair was released and fell around her shoulders.

"Do you know me, mierda?"

"No."

"I am the one sent by God to kill you, mierda. I am not a nun."

"Mamma?" They both turned to see the

little girl looking through the tent flap at them.

"Go on out, Cielito. Go help with the people, I will be out soon."

"Come out now, Mamma. Leave him alone. He is a mean old man and he just needs to pray and tell God he's sorry and maybe when he dies he'll get to heaven."

Rebecca saw her mother stiffen, knew her mother's body language, was well aware of her resolution and tenacity.

"Mamma, please, come away."

Chica exhaled through pursed lips, she looked at the dying man. "Perhaps it is best." She leaned a little closer to the old man, whispered into his ear so that Rebecca could not hear.

"You know that smell, mierda? Your leg, it is mortified."

She smiled. "I did that to you, mierda. I shot you in the ass when the Indian was trying to give you so many riches. Now, you have nothing but a rotten leg and a hot tent in the middle of nowhere. You have nothing, mierda, and it is all because of me. You tried to take all that is dear to me, mierda. You tried to take my little girl, but I have taken everything from you. And now, we will leave you to rot, to die slowly. But before we do, I will go out and recapture those scorpions and snakes so that you will not be alone in your bed. You understand, mierda?"

The old man looked dazed, as if he were in some otherworldly place.

"Wake up, mierda, wake up." She squeezed his fat sweaty cheeks and he came to his senses. He began to breathe with difficulty.

Chica stood up slowly. "Don' worry, mierda, I'll be back with some friends." She walked out of the tent, her arm around her little girl.

Marta looked at the transformed woman not at all surprised. "I knew you were no nun."

"Marta, this is my mamma. She came to get me."

Chica extended her hand and took Marta's cigarette from between the girl's fingers. She took a long drag and blew smoke into the air. "Thank you for helping us, Marta." She snuffed the cigarette out with her toe. "No more smoking for you, little one."

The tiny bandit's eyes widened. She took a deep breath, "I, I . . . yes ma'am."

Chapter XIV:
Fiesta

Colonel Kosterlitzky sat while Arvel got ready to shave. He liked all the Americanos, but he liked Arvel best. Arvel and his mother had the old world about them and they reminded him of the family he'd left so many years ago in Russia, when he deserted from the navy and eventually made Mexico his adopted home.

Billy was sleeping and Arvel went about preparing on his own. He didn't want to wake his friend. A woman appeared before him. She was so strange looking, like a cross between a priestess and a gypsy and Arvel nodded to her and gave her a crooked smile. He looked on at Kosterlitzky for an explanation.

The colonel grinned. "Ah, our resident corandera has learned that you need medical attention, Captain."

The woman looked on, proud, chin forward. She was a beautiful old woman, her long hair braided around the crown of her head with little bits of ribbon and string interwoven. Billy Livingston woke at the sound of the healer. He watched Arvel who gave him a little wink. Billy relaxed and let the old lady perform her service.

She worked quickly, all the while performing incantations and various symbolic gestures. In short order, Arvel's head was bound around with a white band of cloth. Protruding from this, over each temple was a pointed leaf. She gave him a charm and was soon gone. She would check on him the next day.

Arvel looked at her handiwork in his shaving mirror. "How do I look?"

Billy Livingston looked on at Kosterlitzky and gave a little grunt. "Like a deranged Caesar."

"Well, I feel better all ready. Might have to fire you." He smiled back at his reflection. "You never say any nice prayers over me."

He went back to his shaving as Billy turned over to finish his nap. Arvel took care not to get shaving soap on his leaves. He was getting good at shaving with his left hand, even though he could have probably gotten away with using his right by now.

He had a good bit of strength back in the

right side of his body, thanks to Billy Livingston. He looked at Kosterlitzky's reflection in the shaving mirror and spoke into it. "Is Gold Hat's fort anywhere near as formidable as Baluarte de Santiago, Colonel?"

He waited for the man's response and was interrupted by one of Kosterlitzky's sergeants who whispered into the colonel's ear. Arvel waited for him to finish.

In short order, a scrawny and disheveled bandit was brought into the room. Kosterlitzky addressed Arvel. "This is one of Del Oro's men. He was captured a few miles out of town. I thought you'd like to hear what he has to say."

He nodded to the sergeant who recounted the bandit's report.

"This man was found wandering in a panic. He says Sombrero del Oro's camp was attacked by something."

Arvel looked on with great interest, then at Billy who'd by now given up on his siesta. "What does he mean, something?"

The sergeant looked at the man and gave him a command. They spoke quickly, the man was highly agitated. "Something! Angels from heaven, demons from hell, no one could tell."

"How were they attacked?"

"One of the men was crucified, two others killed in some way, no one knows, and snakes and scorpions ran out of their bodies." The man crossed himself.

"Did you see a little girl, blue eyes, black hair, about eight years old?" Arvel got up, stood over the man with his soapy razor in hand, threatening, assuring the man that he should not lie.

"Sí, sí. She was there."

"Is she all right?"

"Sí. She is okay. She was left with two nuns."

"What of Sombrero del Oro?"

The bandit made a little sound, like whistling through his teeth, he shrugged, "Probably dead. His leg was black and rotten. We left him in the desert to fend for himself. He cannot be still alive."

Arvel rushed from the room, found his Uncle Bob and del Toro. "Chica's got her. Chica's got her!"

He was so happy he couldn't stop crying and Billy Livingston had to help steady him as he fairly danced about the room. He ran from place to place, summoning Dick, then Dan and Will and the cowboys and vaqueros. The excitement was contagious and it seemed the whole town had, at the same moment, learned of his good fortune.

Everyone came to see him. Everyone

heard the rumors of the event, the miracle at the camp. Many believed it was a divine intervention and were happy. Finally, something was being done about the demon who'd terrorized them these many years.

Ultimately, he burned himself out and lay exhausted and happy in his room. He suddenly realized that he'd not told his mother and, as if his thoughts of her conjured her up, she was standing by his bed.

"Oh, Mother." He reached out for her, much like a babe reaches from the crib to be picked up and held. She sat next to him and kissed him gently on the cheek.

"She did it, my boy." Alice Walsh was beaming. She never doubted Chica, but was no less overwhelmed by the news.

Arvel read her mind. "Never doubted her for a moment."

He was calm now. He sat up next to her and finally looked her over carefully. She was a tough old gal. He was so proud of her, proud of the two best women in his life.

"I guess Dad's spinning in his grave."

She became a little tense at her son's mention of the love of her life. "Don't say that about your father, Arvel."

He saw it, heard it in her voice and he was immediately sorry. "You're right."

Alice thought it was finally a good time to set things right about the memory of Arvel's father. She walked over to the corner of the room, picked up a chair and placed it next to the bed. She sat down and looked at the broken man lying beside her.

"Your father was always so proud of you and you never saw it, my boy."

Arvel looked up and gave her a hesitant grin.

Alice continued. "You never knew your father the way I knew him. That's not your fault. Your father was a very private and austere man. Showing emotion was not in his nature. He used to tell me how pleased he was that you could be so free with your emotions. He said that you, thankfully, got your kindness from me."

"I never knew."

"Your father didn't have money, Arvel. You didn't know that, either. He came up from humble beginnings and he kept that a closely guarded secret. He was not necessarily ashamed of coming up from nothing — I think he was actually proud of being self-made — but he didn't want others to know anything about him. I guess that was the lawyer in him. He never wanted anyone to have anything they could perhaps use against him. It was my family with the pedigree, for all that it matters, and it was my family with all the money."

"How did that go with your parents, Mother?"

"Not at all badly, Arvel. Your grandfather, my father, God bless him, lived what he preached. He was a good and kind soul and he didn't push us, my sisters or me, to marry for social or financial gain. He saw that I loved your father and he saw a good man in your father; a hardworking, proud and ambitious man, and he knew that your father would make me happy. He gave us his blessing. Oh, Arvel, I wish he had lived long enough for you to know him. He was a fine fellow, my father."

"I remember the stories, Mother. I could tell how much you loved him from all the stories. But Dad, he always seemed so angry at everything I did, or didn't do."

Alice smiled. "Yes, you're right. He was stern with you, and then he'd brag about you. He always knew everything you were doing, Arvel. He followed everything you did through the war. His colleagues would talk about you. They all were so proud. Many of them were too old to go to fight but they believed in the cause, and they lived the war through your exploits. Your father was very proud of that, too. He'd talk about what you did in Tennessee with Rebecca's family and then when you went to Arizona. He secretly liked Robert, too. He used to call him the great adventurer. But he liked Uncle Bob."

"Well, I'll be."

"Your father was initially disappointed in you. Your father only valued things for their practical implications. The man didn't know how to have fun. Actually, I guess that's not true. Working constantly was his fun."

She laughed at a particular memory. "You should have seen us on our trips to Europe. He only went for me. He used to pace about and go through the exhibits practically running. I used to grab him by the arm and hold on, just to slow him down a bit. But he was a good soul, Arvel."

She remembered her original point and continued. "You were sent to the best schools, so naturally, you should have been a lawyer or businessman or banker. To his mind, it didn't take an education to breed mules. And then the rangering, oh, my. You were going in the wrong direction. Do you see what I mean?"

"And he wanted me to be better than him. Better, according to his own sense of accomplishment."

"Oh, yes, and he did well. He added so

much to our fortune, Arvel. He was not a kept man, I can tell you. It was he who made us really wealthy. And, one time . . . I remember him on a particular tirade about you. He said that if he had one tenth the opportunity that you had when he was growing up, he'd have done even greater things. That was your father."

"And the war?"

She smiled at that. "Well, we were both unhappy about that. That was the biggest dunderheaded thing we believe you ever did. Becoming a private soldier when your father could have gotten you a commission with the stroke of a pen. Or kept you out of it all together."

Arvel grinned at his mother's candor. "But you know now why I did it?"

"Of course I know why you did it, my boy. I did then. Arvel, you've lost a child. When Kate died, what did you feel?"

He welled up at the memory of his little girl. "Like all the power to live left my body, Mother."

"We had the same anxiety for you. You were the most important thing in our lives. Your father actually cried."

Alice was very serious as she looked at Arvel. "Your father never cried, Arvel. But the day he discovered that you went off to war, he did. Then later, when he found out how much fighting you had done, and when you nearly died from your wounds, he broke down. I thought it was going to kill him."

"Well, I'll be." Arvel looked down at his lap. She'd never told him these things and in his anxiety over the years, he'd harbored many ill feelings toward his father. He was ashamed of those feelings now.

He looked up at her. "I just never knew, Mother."

"Well, that's my fault, Arvel. I should have told you a long time ago. It was very private for me and I did love your father very much. He was the best of men, despite his inability to show it. He never stopped loving you or being proud of you."

She grinned a little sheepishly, "Do you remember him at your wedding to Maria? Your very Catholic wedding, with Maria in her white wedding dress and swollen belly?"

"Oh, my God, do I! I thought someone had replaced his cigar with a pickle." He managed a weak grin at the memory.

"Well, my boy, let me tell you what he said on his deathbed."

She shifted on her chair and looked at her hands, then back into Arvel's eyes. "He said, 'that Chica is a peach.' " She smiled and now the tears filled her eyes. "He called her

Chica, Arvel, not Maria. He called her Chica."

More electric lights had been strung. Everyone was out in their best, most festive clothes. There was no reason now for the Americanos not to celebrate, and everyone was ready for a grand time.

Food was being prepared and served everywhere, and soon the entire town was heady with the aroma of wonderful foods: chicken, goat, pork and beef, all prepared in the way of the local custom.

Some of Kosterlitzky's men played La Paloma in the little bandstand at the center of the town, and soon after, other bands could be heard repeating the popular tune.

The priest gave an open mass in the courtyard in front of the little church. The rurales and vaqueros and Catholic cowboys and rangers all took communion in preparation for their battle the next day.

Every other person seemed to be either playing guitars or singing. Already a corrido had been created, the folk song of the people, all about the protectors who had come from el Norte to help them put an end to the infamous Sombrero del Oro. Everyone seemed to know the same song as was the habit and custom of the people of the land.

Children were allowed to stay up as late as they wished and many of them helped with the fireworks. Young girls were giving out little cards with the image of Jesus or the Virgin of Guadalupe on them. They placed them onto the brims of the hats of the warriors; the rurales, the Americanos, and vaqueros.

Alice Walsh walked through the streets on the arm of Del Toro. The big Jefe was dressed in a black vaquero outfit and his finest beaver sombrero. His red brocade vest stood out, the girth of his paunch acting like a beacon in the night. They were all happy, happier than they had perhaps ever been when the news had finally come. It was news they knew would come, never doubting that Chica would do it. But the actuality was a gift, an early Christmas present.

Billy and Dan and Dick strolled through the streets, a beer in one hand and a bottle of mescal in the other. Some of the less than honorable women of the town eyed them. They swarmed the little party and soon had Dick Welles's complexion as red as Del Toro's vest.

They looked at Dan and laughed, "You are the prettiest man ever to come to our town, Señor."

One older prostitute stroked his hair and, before he could react, grabbed him by the back of the neck and gave him a long passionate kiss on the mouth. He smiled slyly at her. "Why don' you come with me, Indian. No charge for you!"

Dan smiled and waved her off, "No Señorita, muchas gracias, but I need all the strength in my legs for tomorrow's fight. You are too much for me, I would not survive."

They all cackled and another one looked at Dick Welles, "How 'bout you, Señor, an old violín is what I like, it play the sweetest música."

Dick looked at Dan and Billy, "No, ma'am, no ma'am," was all he could say. He was flattered and embarrassed at the same time and turned a little redder than before. They all laughed again and looked at Billy.

"An' how about this one? He looks to be ready for some fun. How 'bout it, medicine man, you have what will cure our little itch?"

They eventually wandered off, but before leaving gave each man a good kiss and a hug, "You come back when Sombrero del Oro es finito, caballeros, and we will show you a proper thank you."

Uncle Bob ducked into a side street and found some elderly señoras selling rebozos and beautifully embroidered blouses and skirts. He picked the finest of the lot and carried the garments draped carefully over his arm.

Alice caught up to him and smiled. She gave his arm a squeeze and spoke into his ear, "Pilar will look lovely wearing them, Robert." He blushed and looked away.

"So you know our little secret."

"Oh, yes, Robert. It is the biggest open secret on the ranch."

"I'm not ashamed of her, you know."

"Of course I know."

"She won't marry me. She says I'm too damned old, and all her husbands die. She thinks if we marry, it'll jinx us, and I'll die, too. I've asked her, Alice. I have."

Even Will Panks's sullen demeanor began to change. He'd had a shock but it was finally wearing off. He felt better now that he'd talked to Arvel. Felt better knowing what was expected of him the next day and was confident that he would be able to carry it out. He was more than willing to do so.

He, too, wandered about the festive town alone. He didn't really want company this night. He sauntered in and out of little side streets, each one with a significant party going on.

He was distracted and tripped over an object in an alley, caught himself and grabbed the little form he'd knocked to the ground. An old woman in black rushed up and scooped up the child, pulling her out of the way. Will bowed to the two figures and offered an apology.

The child was blind and crippled. He reached down to help the old woman lift the child and realized her terrible condition. He gasped at her destroyed legs, and was shocked at her pleasant demeanor. The poor thing seemed oblivious to her own debility. He looked at the old woman and asked; "How did she come to this, Señora?"

The old woman looked away as if uttering the reply caused her pain. "Sombrero Del Oro."

"Que?"

"He sometime purges his fort of the ones who are too weak to be of use. He left this little one in the desert to die. I found her and she is now my little angel." She patted the smiling little girl on the head and reached down to give her a kiss on the forehead.

"And how . . . what happened to her legs?"

The old woman shrugged. "Something,

some manner of evil by the bandit."

Will sat down beside them. The little girl sensed the air displacement and found Will. She pulled herself onto his lap. He held her and soon tears were running down his face.

He grabbed her up in his arms and held her desperately, cried and shook and tried his best to control his sorrow. The old woman spoke quietly to him and attempted to comfort him in his despair.

The little child put her hand up to his face and wiped his cheeks. "Don't cry, caballero, don't cry."

He smiled and slowly regained his composure. He gently put her off his lap and stood up, unbuckled his money belt and handed the old woman all of his folded bills. He stood up and kissed them both on the head. He knew now what he had to do.

Chapter XV:
Chica's Ride

Rebecca and Marta rounded up as many mounts as they could find and Chica rode into the desert to find some more, but not before donning her nun's garb one more time. There was a chance she might encounter some of the bad men.

Within a mile she managed to pick up a couple more horses. They didn't have enough for everyone but the children could double up.

Off in the distance she noticed a small figure sitting in the sun. Whoever it was seemed to be alone. It was difficult to tell for sure because of the shimmering heat waves that lay between Chica and the small form.

She rode closer and recognized the child from the train, the boy with the red rubber ball. She urged her pony to move into a gallop and when she reached the boy, gave him her canteen. He drank deeply, nearly emptying it.

She pulled him onto the saddle and held him gently as they rode. Suddenly she remembered and reached into her pocket. She grabbed the rubber ball. She didn't know why, but it seemed like a symbol to her, something tangible from the normal world, the world before the attack on the train. She'd carried it with her ever since she found it at the crash site. Now it had a particular purpose and she handed it to him just as she had the day they'd met on the train.

He looked at the ball and wondered how the nun had gotten hold of it. He turned and looked into her eyes. She had pretty eyes and he remembered from earlier, the day he'd first seen her in the desert, before she'd been caught, that she had a destroyed face around the eyes. But they weren't destroyed now.

Chica read his mind and pulled back her veil. She removed her wimple and, shaking out her hair, smiled. "You remember me, mi minito?"

He smiled weakly. "I do, ma'am."

"I am taking you to your mamma. She is good and all the bandits are gone." She rubbed his shoulders as they rode and she hummed in his ear. He pushed himself against her, snuggled against the woman who was so beautiful and lovely and nice to him.

"Your mamma will be so happy to see you, little one."

"I don't think so."

"Oh, she will. She has been treated bad, just like you. You both need to take care of each other for the rest of your days. You needa do this thing, little one. Don't forget, okay?"

"Yes, ma'am." She made him feel all tingly in the pit of his stomach. She was a lovely creature and he wished for a moment that she was his mother.

The old nun prepared the captives for the journey home. It all seemed too easy to the old woman and, when the two riders appeared in the distance, she was certain their ordeal wasn't over. She searched desperately for Chica who wasn't back from rounding up the extra mounts.

She moved off in the direction her companion had gone, but hadn't gotten far when the first bandit called out to her.

They were two stragglers and had not seen the mock crucifixion, the supernatural vengeance heaped upon the bandit gang.

They'd heard from some of their companions in the desert that something evil had occurred, but like a pair of doubting Thomases, had to witness it for themselves.

They were encouraged to see so many useful animals left, and the marquee tent was still standing. There were a few captives left as well, and some of these were still attractive, despite their past mistreatment. They both looked at the redhead. She still had some appeal and they grinned broadly. They'd save her for later that night.

They ordered everyone to dismount. The Mother Superior looked at them and began to pray. They told her to shut up and began poking and prodding the women. They ignored Rebecca and Marta. One bandit walked into the tent and returned with a broad grin on his face, a small chest tucked under his arm.

This was a worthwhile venture.

They found a jug and began pulling on it as if they had not had a drink in a year. It was quickly having an effect. In short order, they were prepared to get down to business, and pulled two young women from the group. They backhanded one woman's child when he protested, but before they could do any further harm, Chica was amongst them.

She jumped off her horse and ordered them to stop what they were doing.

"What are you going to do if we don't, little nun?" The man speaking looked at his partner, proud to have come up with a clever name for the figure standing resolutely before them.

"It would be healthier for you two to go away." Chica hid her hands in her robes, readying the shotgun she had secreted there. She did not want to kill the men in front of her little girl and all the captives. They'd been through enough. Unfortunately, the bandits were especially stupid and they looked at each other, then back to the little nun.

"You are a stupid bitch." They started to pull their six shooters and Chica swiveled the shotgun on its shoulder sling. She had some difficulty.

For the first time in her life, Chica did not have the upper hand. She was tired, nearly exhausted from stress and lack of sleep. She was convinced that the fighting was over for now and she'd not anticipated these two. This battle would be touch and go. The black robe of her nun's costume felt like it had been woven with lead and was an overwhelming encumbrance.

Before anyone could react further a shot

was heard, then another, then silence. The bandits sat on their horses, a weighty expression on each of their faces. They no longer went for their guns.

The first one had a strange wound, like a plug the size of a quarter, dug from his cheek just below the left eye. Suddenly a torrent of blood flowed down his face. He reached up, felt the wound carefully and, as if he were taking inventory of a newly discovered blemish, he pitched onto the desert floor.

The second bandit looked down and desperately tore at his shirt just below his chin. He looked as if a yellow jacket had worked its way inside his shirt and was stinging him. He looked at the little nun and then, he too, fell over.

Little Marta stood behind them. She looked around, as to assure herself that no one else needed shooting and, satisfied, replaced her miniature six shooter in its holster.

Everyone was silent. No one dared move or say a word. Then, as if a signal had been given, the captives began clapping. The little bandit remounted and stood up in her stirrups. Her pony pranced around in a circle and Marta looked proudly at the little nun and the adoring crowd, a little embarrassed by so much attention.

Chica walked up to the redheaded woman. She took her by the hand and led her to her son. The woman hadn't looked up from the ground in many days and hadn't noticed the little fellow sitting in the saddle.

"Look, lady. Your son is alive."

The redhead looked up at the boy. She stood, as if in a trance. The Mexican children and now this Mexican woman had shown her the only kindness she had known since this hell began. Cautiously, she reached for the boy and slowly, awkwardly, pulled him from the saddle. She took him in her arms and hugged him. She looked at Chica and whispered, "Thank you, Miss, thank you."

Chica watched as the surviving women stripped the guns from the dead bandits. They knew how to use them and armed themselves. They nodded to Chica. They would not be molested again.

Chica smiled at them as she got back on her horse. "That is good, ladies, you kill anyone who tries to hurt you. You kill anyone who tries to do this again."

She rode up next to the big redhead and reached down to touch her cheek. "Is okay now, lady. You take care of each other. You two needa take care of each other for a long time."

Mother Superior called out to everyone. "We will leave this unholy place, now, before any other calamities can befall us."

Chica smiled at the little girl. "You are in charge, Marta. I am counting on you to get everyone home, back to Bisbee to the convent. Will you do this for me?"

"Sí, señora, sí." The little girl sat straighter in the saddle. She wished she had a cigarette.

Chica looked at Mother Superior, "Madre, wait for us there. Ride hard north, the next village will be a better place to rest than out in the desert. No more bandits should bother you. I am guessing they will be running south."

The old nun smiled at Chica. Her demeanor became serious and she said, "Come with us, my child. You have your girl, we've done enough. Come along with us."

Chica turned her horse and began to ride off, "I have to get my Arvel. Adios, my lovelies. Adios, Rebecca. You all take care of each other."

"I love you, Mamma," Strangely, Rebecca wasn't sorry to see her go. "Bring Daddy back. I love you!"

■ ■ ■ ■

The two girls rode at the front. Everyone was happy now. The mounts were good, everyone had big sombreros to keep off the sun, and no one bad was in the desert to torment them. Marta was in a chatty mood.

"What will your mother do when she gets to San Sebastian?"

"I don't know. She'll get my daddy and all his friends. She said something strange. I heard her tell the Mother Superior that she would raze the fort to the ground."

Marta rode on, saying nothing.

"Is the fort in a hole, Marta?"

"No." The little bandit grinned at the thought of a fort being below the ground. "It's a fort. It's big, with big walls."

"How can you raise something that is already up high?"

The old nun overheard the children chatting. She laughed and rode up next to them. "To raze means to knock down. I know that sounds silly, children. But that is what it means."

Marta became quiet and rode on for a while. Then she kicked her mount into a trot, away from Rebecca and the nun. She suddenly wheeled and galloped past them.

Marta yelled, "I'll catch up."

Before they could inquire or protest, the little bandit was far away, riding back in the direction of the Marquee tent.

In short order, she was riding up to Chica who'd seen her off in the distance, recognizing the slight silhouette and the horse's stride. She stopped and lit a cigar as she waited for the little bandit to arrive.

"What is this, Marta?"

"Señora." She cast her eyes down. She didn't even know why, but she was respectful of this woman, always. "I need to ask you something."

"Que?"

"Will you kill everyone in the fort?"

"No, Marta. I do not kill innocent people or women or children."

Chica smiled at the little girl's sudden concern. "Why do you want to know this?"

"There are people there. A man. They should not be killed."

"There will be much fighting, Marta, you know this. We will not let innocent people die if we can help it, but we cannot make sure, you understand." She saw the child deflate.

"Tell me, little one. Tell me who you are afraid will die?"

"There's an old man, Señora. He is blind

and he used to be the carpenter, but he can no longer see and he's . . ." she could not come out and say that he was good and that she loved and cared for him. It was too much to show, too much emotion to allow.

"I see." She pulled her mount up next to the child. "What is his name?"

Marta looked up at Chica, mortified. "I . . . I don't know, Señora. I just called him old man all the time."

She was ashamed of herself for never learning the man's name. She was ashamed of herself so much these days, ever since meeting Rebecca, the old nun and Chica.

Suddenly she brightened. "He lives above the dungeon. You will see it."

Jumping off her horse, she found a stick and traced the layout of the fort in the sand. She showed Chica the location of the well, the blacksmith shop, the armory, where the cannon were located and, finally, where the old man lived. He had a craggy little dugout room, up high in the side of the mountain. It was accessible only by climbing a ladder. He stayed there, often for days and days. Marta took care of him because once he became blind, he could no longer serve the maestro and was at risk of execution or, worse, banishment to the desert.

"Sí, I understand, Marta."

Chica dismounted and walked to the girl who was still squatted down in the dust, looking at her map. Chica reached down, raised the girl up with a finger under her chin. She looked into Marta's face and saw herself looking back from twenty years or so ago.

She brushed the hair from Marta's eyes and placed her hands on her shoulders. She felt the girl stiffen and want to pull away, just like a spirited puppy whose owner had placed it on its back.

Chica knew what the girl was feeling and proceeded, nonetheless. She hugged the girl and kissed her forehead. "You don' worry 'bout the old man, Marta. He will be alive when we are finished, I promise you."

On the ride back to the captives, Marta thought about the old man. He taught her everything good. He was responsible for teaching her to read in both English and Spanish. One day, she was reading a tattered copy of a book the old man had in his collection. It had been written by an Italian man. It was called The Inferno. The old man took it from her, replacing it with the Bible which he liked to use for her lessons. He was funny. He didn't want her to read The Inferno because he was afraid it would give her nightmares. Marta thought this was very funny because the fort was much worse than the world in the book.

She liked the story very much. She liked each circle of hell and she loved the man called Virgil. She imagined that she could go down to the deepest part of the dungeon and find the gates to hell. In fact, one day she did. She went to the deepest part and found a rock and scratched out a little doorway. Then she wrote over the doorway the words from the book, Abandon all hope ye who enter here.

When she was finished, she liked to pretend that she could go down there and find Virgil standing under her sign. She'd ask him to come up and grab the maestro and his assistant and take them down to the deepest circle of hell where they would stay for all of eternity and would never be seen or heard from again.

She told the old man this and he really laughed. He loved the little bandit so much. She never understood why until one day he told her, before he'd become blind and worthless, that he could see a light in her. She remembered looking down at herself to try to find the light but there was nothing there. The old man laughed again and said that it wasn't a light that was like a fire or a torch or a star, it was an invisible light and that Marta had the best mind of any creature he'd ever known. He told her that she needed to learn as much as she could so that one day, when she left the fort, she'd be able to live well in El Mundo.

He always called the area outside the fort El Mundo. One day, when she asked him why he said that, and why he didn't call the fort and the ground that he stood on El Mundo, he gave a laugh and told her that this place was unnatural, evil, and it was the mouth of hell. It was not El Mundo and she'd understand him one day.

As she rode north, she thought about Rebecca and wondered what it must be like to live like her. Maybe she lived in the El Mundo the old man referenced. She was excited now. She thought about the beautiful Señora and how she got the big flutter in her stomach when the lovely lady kissed her on the head. She loved that feeling more than the feeling she had when she shot the dark Jesus in the face or when she shot the two bandits. She loved it more than when she rode a good horse fast or when she made fun of the bandits and they would look at her with so much anger, when they wanted to beat her or kill her but dared not touch her.

She loved it more than when she and Rebecca helped the captives and gave them food and water when they were forbidden to do so. She loved it more than when she did the tatting and got all the knots right and didn't have to tear her work apart because she'd blundered.

At one point she stopped her horse and wanted to wheel around and go back to the beautiful Señora so that she could be hugged and kissed by her again. Then she remembered that the Señora had given her the task of getting the captives and Rebecca and the old nun back to Bisbee.

Bisbee, it was fun to say. It sounded funny, like the buzzing of a bee. She thought that maybe Bisbee was El Mundo, too, and she could not wait to get there.

She tapped her mount's sides and got him into a canter, then a full gallop. She tapped him from side to side on his neck with her reins; not painfully, just to urge him on. They were galloping and galloping. In short order, she could see the prisoners and they were all happy. She felt good. She felt the best she'd ever felt in her entire life.

Once Marta was out of sight, Chica rode hard back to the place where she and Mother Superior had first encountered the bandit gang. She gathered her traps and was back to the marquee tent before sunset. She crept inside and looked the maestro over. She was initially disappointed, the man appeared to be dead. She was relieved to see him breathing.

He slowly roused from his fitful slumber and looked at Chica smoking a cigar at the foot of his bed. He remembered her promise to bring him some companions and looked at his bed in a panic.

"I could not find any friends, mierda, I am sorry." She casually pulled up a chair and sat next to him. She saw that he was lying in an awkward position and she helped him sit up so that he breathed better and was more comfortable. He could not comprehend her kindness. She wrung out a rag and wiped his brow. "Are you awake?"

The old man nodded. Chica gave him a drink. He was finally fully conscious.

"Good. I have a story to tell you." She poured herself a mescal and sipped it. "This is good mescal, mierda."

She placed her cigar on a plate on the little table next to the old man.

"One time, many years ago, I met a bandit who looked very much like you. He had the same face as you and he wore very fancy clothes like you. He had two gold teeth, right here." She pointed at her own mouth. The old man gasped.

"Ah, sí, sí, mierda. You understan'. You are not so estupido as you look. Sí, it was your brother. You were always known as Sombrero del Oro because you always wore a gold hat, and he was known as Gold Tooth, no?"

She watched him, waited for his acknowledgement. "Well, one day, Gold Tooth came to my village, and he hurt a little girl. A beautiful sweet, innocent little girl, and guess what, mierda?"

The old man looked on at her, vacantly.

"I cut his goddamned head off."

Chica smiled as she picked up her cigar and blew a plume of smoke over the old man's head. "Then, I carried the head around for a few days and I sold it to a prospector, and guess what, mierda?" She waited for some kind of reaction. "I thought that would be the end of the head, but later, I went to a traveling show and I saw the head again. My head, your brother's head, and it was in a jar full of spirits, and it looked estupido. He was in a jar and all the gringos all around the world got to look at his estupido head, floating in a jar."

She stopped and looked more closely at Gold Hat. Great tears were running down his fat cheeks.

"Awe, it makes you sad, mierda? Your brother, you never seen him for years and years, you thought perhaps he was in California or maybe down south in Columbia or Bolivia living a good life and now you know he is dead. And not just dead, but his goddamned head is off, and his body wanders around hell and cannot see little girls to hurt anymore."

She poured another mescal.

"Don' cry, mierda. Soon, all your troubles will be over." Then she smiled. "Or, maybe, they will be just beginning. That is if you believe in heaven and hell. And, mierda, I think you do. You very much believe in heaven and hell, don' you?"

He looked down at his rotten leg. It no longer hurt because the nerves in it were now dead.

Chica smiled slyly, "Oh, no, mierda, the leg will not kill you." She moved her head solemnly from side to side.

She stood up and pulled the big knife from its sheath on her belt. She pushed it against his round belly, slowly, with increasing force until it entered, puncturing his skin, then going deeper.

He cried out, humping his back and trying to recoil. But there was nowhere to retreat. "This is for all the poor women you abused, mierda." She slowly sunk the big blade to the hilt, carefully, with surgical precision, avoiding any arteries or vital organs.

"This is what it feels like to a woman who gets penetrated by a pig like you. Not funny is it, mierda?" She retracted the blade, blood and offal pouring freely from the wound. She picked another spot and jammed the blade in again.

"This is for all the little girls you abused."

And finally, she struck again, a third time, slicing into his liver. "And this is for my little girl and for my Arvel and for Abuelita."

She pulled the knife out and cleaned it off with the big gold sombrero sitting next to his bed. "Such a nice sombrero, and now it is ruined with your blood and shit."

She watched the life go out of his eyes. "One more thing before you go on to hell, mierda." She leaned in close, "you will walk around hell with your brother, but you won't see nothing either." He was dead.

Chica rode hard, well after dark, heading south. Her eyes were wet and she felt herself crying hard, harder than she had ever cried before, harder than when she was lying in the little cell of the convent, the darkest time of her life when she knew Rebecca was in the hands of the sadist, Gold Hat.

Now her little girl was safe, the worst bandit of her life was dead, and she was going to see her Arvel. She was emotionally spent; excited and exhausted all at once.

She did not like this horse, she did not trust him and the saddle was not a good one, yet she rode him hard, over unknown terrain. But she could not stop herself. The horse fought her, he didn't want to gallop so fast and Chica quirted him hard on the flanks. He responded, flying across the dark desert far too quickly.

She wished she had Alanza under her. Her pony, her constant companion, the most perfect creature she had ever owned, ever ridden. She wanted so desperately to get Arvel and Abuelita, Uncle Bob and Uncle Alejandro, Dan George, Dick Welles, and all the good men who'd come to her aid back home, back to safety.

She would do this and she would never ever again leave her ranch. She'd live out the rest of her days caring for her family, keeping them safe. She would raise Marta. She laughed out loud, into the desert night, when she thought of the wild little girl.

Marta reminded her so much of herself when she was a young girl and thought of the effect Rebecca had on her, as if two little Chicas shared the same universe; the pure and the impure Chica. Little Marta would be good. She was inherently good just as Chica had always been. Rebecca, who was good and pure of spirit would cleanse little Marta, cleanse her of all the evil and impurity and depravity she had known.

Chica was happy and excited, swept up in a sort of euphoria that could not be contained. She suddenly felt alive, free, liberated. She touched the old gelding's flanks, urging him on faster, recklessly, into the night. When the inevitable misstep brought her crashing to earth, she tumbled, headlong, over the horse, onto the hard rocky floor of the Mexican desert.

The magnificent, incorruptible, valiant Chica was down.

Chapter XVI:
Sappers

Will Panks rode south through the night. He led an unlikely war party: Old Pop, Young Pop (Will was never creative with naming his mules), and a young Mexican boy who instantly attached himself to the old prospector when the Americans first arrived in San Sebastian.

The boy lied and said he was seventeen. Will was certain that he'd not yet reached his fourteenth year, but he was a strong boy and quick both in mind and body. He could not stop asking questions about the dinamita Will was toting. He wanted to know everything about it and soon Will was patiently showing him how it worked; what the copper wire was used for, what the funny box with the plunger did. As they rode, Will looked back at the boy, proudly riding the little roan that Will had selected for him. The lad looked odd in his white peon clothes with his huaraches stuffed precariously into the stirrups.

The lad would prove useful in escorting Will to the old fort as well. They made it to their destination with two hours to spare before sunrise. The fortress was formidable from a distance; incongruous in its man-made form, pressed against the side of a giant mountain. The Spaniards who built it were a resourceful lot. The base of the mountain held good water and the fort's occupants would be able to withstand any sort of siege for many months. The mountainside itself was honeycombed with little cells throughout. It was easy to excavate and with a minimum of effort, a horrific dungeon had been created.

Only three sides of the fort had needed to be constructed, thereby saving one entire side from the labor required to build it. It served the Spaniards for as long as it took them to extract every last grain of gold from the region. It was strategically placed in the center of the country.

Sombrero del Oro had known the place since childhood. He used to play amongst the ruins, even before his aspirations to become the meanest and cruelest villain and slave trader since the conquistadores roamed the land. He had wandered about the place for hours; deep into the recesses, to the dungeons where unspeakable cruelty had been meted out. It was one of the many experiences that helped corrupt his diseased mind, the training ground for his malice toward humanity.

By the time he was twenty, he was regularly retreating to the fort with his various riches; his slaves and his growing gang after he'd carry out his attacks on the villages. Later he began attacking towns and then cities as far away as Texas, Arizona and New Mexico. Eventually, with the wells cleaned and good water to hand, he accrued livestock, a blacksmithy, carpenters, and a remuda of some of the hardiest mustangs found in the desert. By his mid-twenties he had a harem of twenty concubines and a burgeoning family.

As expected, the bandits were casual in their security while the maestro was gone. He'd been a task master for years, forcing them to secure the walls of the fort through the night, yet for years, no one ever needed to raise an alarm. No one of any consequence, such as Colonel Kosterlitzky, bothered with them and other bandits or Indians hadn't a prayer of ever penetrating the thick walls. So the bandits fell into a kind of complacency, and now that Del Oro was not around to enforce his policy, most spent the nights snug in their cots and hammocks.

Will and the boy hobbled the horses and mules some distance away. Will looked at his companion and noticed the boy literally glowed in his white peon suit in the moonlight against the blackness of the desert floor. This wouldn't do. He thought hard about it for a moment and called to the boy in a hushed tone.

"Raphael, get the lamps off of Young Pop."
"Sí, Jefe."

In short order they were stripped of their garments and smeared liberally with the lampblack rubbed from the lid of the old coal oil lanterns. Raphael was amused. He watched everything the old miner did and mimicked his every move.

Once they were camouflaged, they made their way silently to the base of the fort wall nearest them. Will was pleased when he picked at the mortar holding the stone wall together. To his delight, three hundred years of desert wind had undermined the base and there were deep crevices periodically in the wall.

Will patted Raphael on the back and gestured with his hand. The clever lad understood.

Back at their base of operations, Will pitched his little canvas tent and covered this with blankets. He lit one small lamp for light and they both squeezed into the space together. They prepared eight charges of the dynamite. Will was delighted to see his prodigy learn so quickly.

"Now, the trick is," Will started with the first charge, opened one end of the cartridge making a hole in the end with a hard wooden instrument, "to get the hole the right depth."

He looked at his handiwork and showed it to Raphael. The boy was fearless, not because of ignorance — he knew that he was quite literally handling dynamite — but because he had a resolve and confidence shown by few men twice his age.

"There now, for the fuse." Will held up an implement, "This is the most important tool you'll ever use, my boy."

Raphael picked one up from the pile of tools and material at their feet and worked it deftly. Will snipped off the end of the fuse. "There, nice and square." He looked at the boy and grinned, "Even though all your work is going to be destroyed, it has to look pretty, Raphael. It has to be perfect."

Next, Will placed a copper capsule on the end of the neatly cut end of the fuse and used the fuse cutter to crimp the cap on. He waved a finger in front of the boy's face, "Never, never, never bite a cap to crimp it on a fuse, Raphael." He gestured, pretending to do what he'd just warned the youth against and made a noise, "Kaboom! No more Raphael." The boy nodded and grinned.

Will drew a map of the fort on the ground at their feet. He indicated the old Napoleons that pointed out from each corner, then the reinforced towers on each side of the great entrance. Sombrero del Oro neglected the stone walls, but with the aid of his carpenters and blacksmiths, he maintained a formidable gate.

He'd constructed two thick oak doors, each eight feet wide with heavy iron hinges. In front of this were two grates, so that during daylight hours, the doors could be left open for ventilation and light into the center of the interior plaza. These great grates were carefully maintained as well.

Raphael whistled low between his teeth when they'd surveyed it and was curious as to why his boss seemed unfazed. The lad thought about this as he finished the last of his bundles. "How will we get through the gates, Jefe?"

Will smiled and patted the lad on the arm.

"You see a lot, lad, you see a lot." He was pleased with the young fellow's quick and curious mind.

When they had fully prepared, Raphael began scurrying back and forth, placing the charges as his mentor had instructed. He packed them tightly into the deepest recesses of the eroded walls and then packed rock tightly around each. He payed out the wire he and his instructor had inserted into each charge.

Will watched him, pleased and amused. The young fellow, wearing nothing but his sandals, covered in soot, ran like a little monkey from one place to the other.

In short order, he was back at Will's side. Raphael was smiling, proud of the work he had done. They looked to the east and saw the slightest hint of the sun working its way above the horizon.

Will looked at his watch and grinned at the boy.

"Just a little more, lad, just a little more to do."

Will went back to the map and showed Raphael the wiring plan for their fireworks display. The boy nodded eagerly and ran off with two coils of copper wire. Will watched him as he worked.

When Raphael returned, Will had already

taken down the tent. He had the animals packed and ready to go. They mounted and rode up the incline away from the fort for another two hundred yards, unrolling copper wire behind them. This is where they would make their attack.

In the dawning light, Will had four Du Pont blasting machines set up, side by side. He connected the first one and then let Raphael handle the rest. "Good lad, good lad."

He poured water into the boy's cupped hands, then did the same for himself. They washed up, dressed, and had a breakfast of cold coffee and chicken. They hunkered down, low, so that they wouldn't be seen on the horizon.

A cock crowed at the fort and soon they could see people moving about. Smoke was beginning to rise here and there as the inhabitants of the fort began to prepare their morning meals. The odor of bacon wafted over them and Will's stomach began to growl. He wished he could prepare a good breakfast for himself and his companion.

Some bandits wandered about along the parapet. They didn't seem to be guarding so much as simply starting out the day surveying their surroundings.

The two sappers sat together, lying on their bellies, enjoying the dawning of the new day. Will would have enjoyed at least a cup of hot coffee but he didn't want to risk a fire. He resolved to wait and relax. He put a hand on Raphael's shoulder and told the lad to get some sleep. The boy didn't need much coaxing.

Chapter XVII: Tarahumara

She woke with a start and recognized where she was immediately. She sat up and lost her balance. She'd been bleeding but was now clean, cleaner than she'd been in many days and lying in a comfortable bed. The Indians who had rescued her were sitting around the little cabin, waiting for her to wake up. She looked at each of them, bowing her head solemnly to every occupant in turn.

Chica loved the Tarahumara. These were the famous runners. They were a proud people with such a strong code of honor that it was impossible for them to lie. She had known many Tarahumara in her life and every one was fine and decent. She'd never stolen from them in her younger days and had always treated them and their lands with the utmost respect.

She'd not had dealings with this particular bunch, but they seemed to know her. They'd been through her traps and recognized the special cargo she was carrying. They'd also encountered some of Sombrero del Oro's band moving through their land, heading back to the fortress, and knew from what they had been told that something serious and terrible had happened to the bandit and his gang.

They knew Chica was not one of the gang and that she had been responsible, at least in part, for the calamity that had befallen the outlaws. They treated her with great humility and reminded her of her indios, up in the red rocks, how they were so similar.

Yet the Tarahumara were very different. They were always fit and the men were always present. They thought too much of their family unit to go off looking for work and resolved, instead, to make the best of what they had. At least they would be poor together.

Chica had never seen an ugly Tarahumara and this group was no different. The children were pretty, the men handsome and the women beautiful; even more so with their lovely, colorful clothes. Their bright koyeras brought out a striking contrast to their raven-dark hair. Chica could have easily been mistaken for one of them.

They weren't violent people, yet they

showed respect for Chica's obvious warrior behavior. She had finally put an end to the one man who, more than any other — the Spaniards, the Mexicans and even the corrupt Jesuits — had injured them in the recent past.

Sombrero del Oro had made their lives miserable for many years, and now, obviously, this diminutive señora was the reason for his demise.

A pretty young girl helped Chica to the edge of the bed, gave her some water and a stew made from potatoes, beans, a little goat meat and apples. She smiled at the child and thought immediately of Rebecca and little Marta. She wanted to cry again.

She patted the child on the cheek, then reached over and kissed her. Without really thinking about it, she hugged the child, squeezing her tightly to her breast and holding her for a long time. The others approached and all patted Chica gently on the back. She looked up and smiled at them with tears in her eyes.

Her horse was dead. He'd fallen hard and broken his neck. The Tarahumara had pulled Chica's traps and saddle off the beast and everything sat in a little pile at the foot of her bed. She looked through her saddle purse and found some old gold eagles that she'd only recently liberated from the bandit boss. She pulled the child's bright skirt up to form a pocket and dropped the pile of coins in, one by one. It was a king's ransom, rather, a villain's cache. It was just a small token to repay them for what they had done for her.

She fell back onto the bed and the child covered her with tightly woven colored blankets, then retreated with the others from the room. The woman needed to rest without any distraction.

In another two hours she was up, dressed and peering out the front door of the little cabin. A fresh mount was waiting for her. While she slept, they'd retrieved her traps and saddle from the foot of her bed and had the animal ready and waiting for her as soon as she was able to move on.

The Tarahumara had anticipated that she would not be with them long. They understood that the resolute young woman would not be kept in any sick bed. The little girl who'd tucked her in approached with a scarlet koyera. Chica knelt and, like a warrior being knighted, the child deftly, ceremoniously, tied it around Chica's head. She was now one of them. The little girl looked her over and nodded approvingly.

They told her about the army of rurales

and some Americans who were closing on Del Oro's fortress. It was not more than ten miles away. She looked at the sun and her pocket watch. It would be noon shortly and she hoped she hadn't missed the battle. She thanked the Indians and urged the pony on. It felt good to have an animal that fit her and Chica thought how the mare was not unlike her own beloved Alanza.

Chapter XVIII:
Attack

They arrived at noon, greeted by Will Panks and little Raphael, the two smiling broadly. Will swept his hand across the horizon behind him, indicating the ground he stood upon.

"Pretty good base of operations, eh?" And it was.

They stood on a rise. Terrain-wise, it placed them a good thirty feet higher than the top of the old Spanish fortress's parapet, five hundred yards south, out of reach of the poorly trained bandits manning the Napoleons with their bronze cannon balls.

Del Oro was not savvy in the ways of military strategy. He thought the bronze balls were more effective than iron because they were more attractive, a pretty orange and green color, compared to the boring old dark grey of the iron.

None of his gang really ever expected that the cannon would have to be used, anyway.

It was more a show of force and, every now and again, when Del Oro was in a particularly festive mood, he would have his men fire a few rounds, just to enjoy the noise and smoke.

Kosterlitzky set up his French guns. They were fierce looking contraptions. They looked new; modern and deadly, which they were. He'd trained his rurales well. They could hit a man-sized target at twice the range their enemy now was.

Will smiled at Arvel and Dick Welles as they rode up. He looked lovingly at his plungers. "You just say the word, Arvel, and I will give you a show."

Arvel cast his eyes about the site, he was looking for Chica. He felt in his bones that she was nearby. He wanted to ask Will about her, then realized it would be a stupid question. If she were there, Will wouldn't have kept it a secret from him.

He smiled at Raphael, still wearing the vestiges of lamp black around his eyes and in his ears. He was a mess. "Old Will hasn't blown you up yet, I see, Raphael."

"No, no Capitan, he is a good teacher."

Kosterlitzky established his men's positions, fanning them out at about three hundred yards. He had them dismount so they could shoot their Mauser rifles with better effect. It was Arvel's turn to make a move.

Arvel said, "Colonel, I'd like to have a parlay with them down at the fort."

Kosterlitzky smiled. "I think that is a bad idea, Captain, but it's your funeral. I'd sooner just let the miner give us a display of his expertise and let my boys reduce the whole mess to rubble with the French guns."

"Let's see what we can do without shootin' up the place. Now that Del Oro's finished — and they're sure to know it by now — maybe the rest'll give up easy, maybe they won't want to fight."

Kosterlitzky smiled as he lit a cigarette, "As I said, Captain, it's your funeral."

Dan prepared to follow as Arvel worked on removing his old Henry rifle. He got Billy to tie a white flag to the muzzle. Arvel looked at Dan and smiled, "No point in asking you to stay back, I guess."

All the Indian said was, "No." He sat resolutely on his horse until Billy finished. Arvel looked over to his captain partner. "Dick, get the boys with those big Winchesters ready. If I need your help, you'll know it. Just come ridin' as fast as you can."

Dick nodded and looked at the ground.

The guard at the parapet spoke up first. "Alto!"

They stopped short and waited.

"What do you want, gringo?" The man was a younger version of Del Oro, he was one of the old bandit's many sons. He looked primordial, like a version of a human being who'd not fully developed.

Arvel looked at Dan George and whistled quietly between his teeth, "Je-sus! Contact Dubois, I've found his missing link!"

Dan George chuckled, "Amen to that, Arvel, amen to that."

Arvel lit a cigarette and smoked as he spoke to the ape on the wall, "Sombrero del Oro is dead. We have eight hundred men and thirty cannon ready to reduce you to rubble. Surrender now and we will go easy on you."

They were met with silence; a group could be heard speaking in a muffled tone, conferring behind the wall. One stuck his head up and shouted, "Sombrero del Oro is not dead, and you have nowhere near that many men and guns. What business does an old man, and Indian, and a whore have in making such bold demands?"

Chica was suddenly there, off to Arvel's right, in his far periphery where he couldn't see her. He looked on and smiled. He was about to speak to her when she pulled something from a feed bag so quickly that he didn't have time to see what it was. She raised it high above her head, pointed at the bandits on the wall and shouted, "How do you suppose he lives without this, puta?"

A collective gasp came from the wall. Chica held up the severed head of their father and beloved leader. Her horse pranced in circles, as if the animal knew the importance of its cargo.

Arvel spoke out, compulsively, without thinking, "Jesus, Chica, not another head! What is it with you and severed heads?"

"Shush, Pendejo, and don' say Dios' name in vain."

She directed her attention back to the wall, "Well, what'll it be, boys, I am in a head collecting mood today. Shall I take some more, or will you give up to my husband?"

A shot was their reply and Dan George slumped forward, nearly falling from his horse. Arvel reacted immediately, covering him with his body as best he could and grabbing the reins of Dan's horse. He wheeled and began to gallop back to Kosterlitzky and the French guns.

Chica dropped the head and it bounced three times. She fired quickly with her Winchester, covering Arvel and Dan as they retreated. The rurales' Mausers began to thunder on the hillside. Dick and his men came riding and converged on Arvel and Dan George. They fired as they rode.

The ape men ducked behind the parapet. Some fired back wildly, without aiming or exposing their heads, as the Americanos rode back to safety.

Arvel was furious now. He grabbed Dan and tried to ease him from his horse as others came to their aid. He knew he shouldn't have let his friend come along.

They got him to the ground and Dan looked up at each of them. He smiled weakly and looked down at the wound in his shoulder. His clothing was now red, drenched in his blood, he was ghostly pale and this made his long raven hair look unnaturally dark. He grinned at his friends looking at him with fear in their eyes. He swallowed hard and spoke in his most articulate voice, "Well, I guess that's the end of this suit."

Chica bent over him, held his hand and looked him in the eye. "You listen to me, Dan."

He looked up at her, trying to remain calm, trying his best to be the quintessential Dan. He hid his terror well. He was a brave and stately man, even with a big hole in him and he was very much afraid to die. He managed a little grin, "Yes, Chica?"

"You will not die. You hear me, Dan? You will not die. I am going to go get some more heads now, and I expect you to be just as alive as you are now when I get back." She pressed his cheek gently with the palm of her hand. "Even shot up, you are the prettiest man I ever seen." She reached over and kissed him.

The wound was a dandy, it was big, a big slug from a shotgun which had gone through the meat of his chest and punched a nice hole through his left scapula. He was even paler now, pale as face powder.

He began to drift away. Alice Walsh held him and got the men to move him to a comfortable spot where Billy Livingston could do his best. The aborigine was all over him, pouring potions and preparing bandages. He looked at Dan and gave him a confident grin.

"Don't worry, mate. I'm just going to patch you up well enough so that Ging Wa can put you back together again when you get back home. No worries."

■ ■ ■ ■

Arvel was now possessed with his usual battle mania. He'd remounted and ridden to Dick's aid as his ranger partner brought up the rear, firing as they moved back to their base of operations. That was the way when Arvel was in kill mode. He was narrowly focused and could think of nothing but going into battle. He was ready to go do some killing.

There would be no stopping him now and just at the most inopportune moment, one of the Americans who'd followed on the expedition came forward, white as a sheet and unnerved by Dan's wound. The man touched his trembling lips with his shaking fingers. "Arvel?"

Arvel turned his head and barked a reply. He suddenly looked into the man's eyes and was brought back to reality. "Chica! Where's Chica?"

"I am here." He took solace in seeing his wife safe for the first time since the ordeal began. She was beautiful in her lovely koyera and looked more deadly in it than in her sombrero. Arvel tried to focus, get back to the task at hand, he looked on at the rattled man, "Sorry, Tom. What's the matter, my friend?"

"Arvel, it's, it's just, my boys and me," he pointed to two young men who looked like younger versions of the spokesman, "well, Arvel, your little girl's safe now, and well, this ain't really our fight. We'd ride through hell for you, Arvel, if it was for your little girl, but like I said, this really ain't our fight. Arvel, these boys, they're the only thing their mother's got."

Arvel smiled, "Enough said, Tom. You and your boys hang back here, no harm done."

He was distracted with the task at hand. He looked at Kosterlitzky.

"Colonel, do your worst."

Kosterlitzky smiled and saluted the Ranger captain. He nodded to Will Panks who directed Raphael to the mechanisms. The boy pushed one plunger, then the other in quick succession and a pair of unimpressive explosions went off at each far corner of the fort.

Will smiled at the obvious disappointment amongst his party. He nodded to Raphael who hit the remainder of the machines. There were two more explosions, even less impressive than the first. Will smiled again and waited.

Will watched, and suddenly, as if a lead domino had been set in motion, the great front wall imploded on itself, dropping into a heap of rubble, trapping everyone who'd been on or near the fortress walls.

The great wood and iron doors continued to stand, as if by magic, for several moments, then came crashing down. Dust rose all around the destroyed walls and for several moments, the entire scene was occluded by the red dust of the desert floor. The surviving bandits began to scurry uneasily about their destroyed fortification. Many were now caught in the open and the rurales' Mausers began to find their marks. At this rate, it would be an even battle in short order.

Kosterlitzky smiled. "You are going to disappoint my boys manning the French guns, Mr. Panks.

"Well, Colonel," Will replied, "if you'd shoot your guns up high, there along about thirty feet from the top of the mountain, that's some good limestone and it'll peel off and fall right on those bastards' heads."

Kosterlitzky gave the order and soon most of the mountain began to rain down on the remains of the bandit fortress. There was more dust and confusion and, added to that, a chorus of cries of fear and pain could be heard. The sheared rocks became a thousand small bombs, dropping and cutting and smashing into the miscreants' heads, torsos, and limbs. They were being cut to pieces and Kosterlitzky had not yet unleashed his exploding shells.

He ordered his men to remount and they began to charge headlong into the center of the bandit stronghold. Arvel was with them and Chica quickly followed. Alice Walsh called out to her.

"Maria, would you rather ride Alanza?" Her pony stood beside the old woman. She'd barely been able to control the animal ever since Chica'd arrived. Chica grabbed the reins from her mother-in-law and switched her guns over as Alice put her hand to the pretty face, "It's good to see you child. Be careful and take care of Arvel for me."

"Sí, Abuelita, he will be okay." In one motion she threw herself on the animal. It felt good as she became one with Alanza. Her pony was happier than she'd been in months. They rode into the fray, excitedly, fearlessly, as if Chica was off riding to nothing more than an afternoon of foxhunting, without a worry or care in the world.

She soon overtook Arvel and nearly caught up to the rurales now fully engaging the bandits, who still had some fight left in them.

At two hundred yards, the bullets began to pass over their heads, past their cheeks, between, over, under and all around them. It was as if they were protected by some great invisible shroud, a magic spell; nothing could touch them. Nothing could impede their attack and they came on with a resolute energy. They rode with their shotguns drawn and ready to unleash the fury, the anger and vengeance that had been pent up in them these past days.

At fifty yards Chica began to fire, the shots hitting their marks, pattern wide and still a bit too far for good effect. Several bandits, hit with the little balls, jumped back here and there, feeling the spots where the buckshot had entered through muscle, smashing bone, into gut, into arms and legs and torsos. They experienced blinding, searing pain, but only enough to maim, cause distraction. Not enough to outright kill.

The riders were upon the bandits now, guns blazing. Chica shot men at point blank range, the shotgun doing its horrific worst. Great chunks of flesh were torn away, men dropped, toppling like ten-pins, all life leaving their bodies. This was a slaughter.

The rurales were getting their revenge. For years, Del Oro's bandits had given them hell, made them look foolish, picked them off one by one whenever they got one alone or in a small group. The rurales were taking full advantage of this opportunity and now that the fighting was close, many put away their Mausers and used their swords to good effect. They slashed and cut and lopped away. Chica would have many heads to collect when the orgy of destruction was complete.

A half dozen of the Mexican soldiers made their way up high on the destroyed mountain and fired with precision at the bandits occupied by the onward attack. Soon bandits were fairly spinning about, not knowing which way to face. They were completely surrounded, many were shot multiple times, every side of their bodies riddled with bullets. Some simply stood still, not fighting or running or trying to surrender. They waited like animals in a slaughter yard for their turn to come.

The soldiers on the hill watched Chica riding and firing. She was like a Centaur, welded, enmeshed as if she and her beloved beast had grown into one. Alanza knew the direction to go, which one to attack next and she took Chica to one destination after another so that her Love could deliver her many kisses of death. Chica looped the reins around the saddle horn. She didn't need them to guide Alanza and she fired deliberately, both hands unencumbered, working the slide on the shotgun so fast that the gun appeared to be firing itself. The spectators called out, "ole, ole," as if they were watching their favorite toreador.

Dick Welles and his cowboys flanked wide and took the attack to the west. They were in open terrain but the ground was hard and flat and they made good progress. Dick looked left, then right, his men looked good and he was proud of them.

They received no opposition until they hit the downward slope of a small rise and then all hell broke loose. Suddenly, as if they'd been pulled down by a great invisible rope stretched across their paths, horses and riders were tumbling to the ground.

A staccato of noise blasted above the cacophony of Kosterlitsky's French guns. The men rolled onto the dusty desert floor, regaining their bearings. Two men and ten horses were hit bad. Dick Welles looked about and over to one of his companions.

"What the hell?"

An Englishman, a former British soldier riding in the posse, spoke up. "They've got a Maxim."

"A machine gun? Holy hell!" Dick looked

himself over for holes. He ducked down as the firing continued, kicking up dirt and rocks all around him. The bandits had loaded the Maxim's belts with Dum Dums and the carnage was appalling. The bullets cut through them like razors, tearing out great hunks of flesh and bone as they exited the defenseless bodies.

Dick's favorite mount, Rosco, lay screaming in pain, his forelegs broken in two. Dick comforted the poor beast as best he could, cradling the animal's great head and whispering calmly into his ear. Pulling his six shooter, he pressed the muzzle to the old gelding's head and fired.

Just as quickly, he turned his attention to the task at hand, thought hard and was suddenly back in Gettysburg. He called to his men, focused, ready to handle this tactically.

Out of the corner of his eye he saw a man riding hard, a circus rider, like the one he'd seen with Arvel and Chica and little Rebecca at a traveling show up in Tucson two years before. One man was riding and another was standing upright on the back of the horse, both hands full of something that smoked and hissed.

Will Panks rode so quickly that the bandits with the Maxim couldn't traverse fast enough to pick him off. Raphael stood upright, pressed tightly against Will's back, a big cigar burning between his clenched teeth, ready to light another fuse. He waited until they were within thirty yards, threw the first stick of dynamite high, in a graceful arc, right into the gunner's lap.

Everything exploded; men and gun and cartridges went flying into the air. A second stick wasn't needed but Raphael threw one anyway. Will smiled at the cowboys, waved his hand and they remounted the best they could. Those riders whose horses had been killed carried on the fight by foot. Dick took the mount of one of his men who was too badly wounded to continue. He tipped his hat to the two bombers as he galloped by.

"Much obliged, gents."

Will patted the lad on his leg, grinning broadly. "Our pleasure."

Will wheeled his horse and the two were off to see what more damage they could inflict on the fort. Now and again an explosion could be heard, measuring their progress.

Dick and his boys made it over the destroyed wall of the fort. The men picked their targets from amongst the piles of rubble. Many of the bandits were stunned, blood pouring from their ears as the French guns were now loaded with exploding ordnance. Colonel Kosterlitzky and his gunners were firing so accurately they could avoid hitting their fellow combatants. The sound was deafening.

Dick made it into the center of the square, near the dungeon's entrance and found many dead children. They were killed by small arms fire, six shooters, and soon it became apparent to Dick that the bandits were executing witnesses. He heard muffled shots and cries inside a building and dismounted. He ran inside just as three bandits finished executing some nursemaids, old women who'd died shielding the bodies of their small charges.

The bandits were now preparing to dispatch the occupants of the nursery. Dick would have none of it and began firing his Winchester as fast as he could work the lever. In short order, the savages were all dead. He called to one of his Texans who'd been wounded but was still strong enough to act as a sentry. He got him to stay with the babies. "Kill any son of a bitch who tries this again."

The man nodded and filled his Winchester's magazine. He'd never seen his boss like this: wild, angry, terrifying. Like Arvel, Dick was in his own manic state. His blood was up worse than at any time during his years fighting the rebels; it was up higher than it had been at the height of the Gettysburg battle, when he'd lost more than three quarters of his men repelling a charge on the little round top.

He could not comprehend how another human being could bring himself to shoot a little baby. These were the most evil animals he'd ever known.

He calmly, as if delivering a summons or collecting taxes, took careful aim and killed every bandit in his path. He didn't run or duck for cover or try to avoid being shot. He walked, standing upright and firing, until his Winchester was empty and the cartridges all gone from his gun belt. He careful put his rifle aside and began to pull his six shooter when he saw the Maxim that had recently been put out of commission by Will Panks and Raphael.

He ran to it and saw his British soldier off to the right, shooting bandits from a rubble wall.

"James!"

The man dutifully reported. "Can you work this thing?"

The Englishman could. He showed Dick how it operated and picked up the long belt still full of the hellish Dum Dums. The device was heavy, too heavy to be carried about and fired in such a way, but Dick was too full of adrenalin to know any better and he managed it without a problem. He soon had it thumping away, the Englishman in tow feeding the deadly machine. They fired with horrific effect. One bandit was literally cut in two and Dick looked over at the Englishman, incredulity in his eyes. "I guess that was a bit too much."

They continued until the water cooling the barrel evaporated and the gun burned up. They went back to using their own shooting irons and, soon, there were more rurales and Americans and vaqueros inside the fort than living bandits.

Further on, toward the center of the fort, Chica was giving her new shotguns a thorough workout, firing as fast as she could. Arvel worked more deliberately with his Greener.

Chica said something to him in her matter-of-fact tone. Arvel called out to her, "What are you saying? Can't hear you!"

"I said I like this new shotgun, Pendejo." She held the Winchester up to show him. "It is very fast."

He turned to shoot a bandit and when he looked back, Chica had ducked and ridden Alanza through the portal to the dungeon.

He started to follow with Tammy, then thought better of it, staying at the entrance to guard her rear.

Alanza picked her way down the old stone steps, here and there a bandit cowered in a corner or tried to take up a shooting position but was cut down by the señora. She cleared the place and saw several cells that were securely locked. She dismounted and found a dead guard, one of her victims, with keys still stuck in his belt.

She began opening one hellish nightmare after the next. Slowly, as if she'd awakened the dead, living corpses began to emerge from their captivity. Even Chica had never seen such things.

She eventually came back up to daylight and found Arvel. The fighting was beginning to slow. She looked at him and saw the shotgun in his hands. "Pendejo, wha' did you do to my Greener?"

He looked down at the fine English shotgun that he'd had the muzzle and stock cut down on. "Oh, I'm sorry, Chica, it's the only shotgun we have with ejectors and I had a hard time handling a shooting iron at first." He grinned and showed her the strength in his right hand. "I'm much better now."

"You are such a Pendejo. I waited two

years for that shotgun to be made and paid a lotta money for that wood and now you ruined it." A bullet zipped between them and Chica shot the man who'd delivered it. She went back to lambasting Arvel for ruining her gun.

"Is this really the best time to be discussing how I ruined your shotgun, Chica?"

He looked around for any other assassins. She didn't answer him, instead searching for more bad men to kill.

She rounded a substantial pile of rubble and saw three strange looking bandits staring at her menacingly. They were remarkable in their likeness to Sombrero del Oro. They were younger images of the man, but with breasts. They fired on Chica ineffectively. Alanza was too quick and Chica rode around them in an arc, shooting the nearest one, then the next and finally the last.

Arvel came up alongside her.

"I guess I can no longer say that I do not kill women, Pendejo." She loaded the Winchester's magazine and let it hang from the sling on her shoulder. She took the other one from its scabbard and loaded it as well.

Arvel looked down on the slain banditas. He snorted. "Can't really count them as women, darlin'. Can't really count them as human beings. More like shootin' vermin, to my mind."

"So I can tell Marta that I do not shoot women, still?"

He was confused by the question and was ready to ask what she meant when she rode off again, after more bandits to kill.

Kosterlitzky stopped the French guns and the shooting began to slow. It was strangely quiet, just sporadic shots here and there. The cacophony of explosions had temporarily deafened the avengers, and now the silence put them into a strange state of mind; the buzzing in their ears mixed with coming down from the battle high, the adrenalin rush. Everyone felt a little drunk, disoriented, unreal.

The less aggressive bad men began to surrender and Dick started to come down from his mania as well. He only killed three of the men trying to surrender and suddenly laughed out loud. The Englishman looked at him, confused. He didn't know the joke that had Dick so amused. The old Ranger Captain was thinking of Arvel.

He made it back to the nursery. The tough Texas Ranger was sitting among his little charges. He'd found them milk and was moving from one to the next. He burped them in turn. He looked very strange, blood and dust covering his face and clothes, with a little blanket over his shoulder to protect the babies from his outfit.

Dick smiled broadly at him. "All okay?"

The Texan smiled, "All okay, boss. All perfectly okay."

Dick and his British companion now turned their attention to the inner recesses of the fort and began searching the buildings one by one, kicking in doors, looking for any holdouts or further acts of barbarity. They came upon a group of captives, women and children, cowering under tables in a room. They were coated in dust and crying, terrified. They looked at Dick and James, waiting for the worst.

James called out to them in his perfect Castilian accent. He assured them that they were all safe now and the women believed him. No one with such queer Spanish was part of the bandit gang. They recognized the two men as their rescuers.

Chica rode up another staircase to Sombrero del Oro's hacienda. Arvel followed on Tammy and soon they were in the old bandit's home. They dismounted and Chica finally approached her lover. She grabbed him and hugged him.

"Rebecca is good, Pendejo, you know this?" She kissed him hard on the mouth.

"Your face is all crooked." She grabbed his jaw and moved it about. She grabbed his right arm, moved her hand down over it and picked up his hand. "You are a mess, Pendejo."

"I'm getting better." He grabbed her around her tiny waist with his left arm, pulling her tightly against his chest. He breathed deeply, taking in the scent he'd missed and thought he'd never know again, and gloried in having his love back in one piece. "I've missed you, Chica. I've really missed you."

She pulled back and examined him further, checking him for any other debility. She slid her hand down below his belt and grabbed him firmly, "Is the most importante thing working still, Pendejo?"

She looked him in the eye with an impish grin. "Oh, sí, it is good, it is very good."

She led him into Sombrero del Oro's bed chamber. Two bandits were hiding on the floor on either side of the frilly bed. Chica chose not to shoot them. She looked at them and told them to get out. They slunk away like a couple of scolded dogs. The rurales would deal with them.

She tipped Arvel off balance and onto the bed, turned and latched the door and was on top of him instantly. "I like you this away. You are easier to pin down." Straddling him, she kissed him hard on the mouth and made love to him with a recklessness, a desperation he'd never before known from his wild wife.

In short order, Dick Welles was calling for them. Arvel didn't want to answer, yet didn't want to worry his old partner. He finally called out. "I'm okay. In here, Dick . . ." Welles was soon on the other side of the door and reaching for the handle, "with Chica."

"Oh . . . oh!" Arvel could nearly feel the man blushing through door. He looked at his wife and they laughed together for the first time since the beginning of the nightmare. He hugged her tightly and felt something strange, something wet on his face, something he'd never seen in all the time he'd known her. She was crying.

He tipped her face up by the chin and looked her in the eye. She was smiling and crying all at once and his tears started flowing, too. No words were necessary, they held each other and cried and rejoiced that they and their little girl had survived.

When the smoke cleared and the bodies were removed, the extent of the fortress of horrors could be fully comprehended. Alice

Walsh walked amongst the victims of the bandits' brutality. It was heartbreaking. Many of the residents of the dungeon were children, born into the squalor and never even seeing the light of day. Their eyes were not accustomed to the daylight and many wore rags over their faces to block out the sun. Some had been kept in quarters so small that they had never stood upright. Their little backs were permanently bent. It was doubtful they would survive or, if they should survive, ever live a normal life. Some had been blinded completely because of a poor diet. Not because there was no food, but simply because of the diseased mind of the man who'd made this hell on earth for so many decades.

Alice Walsh looked up at Kosterlitzky as he rode about. The colonel was pleased. He'd run a good campaign with the aid of his friends to the north and suffered only minor casualties. They'd killed three hundred bandits and two hundred had surrendered. These would later be hanged in San Sebastian.

"You should not be so proud, I think, Colonel." Alice was overwhelmed with grief. She could not believe the inhumanity. Kosterlitzky was a little surprised at the woman's stern words.

"I am sorry, Mrs. Walsh, I don't understand."

"All these years, this has been allowed to go on, and all these years, you've been an official of the government and you've let it continue right under your nose."

"My dear madam," the colonel was patient with his guest. "I understand completely." He dismounted and took her by the hand, led her to the remnants of a wagon and handed her a flask. She drank and suddenly was sorry for her terse comments.

"With due respect, madam, I have two things to say to you. One, Guggenheim and two, U.S. Smelting."

"I don't understand, Colonel."

"The vast majority of this country's wealth is its natural resources, and ninety percent of the mining is owned by US interests, Mrs. Walsh. That means that persons such as you, the stock holders of these companies, are receiving great riches on the backs of the poor people of Mexico." He removed a cigarette from a gold case and placed it in an ivory holder. He lit it and drew deeply. "That leaves little for our government, and little for my rurales; little for the protection of this great land."

He looked on at Alice Walsh and continued. "As you know, I am not from this land, but I fell in love with it a long time ago. I knew the limitations, I know the leaders of the government are far from perfect, but I do what I can and . . ."

Alice looked him in the eye, "I apologize, Colonel." She looked at her hands. "My husband bought stock in both of those companies. I've benefited from them since his death, and I've lived comfortably. While all this," she looked on while a rurale helped a young blind girl to some water, "has gone on."

She started to cry and caught herself. She straightened her back.

"You are a good man, Colonel, and I aim to do something about this. This is a good land with good people, and they deserve better. You know my country is not perfect. We've had human trade for longer than any other civilized country in the world but we are getting better every day. There is no reason to believe that this land cannot become better. Would you accept my help if I offer it to you?"

"Of course, madam, of course." They sat together for a while and Alice Walsh even had a cigarette, just to calm her nerves. She'd been through more strife these past few days than she'd been through her entire life.

She suddenly felt alive, energized, as if she could jump up and run a marathon. She looked at her surroundings, noticed a little commotion and saw her boy emerge, his lovely wife in tow. They'd survived without a scratch and both looked radiant.

She gave them a little smile and nearly snuffed out the cigarette before they'd had a chance to see her engage in such scandalous behavior. She stopped herself and looked both of them in the eye and took a long drag.

Arvel smiled at her, Chica didn't see anything out of the ordinary. She looked on, indifferently. She was proud of the old woman.

"Abuelita," she walked up to the old lady and the colonel sitting together, "I think we all needa little trip to Maryland. What you say?"

"I think that's an excellent idea, Chica."

His rurales delivered a great prize in the form of the commander of the fort. The man was yet another image of Sombrero del Oro; younger, uglier, inbred, as if he was a kind of strangely manufactured being, a clay statue of a man that had not spent enough time in the kiln. His left ear was gone, sliced off by a rurale's sword and he was covered in his own blood.

The rurale captain pushed him forward. His hands were manacled and he had a malicious sneer on his face. The captain knocked his hat from his head and pushed him to his knees. Dick Welles spoke up first.

"Did you order those little children and babies killed, you bastard?"

The man would not look up. He was evil and defiant, but not so stupid as to incur their wrath any further.

Alice Walsh looked Dick in the eye. "Children? Babies? What are you talking about Captain Welles?"

"We saw 'em." He motioned with his head to his English companion. "Killed little children, over there, a pile of little children. And babies. We got to 'em first, but they were fixin' to kill babies in the cradle." He smiled proudly, "But they didn't get a one of 'em."

This was too much for Kosterlitzky, who'd been too far off directing the attack to see the particulars of the barbarity. He stood up and removed his pistol from its holster, pressed it to the man's temple and fired. The bandit leader pitched forward, dead.

Arvel breathed smoke through his teeth. "A good riddance to bad rubbish."

Kosterlitzky smiled, returning his gun to

its holster. He was very calm. The execution had no apparent effect on him. "Ah, you are fond of the writings of Mr. Tobias Smollett, Captain Walsh?"

Dick Welles interjected, breathing his answer through a plume of cigarette smoke. "Even though he was just a minor poet."

Most of the rurales were gone, off to escort the prisoners to San Sebastian. The Americans and Alejandro del Toro and his vaqueros made camp at the ruined fort. Dick Welles approached Arvel sitting on a pile of rubble. He was all alone.

"Where's Chica?"

"Off looking for her head. What's with that girl and heads?" He shivered, thinking about Chica cutting away.

Dick smiled and watched Arvel massage his right hand. "She had another tied to that Indian horse she rode in on. Saw it bouncing around in a feed bag, definitely a head."

"How was Dan when you checked on him, Dick?"

"Billy's got him in good shape, bleeding's stopped, he'll be okay."

Arvel ran his left hand through his hair and Dick could see it trembling. He smiled and lit a couple of cigarettes, handing one to his partner. He lay back on a pile of rubble next to Arvel, "I think this is the end of my adventuring, Arvel. Think I'm . . . we are too old for this shit."

"I will not disagree with you, Dick, I will not disagree one bit." He looked at a group of former captives. They'd been washing and Chica had found them clean clothes. They didn't know they had an audience and, for the first time for many of them, they chatted and even laughed a little, freely, without repercussions. Dick watched them and Arvel could just make out a little smile.

The smile turned sad and Dick looked at the end of his cigarette. "Lost Rosco."

Arvel looked his old partner in the eye, "No!" He thought of Dick's favorite mount. "Goddamn, Dick, I am mighty sorry. He was a good lad, a damned good horse." He fought back the tears again, cleared his throat hard.

"Got to admit, Dick," he nodded at the group, "we did good again, didn't we?"

Arvel looked at his partner through a haze of his cigarette smoke. Dick looked bad. The tumble from his horse had opened a big gash in his forehead and dried blood still covered his cheek and ear. His shirt was stained as well. He looked like a very old man to Arvel now. He moved about on the rubble seat as if every fiber in his being caused him pain . . . and it did.

Chica found her head and now focused on finding the old man. Marta's map was clear and Chica looked up, over the entrance to the dungeon and could make out the cave where the old man lived. Kosterlitzky's guns had dropped so much of the mountain top down into the fort that there now existed a ramp to the entrance and Alanza negotiated this with little difficulty.

Half of the cave was now exposed, and the deeper recesses were open to sunlight. She looked in and could see the old man clearly. He was sitting on a little wooden chair paging through a book. He looked in her direction when she entered his abode.

"Hola, Señor."

He looked up with vacant eyes and smiled in her direction.

"Ah, a visitor."

"I have come at the request of Marta."

"Sí." He motioned for her to sit down. "You are one of the fighters?"

"Sí. I am Maria, wife of Arvel Walsh." The old man acted as if this had no meaning to him.

"Come close, my dear." She sat beside him and he reached out, gently running his hands over her face, touching her koyera. He had smooth, gentle hands. They were completely clean, the cleanest thing Chica had seen that day. "Ah, Tarahumara." He felt some more. "What a lovely."

He moved his fingers over her eyes, then her cheeks and lips. "But you do not have the right accent."

"The Indios gave me the scarf when I moved through their land, Señor. I am Mexicana, and now an Americana."

"Ah, I see. And the child, she is all right?"

"Sí, she is in El Mundo."

"Ah, bueno, bueno, Señora." He had a kind face and looked like a living skeleton. He was all bones barely covered with skin. He had a long white beard but no hair on his head, his moustaches started up his nose and flowed downward to his chin.

Chica liked the old man. She looked around his little half-cave and saw the remains of Marta's ministrations. She'd stored plenty of food and water for him. He had a little cook stove and plenty of coffee.

"She will live with me, now."

"Sí, sí." He was pleased to hear this news. He went back to paging through the book. Chica figured it was just a method of keeping his hands occupied. It made no sense for a blind man to page through a book.

"And she wants you to come with me, so that you will live with me as well."

"Oh, no Señora, no, no." He smiled broadly and answered in his gentle, gentlemanly voice. "I am here, this is where I belong."

She was tired and answered him a little too tersely. Chica was not used to being refused. "Old man, the fort is no more. We are going to make it a pile of rubble and ash. Sombrero del Oro is no more."

"Ah, princesa. I see." This sounded particularly amusing to Chica and she smiled at his lifeless eyes. He grinned a toothless grin. "Sombrero del Oro always has a way of surprising you. He'll be back. He always comes back."

Chica pulled the sack with the head inside from Alanza's saddle skirt. She dropped it into the old man's lap. "Well, that'll be a good trick, old man, without this."

He felt through the burlap and knew at once what it was. He grinned broader still. "So this is really the maestro?"

He leaned forward and sniffed around the head's mouth. "Ah, yes, it is. He had peculiar breath." He drew in deeply, a great lungful of air and spit on the head's face.

He nodded at Chica and smiled. "Hah, it is so, Señora, it is finally so. I think you are at last the one to do it. You are a great warrior, little Artemis, a great warrior, indeed."

"Sí," Chica looked down at him as he ran his fingers over the head, "I've heard this before."

Will Panks and Raphael dynamited the dungeon closed, then methodically destroyed every structure that could serve in a capacity for defense, reducing the fort to rubble so that it could never be used in such a way again. Sombrero del Oro had produced many monsters and some would undoubtedly slip Kosterlitzky's noose. At least they would not be able to revive this chamber of horrors for any future enterprises.

Alice Walsh took Kosterlitzky's comments to heart. She worked tirelessly to get the survivors the help they needed and moved everyone, at her expense, to San Sebastian where she got those who needed it medical care.

As soon as was practical, she would contact her attorneys back in Maryland and have reporters brought down from San Francisco to chronicle the horrible conditions in the region. She'd have copies sent to the various American mining companies and would offer them an ultimatum:, either make living conditions better in Mexico, or suffer the consequences once the photographs and accounts got into the newspapers. She would do whatever was in her power to make things change.

She made it back to civilization, back to the Presidential Suite of the San Sebastian hotel. They had indoor plumbing and electric lights. She felt that she'd been away from such things for a decade instead of just one day.

She stripped and threw her clothes in a pile, ran the tub until it was nearly full of the hottest water she could bear. She soaked and worked the knots out of her old muscles, rubbing at the worn out joints. She brushed her teeth three times, washed her hair four and got into her comfortable bed to settle down to a good cry.

She cried for her family and for all the good men who helped them. She cried for the brutality of this cruel and ugly world. She cried for her own ignorance and innocence as she'd been on this earth for many years and never knew, never imagined, anything like this could exist.

She cried for her little Rebecca and wondered what she was doing now. She imagined the child in the safe convent and knew that soon they'd be together. She cried for Arvel and his broken body and Chica for whatever horrific life she must have led to make her the terror that she was. She was proud of her and sorry for her at the same time.

She cried until she had no more tears and lay back in her bed and looked up at the fan turning above her head. She listened to the sounds brought in by the cool breezes of the lovely Mexican night. They were happy sounds: music in the distance and people laughing, singing, and talking. She smelled the wonderful odors of food cooking, and she thought about the young people enjoying the community, enjoying their youth and the promise of good things to come.

She thought back to the celebration the night before the big battle. Of all the fine people and how they loved and cared for their children and each other. How they managed, many of them so poor, to make the best of things, how they had each other and led fulfilling lives.

She heard another sound, a cat meowing, down on the street below. A man was talking to the cat. He spoke lovingly and she could tell that they were great friends. He was kind and decent and she knew from the sound of his voice, that he had love in his heart.

She heard something else. By straining her ears and listening hard, she heard on the balcony one floor down, just beneath her window, a honeymooning couple. The woman's voice was lilting and happy. The man's tender and consumed with his new bride. They were speaking Spanish to each other in hushed tones and, even though Alice couldn't understand the words, she understood the meaning.

She took a deep breath, held it and listened. She surmised they'd just consummated their marriage and hoped that they were both virgins, not out of prudish moralizing, but in the hopes that it would have been the first time, the best first time for both. They were taking a little break, basking in the glow, excited for their future together and it suddenly seemed right. All was right in the world at this moment and, sighing, Alice felt the lessening of her despair and the beginning of hope. She fell into a deep, restful sleep.

Chapter XIX: Coming Home

Will Panks rode along half asleep with Raphael by his side. The young fellow was good company. Will never had a son and never had an apprentice. He was thoroughly enjoying his new role as Jefe.

His little horse hair cross was tapping along, a constant reminder of the young señora he'd helped rescue from the barbarous Dutchman. He'd sweated both cross and chain up so much now that it had become soft with the oils of his skin and didn't chafe him anymore. Even when it had, he wouldn't take it off. His bony chest was sore for the better part of a week.

He chose to ride back home alone and Arvel was not much surprised. Old Arvel could see into a man's soul. He certainly could see what Will was up to. Will even tried to get Raphael to go on with the party, but the young Mexican would have none of it. "I go with you, Jefe," is all he would say, and smile broadly. Like a loyal canine, he did not want to lose sight of his new master.

He thought about what he was going to say. What would she want with him? He was such an old crippled bastard. His back healed well enough, but in a permanent question mark and it made him look even older than he was.

My God, she was less than half his age. But there was something there, he was certain of it. Arvel was certain of it. Arvel mentioned it half a dozen times. Old Arvel liked a good joke and loved to tease his friends, but he wouldn't joke about such a thing as this. He wouldn't let Will Panks make himself out a fool. Arvel would not encourage a man to pursue a woman if there wasn't something to it.

As he rode, he thought more about it. He suddenly thought it was a stupid plan. He felt all jittery inside and looked north, just through that valley up there, between those mountains, that's where he'd have to turn off, go east and then the boy would wonder why they were going in the wrong direction. He'd smile and not ask, but he'd have the questioning look in his eye.

Maybe he'd send Raphael up ahead with Young Pop and Old Pop. He'd tell him to just stay on the road and he'd catch up. No, that was a bad idea. He didn't want the boy to travel alone and it was stupid to expose him to danger just because Will felt the old fool.

Before he knew it, he was there; the exact spot where the little boy was sitting and crying that day. No one had been by since. The remnants of Billy's little fire was still intact, untouched. Nothing had changed. Will rode past it. He rode past it and was seized by the terrible feeling in his gut that a man gets when he is in love and thinks it is the stupidest idea he's ever had.

He rode at least a hundred yards more and stopped. Raphael looked at him, then up at the sky. There was still half a day left to ride.

"Okay, Jefe?" The boy smiled. He was a delightful companion and Will looked on, then down at the ground.

"We've got to go and check on some folks, lad."

"Sí, Jefe."

Will smiled at the boy. Will could just as well have said, "We have to ride into the bowels of hell," and Raphael's response would be the same. He was completely dedicated to the old prospector.

He turned their little convoy around and got back to the burned out fire ring and then turned left and east and rode on. Will was silently rehearsing what to say when they reached the woman's hut; something that would not make it look like he was sniffing around looking for a woman, looking for a wife. He wasn't looking for a wife, he was looking for her.

His gut was hurting constantly now and before he knew it, before he was ready, he could make out the little hovel in the distance. It looked different now, less dilapidated. In only a few days it looked better, more complete, less dreary. His plan had been to ride in like a knight from Camelot, sweep her up, take her out of this hell, and now it didn't look so hellish. He'd lived in rougher mining camps. How could this be? The woman couldn't have done these things in her condition. She'd likely be moving slowly for many days yet. The child was much too young, much too small to do any heavy work.

Will suddenly knew the answer; this was a man's work. He stopped. Raphael, looking on and smiling, awaited his Jefe's next command. Will had gone rigid when he spotted the neatened cabin and now he started to turn them around, wanting to be invisible, trying to be quiet. He heard the little boy call from a distance.

"Caballero! Mamma, El caballero está aquí!"

There was nothing for it now. He couldn't turn back. He smiled weakly and rode up, stopping outside the shack's entrance, next to where the Dutchman had lost his head.

Will stood up in his saddle and tipped his hat, "Señora."

She looked better. The swelling was gone and her face was purple, the sclera of her left eye still bloodshot, but she looked better. He looked at her a little too obviously, then looked away. Her hair was different. She'd combed it over to try and hide her face while it healed. It was much prettier hair than he remembered. She was a lot prettier than he remembered.

She gave him a strange look. It was the kind of look a woman gives when she is very pleased to see a man but doesn't want the man to know it. This caused Will some confusion.

A man emerged from behind her, out of the shadows of the hovel. This had to be the man who'd done all the work.

Will nodded. "Señor."

The man nodded back. He was guarded, uncertain what the gringo wanted.

She spoke quickly to the man and he suddenly became friendlier.

"Ah, one of my sister's protectors."

Will grinned broadly. He smiled at the lady who beamed back. It was all right, it would be all right now.

Dan George sat quietly in the foyer of his home amongst a few patients waiting to be seen. He shushed them politely when they recognized and attempted to welcome him home. He could hear his wife's muffled voice behind the door of the examination room. He closed his eyes and listened, could make out the lovely pitch, the precise, direct way she spoke.

He changed his focus and listened to his little boy sitting on the floor next to her. He'd learned more words while Dan was gone.

It suddenly felt that he'd been gone a long time, a lifetime. He reveled in the moment and the throbbing in his shoulder stopped bothering him so much. His heart rate quickened when he heard his wife's counseling come to an end. The patient said her goodbyes, the chairs moved, there was a shuffling of feet.

He thought his little drama was now stupid and wanted to hide, run from the room as the door handle turned. He could see the shadows behind the frosted glass separating them. He dared not move, instead, breathing in deeply and looking at his wife as she surveyed the room for the next patient.

She didn't see him at first and he called out. "Is an appointment necessary?"

Ging Wa looked into his eyes. She stiffened, pulled herself together and glanced at him casually. "No, but you will have to wait your turn."

The other patients looked on, mouths agape; watched as Ging Wa led the next person into the exam room. Dan slumped down and smiled; it was going to be all right.

He dozed and, later, awoke to an empty room. Ging Wa led him by the hand to the examination room. She looked down at little Bob who'd fallen asleep amongst his toys. She got Dan undressed so she could see his wound. It was clean.

"Billy Livingston took good care of me."

Ging Wa said nothing. She smelled the wound, breathed deeply, and was satisfied. She cleaned it and redressed it. She looked into her husband's eyes and gave him a long, passionate kiss.

"I hope that not everyone gets that sort of treatment after an examination."

"Only the attractive young men."

He held her tightly and breathed deeply.

"You smell like medicine."

"You smell like a horse." She sat down on his lap and put his head to her breast. "I am glad you're home, Dan. I had a dream that I lost you and it made me very sad."

"I thought I was going to die, Ging Wa, and it made me sad, too. It made me very afraid and I want to tell you I'm sorry. I'll never go away again, I promise you."

She held him more tightly. "You will do what is right, Dan, always." She pulled his head up and looked into his eyes. "We will do right, always, as that is what we do."

Mother Superior sat and sipped tea as her little assistant moved around her bed chamber. The little nun remembered something and ran back to her cell to retrieve it. Like a magpie who had remembered the shiny object she'd secreted in her nest, she looked one last time at the diamond ring the Mexican woman had left in her care and hurried back to the old woman's room.

"What are we to do with this, Mother?"

The old woman looked at it, trying to remember back to the first day the señora entered their lives. She smiled and looked on at her assistant. "Give it to the child, Rebecca. She'll take it to her mother."

"And what of the other child, Marta?"

The old nun smiled gravely. "I believe she's going to be fine." She remembered the little bandit shooting the two bad hombres and could not help feeling a bit proud of the little girl. "She's going to be a handful for the Walsh family, no doubt, but I believe they're up to it."

The little nun lit lamps and could now see the toll this adventure had taken on the old woman. She worried over her sunburned face and hands. She looked the old woman in the eye. "I'm glad you are back home, Mother."

The old nun smiled and leaned back in her chair. "I am, too, child. I must say, I am, too."

They were interrupted by some joyful laughter in the room next door, the room that had once been occupied by the distraught señora. It was good to hear the laughter and the little nun looked at the old woman, "Shall I quiet them down?"

Mother Superior raised her hand, airily. "No, no let them laugh, let them bring some happiness. They've been through a lot and little Marta needs to learn to laugh, needs to learn to be a little girl."

And the girls did bring joy into the place. Marta was quickly transformed. Mother Superior wisely took everything from the child's old life away from her. She stowed away her gun and her cowboy outfit, her sombrero, her gun belt and her daga. Nothing was left to remind the child of her previous life as a bandit.

Rebecca decided she'd take Marta on a shopping spree and the two would be transformed into proper little ladies. Rebecca's plan was to dress her new sister as if she was a living doll and Marta thoroughly enjoyed it. She'd already begun to mimic Rebecca's actions and was very keen to learn how to behave properly.

N.S. Stein immediately came to Rebecca's mind. The little nun had gotten them cleaned up okay, but had purchased the most horrid looking prairie dresses she could find at the nearby dry goods store. Her daddy used to say of both of them, she and her mother, that they were spoiled but not rotten and Rebecca had, at an early age, developed a wonderful sense of style.

She was convinced the dresses must have been made from discarded feed sacks. She wasn't a proud or vain child, but she was used to nice clothing. She looked at herself and her little charge doubtfully.

Marta, on the other hand, was rather pleased with her new look. She liked the way the dress swished when she moved quickly from left to right.

"Come on, Marta, we need to get some other clothes." Rebecca took the little bandit by the hand and announced her intentions to the Mother Superior, who realized at once that they were not attired according to Rebecca's custom. She smiled at the thought of her poor clueless assistant; the young woman was the quintessential nun.

They made it to N.S. Stein in short order and Rebecca was immediately shocked at the cool greeting they received. She didn't realize that no one ever looked very carefully at eight year old customers. Her mamma and daddy were not there to be recognized and fawned over by the staff.

One haughtily dressed man ignored them, seemingly on purpose, and Marta walked up to him in her little general's stride. "We are in need of assistance."

The man looked at her over his spectacles, then at her feed sack dress, then at her little companion. "Go fetch your mother, child. I will help her."

"Pendejo, I have no mother, and this girl with me is a famous person."

Her daddy taught her how to deal with people who were rude or unkind, and Rebecca handled the man in this way. Her daddy always said that she should work to be kind to mean people as one could never know what's bothering them and they might just be having a bad day, or were unhappy in life for some reason. He told her to never take abuse from anyone, but never try to pick a fight or be nasty back to them.

She looked behind him and recognized an old man sitting at an important looking desk at the back of the store. He had his name on this desk which read N.S. Stein. Rebecca recognized him as the man who'd always treated her mamma as a queen. She walked past the officious clerk and up to the desk. The man was working diligently on some documents and Rebecca cleared her throat.

The man looked up and smiled. "Yes, madam, how may I help you?"

Marta was pleased to hear Rebecca called madam. She looked over at the clerk, satisfied.

"I'm Rebecca Walsh, sir. I've been coming to your store for a long time, but my mamma and daddy are not here right now." She looked over at Marta and smiled, "We need some new clothes and things."

The old man jumped to his feet. "Little Rebecca, of course, of course." He extended his hand to shake hers gently. He turned to Marta and bowed. "Madam." Marta beamed.

"I have heard of your troubles, little lady. I hope all is well."

"Yes, all is well, Mr. Stein. All is well. My mamma and daddy are still in Mexico, but we are at the convent. We have no money to pay you, Mr. Stein, but I remember Mamma telling the people here to put it on the account, which always was very surprising to Daddy when he got the letters from you."

The old man smiled broadly. He looked over at his newest clerk. "Welk, whatever the ladies want."

"Yes sir."

The clerk named Welk had a funny look about him. His lips were pushed up, toward his nose, as if he were breathing in an unpleasant odor. Rebecca remembered her daddy would sometimes point out people to her, "Look at that one, Rebecca." He'd then mimic them, screwing up his face and contorting it to make her laugh. "He looks like he just stepped in a pile of dog shit." She'd laugh all the harder at her daddy's naughty words.

This man did look as though he had stepped in dog shit and Rebecca could not help but look down at his fancy black congress gaiters for signs of excrement. Of course there was none. This man obviously worried a great deal over his appearance and he would never be caught with shitty shoes.

Marta found the man very amusing. He'd covered his black hair with too much oil and parted it down the middle, so that his white scalp shone through like a beacon. He looked mostly over his glasses rather than through them and this made his face stretch out all funny. The man was new to the West and Arizona as he had spent his formative years in Chicago. He'd not yet learned to hate Indians and Mexicans, and his negative response to the girls was not due to that prejudice, but rather to a general disdain for children.

Marta had some fun with him and he started to relax. He pretended not to care but, being new to the region, thought it good to learn the words common to the locals. He casually asked her to repeat the name that she used to address him.

"Pendejo."

The man repeated it carefully. "Pen-de-ho," rolling it around, off his tongue as if he were tasting it. "What is the meaning of this word in English?"

"Oh, it is a nice word. It means fine fellow."

Rebecca was trying on an outfit in the little dressing room next to them. She laughed out loud when she heard Marta's explanation. She did not see the clerk stand up a little straighter, pleased with the term the little girl had used to describe him. She dressed quickly, all the while envisioning the poor man using his new word in public at some restaurant or saloon and having his nose properly punched for his trouble. She came out still wearing the new dress.

"Sir, it really is not a nice word. My friend is just learning English herself and doesn't know." She gave Marta a knowing grin and a wink without letting the man see what she was doing. "May we see some shoes in our size, sir?"

When they were finally alone Rebecca chastised Marta in her best Pilar impersonation.

"Marta, you are not among savages anymore. You cannot call men pendejo. You have to act proper."

Marta smiled her devilish smile. "He is a Pendejo."

"That doesn't matter. And he isn't really. He's just different." She loved her naughty new sister, who reminded her too much of her mother. "You are a very bad girl."

The clerk returned with shoes in their size. Marta looked at the top of the man's head while he placed a shoe on her left foot.

"What is your name?" She half questioned and half demanded.

The man did not look at her and kept at the task at hand. "Mr. Welk."

"No, what is your other name?"

He did not understand and Rebecca interjected. "Your Christian name, sir."

He thought for a moment. The impudence of the little girl was astounding, yet there was something about her, something so natural and disarming that he found himself blurting it out. "Waldemar. But I like to be called Waldo."

"Waldo Welk?" Even Marta worked hard to control herself now. She was beginning to like the hapless dude.

"Well, Waldo." She admired the kid-lined shoes he'd placed on her feet, moving them one way, then the other to get a proper view. She leaned in close to his ear so that Rebecca could not hear her. "Do you know where I might get a cigarette?"

They returned from shopping, looking like two debutantes twice their age. Most of the packages would be sent to the convent for them, but Marta insisted on carrying many of the most exciting items with her. The present source of their joy was Marta's interest in looking at herself through the gilt hand mirror Rebecca had purchased for her. She'd look left and then right. She liked the new way Rebecca had fixed her hair. She'd make comments into the mirror about how beautiful she looked, then would screw her face up like a monkey and ask Rebecca how she looked.

She eventually stopped that and went on to her tatting, periodically gazing down at her lap, at the lovely material of the new dress she was wearing. It was so much finer than the one the nun had gotten them, and that one seemed wonderful at the time.

Little Marta was learning quickly. She'd become better at tatting and had created two doilies. She wanted to make something for Señora Maria.

"You know, you could call her Mamma if you wanted?" Rebecca did not look up from her own work.

"Sí, I know." Marta was suddenly overwhelmed. "But, she is not my mother."

"I know. But there is enough of her to go around. And then we could be sisters."

"Could we?" Marta looked at Rebecca who could now barely recognize her. Gone was the fearless little bandit. Gone was the cigarette-smoking profane creature she'd encountered just a few days before, at least from where Rebecca was sitting.

Rebecca looked back at her work. "I think so."

The redheaded lady watched them go into their little cell. She looked back at her sleeping boy, looked around at her small room. It was safe here, safe and cool and quiet. It smelled good. It smelled of fresh bed linen and candle wax and the slightest hint of incense from special mass celebrations.

The nuns were so kind to her and her little boy and the other captives. She didn't want to ever leave the convent. She'd had a lot of time to think here. She'd been so confused over the past days. She'd experienced the worst calamity of her life; the horrible, repeated assaults, the violation of her body, the decadence of the men who'd been her tormentors for so many days.

She wasn't a worldly woman, but she'd had her share of book learning and was a voracious reader. But nothing up to this point in her life could have prepared her for this. Not even in her wildest dreams could she have ever imagined such inhumanity.

She wandered over to the chair and table next to the beds. The boy's nightmares were so intense that she had put the mattresses on the floor, making a large bed so that they could sleep together. This was the first time in her life she let the child sleep with her.

She felt guilty because her kindness to him was so alien, so out of character that he'd stiffen, holding back because he didn't want her kindness to end but didn't want to do anything to set her off for fear that she'd resort to her old ways.

She hated herself for this. She should not have treated the child in such a way just because his father had done her wrong. It wasn't the child's fault and she knew the boy didn't deserve it. She knew what the fat bandit had done to her son the night he'd taken him away, the night that she thought he was gone from her forever, and the thought of this made her especially sad. She'd make it up to him, though. It wasn't really hard being kind or loving to him. He was a good boy and responded so positively to her love.

He was sleeping well now and she wandered out into the courtyard where a brother was working on a small garden. This was the first man she'd encountered since her abuse. She thought she'd not want to see another man, especially a Mexican, and now there was one just a few feet away.

He looked up from his work and invited her to sit down on a bench next to the garden. He was dressed in a plain brown robe and sandals. He looked timeless, old-timey in the backdrop of the plain adobe-walled convent. It reminded her of how she used to be transported to a place in time and history, when she and her sister read one novel after another. She could have been in an ancient monastery in France or Italy.

She sat silently for a while, watching him work. He was an older man, very dark, more Indian than Spanish. He worked the garden with care, gently, so as not to bruise or do harm to the plants. It was especially significant to the woman, as she'd only known cruel hands for so many days. He never spoke to her or even looked in her direction. He thought that perhaps it was just good to have another human being in her presence, so that she wasn't alone but was not obliged to interact in any way.

These were her saviors: Papists and Mexicans and children. It was confounding to her. She finally felt compelled to speak. "How long have you been here, brother?" She'd heard the nuns call him that, and thought it appropriate.

The man didn't look up from his work. "Fifteen years, Miss." He stood up straight and surveyed his work, reached over and pulled a weed that had escaped him. "I lived in a village down in Mexico, but Sombrero del Oro came and," he made a little sound with his mouth and waved his hand in the air, "all gone."

She suddenly felt a connection with him. "You were not always in the church?"

The man smiled. "Oh, no, Miss. I had a family and a trade. I was a blacksmith. I still do blacksmith work here at the convent." He pointed to some iron hinges on the garden gate. "I made them."

He took his gloves off and laid them down.

Without asking, he walked over and sat down next to her. She didn't mind. "I had a wife and two children and my mother and mother-in-law, all living together at our home. And, puff, it was all gone."

"I am sorry." And she honestly was. She never thought she'd feel sorry for any man again, any Mexican or, for that matter, anyone who wasn't just like her. He smiled at her and patted her arm.

"And I am sorry for you, dear. But, now he's gone, no more Sombrero del Oro."

She thought for a moment and looked at the old fellow. He'd survived. He'd lost more than she. She'd been terribly brutalized, it was true, but her boy was alive. She suddenly felt strange, even fortunate.

"Tell me," she was not trying to pick a fight with the old man, but was genuinely curious. "How did you come to join the church?"

He laughed a little. He sensed where she was going, what she was thinking. "You would think that I would be angry at God for my predicament, but," he sat quietly for a moment.

She interjected, "Why would God let these things happen? Why would He allow Sombrero del Oro to exist?"

"Yes, yes."

"Have you found the answer?"

"No, I have not."

Marta woke early and left the little room as Rebecca slept. It wasn't quite daylight but something had been on her mind ever since she'd seen the brother in the garden the day before. She picked her way quietly through the breezeway to the spot.

The man smoked but never stripped his cigarette butts. For some reason, he put them in a little bucket in a corner covered by shrubbery. Rebecca found it after a short search and pulled a dozen little stubs together. She'd gotten some old newsprint and fashioned a cigarette paper from it, creasing it down the middle. Into this she dumped the contents of the stubs and eventually had a serviceable smoke. She lit it with a match she'd taken from the bedside table and smoked and blew smoke up at the sky as daylight began to illuminate the little courtyard. Birds began to sing and lizards appeared amongst the stones on the walk. Everything was moving about her.

She liked this place, but so many images of Jesus and The Virgin made her think a lot about how things were unfolding in her life. She couldn't help but feel a bit strange. She'd never had this uneasy, even foreboding, feeling in her life and she wasn't certain she liked it much.

The Mother Superior was leaning over her shoulder before she could react. She knew the old woman wouldn't like to see her smoking, but the nun said nothing. She sat down next to the little girl and still said nothing.

"Old nun . . ." she knew that was not the right way to address the woman, but was uncertain as to what was correct. She was just learning civility and it was coming to her slowly.

"Yes, child."

"I wonder if I will go to hell when I die."

"Not if you lead a good life and take Christ into your heart."

"I've done bad things."

"I see." The old woman thought back to

the incident in the desert. She decided not to push the girl.

"I don't mean killing." Little Marta was a smart child. She seemed to be able to read the nun's mind.

"Oh, I see."

"I let many bad things happen to people. The red-haired lady. And many others. I would just stand there and let the things happen." She looked into the nun's eyes and was genuinely confused. "Will that make me go to hell?"

Mother Superior took the cigarette from Marta's hand and crushed it out. "Smoking is a vile and filthy habit, Marta."

"The Mexican lady does it."

"Ah, this is true." She laughed a little. It was barely audible. "You like her, don't you?"

"Oh, yes, sister, I like her. Rebecca says I may call her Mamma, but she's not my mamma."

"Would you like it if she were?"

"Oh, yes." She began to fidget as she no longer had a cigarette between her fingers. "She kills men, but she will not go to hell, will she, sister?"

"I don't know, child. Everyone has to stand before God when the time comes and I don't know what is in her heart."

Marta stood up. She was finished now. She felt a bit better. She looked the nun in the eye again and smiled. "I do."

Uncle Bob leaned into the doorway of Pilar's room. He'd gotten in late and she'd finally fallen asleep. He listened to her snoring. It wasn't a pleasant sound, but the best he'd heard in days. He breathed deeply, breathed in the familiar smell of home. He began to turn away, disappointed but willing to wait until morning when she spoke from her bed.

"Do you need coffee, old man?"

"No, no. I'm sorry to wake you, old girl." He took a couple of steps forward and she, without further acknowledgement, held up the blanket, welcoming him into her bed.

He kissed her all over and was pleased to find her without her big sack of a sleeping gown. She pressed herself against him, burying her face into his old boney sternum.

"I brought you some things."

"From the desert?"

"No, no, old girl, we spent some time in San Sebastian."

"Oh, with the whores, no doubt."

"Oh, you are a bad old girl."

"And you are a bad old man." She felt him next to her. "You are like a young colt, old man."

"I've been thinking of you, old girl. I've been thinking of you all the time."

"Everyone is good?"

"Yes, all good. Arvel's better, Chica is all right, Rebecca's in the convent down in Bisbee." He sat up and undressed. The gifts could wait until morning. "And Rebecca's got a new sister."

"Ay, I've heard of this thing." Pilar climbed onto the old man and kissed him gently on the mouth, then covered it with her hand. "No more talking."

"I need to say one thing," he was beginning to become distracted. Pilar was a powerful woman for her age. "I love you old girl. I don't think I've ever said that, but I love you and I think it's time I made an honest woman of you."

She let out a little sound, a happy sound and went back to the business at hand. "No more talking old man."

After awhile she took up the conversation that had been so pleasantly interrupted. "Roberto, I cannot marry you."

"Oh?" He was drifting off to sleep and this awakened him. "This is silly superstition, Pilar. I will not die just because you marry me. It is silly and I expect more out of you." He looked over at his clothes, too far away to get up for a cigarette.

"I am from the land, Roberto. I am a peon, a peasant. I would not be worthy of even a shop owner, much less a hacendado. It is not the right thing, Roberto."

He was getting a little angry now. He sat up and walked to his cigarettes. He found one and a match. He smoked for a moment. He thought hard about what he was going to say. He could see his love in bed, lying on her side, facing away from him, breathing quietly. She was such a hard head.

"You listen to me, Pilar." He waited until she turned to look him in the eye. She'd not heard this tone ever from the kind and gentle Uncle Bob. When he had her attention, he continued.

"You are not in Mexico. You are in my land now. And I don't mean the US. I mean you are on my land, my land and Arvel's land and Chica's land, and your land. I make the goddamned rules here. And what I say is the law around here!

"Hacendado! I cannot believe you'd use that term on me. I am not a hacendado! I am not a tyrant and we do not live like royalty with serfs and vassals. This is not India with a caste system. This is not Mexico. This is the goddamned united states of Robert! Goddamn it, Pilar, you've really made me angry." And he was, but not as angry as he appeared to the woman. A little theatre was in order as far as he could see. He stopped and smoked. Waited.

"I understand."

"Then, what will it be, woman? I am tired. I want to go to sleep. What will it be?"

Dick Welles sat in his new sack suit at the office of the Northern Mining Company. He waited patiently but squirmed on the hard wooden chair until his son sauntered out from a corner in one of the back offices that had no windows. He'd been working here for six years as a clerk. He had not seen his father for more than seven.

"Hello, Father." He was shocked to see the old fellow in such a state. Dick grinned sheepishly and held up a hand.

"I know, boy. I've looked worse."

"Not that I've ever seen." He was able to relax. When his father called him boy, it was always a good sign.

They walked together to the hotel restaurant next door and looked over the bill of fare in silence.

Michael finally spoke up. "I understand you had quite a time in Mexico."

Dick nodded.

"And Captain Walsh's little girl's okay?"

"Yes, all good, Michael. All good."

He shifted on his chair and looked at his son more carefully. He looked good. After six years, Michael had beaten the hold that the laudanum and gambling had over him.

Michael had taken up housekeeping with a retired prostitute and they had a child together. Dick had helped them over the years, but would never come to visit or even acknowledge that he had a grandchild. Even after his wife had died, and he spent many lonely nights at home, he just could not bring himself to get involved. Now everything was about to change. He swallowed all his stoic pride and decided to just come out with it.

"I figured something out down there in Mexico, Michael." His son looked at his father, wondering if it was not some man impersonating his father.

"Oh?"

"I figured out that I'm a colossal ass and I'm mighty sorry for all I've done, or, I guess I should say, haven't done." He looked his son in the eye and really wanted to look away. "That was a damned fool and prideful thing, and I know it now. Sal seems a good lady . . ." Michael snorted and his father held up his hand. "Yes, a lady, and

I'm damned proud of how you and she put yourselves in order."

"That's the first time you called her by her name, Father."

"Well, it's not going to be the last. And little Rick, I've been away from him too long..."

"Actually, you've never seen the boy."

"Fair enough." He managed a weak smile. "Fair enough, Michael. You named the boy after me and I couldn't even give him the courtesy of a visit. I've sent you money over the years, but that doesn't cut it. I'm damned sorry, Michael. Can you forgive me?"

Michael sat back in his chair and whistled low through his teeth. "My God, you must've had a time down there in Mexico, Father." He sat up in his chair and leaned forward. Dick was half worried his boy was going to tell him to go to hell and Dick wouldn't have blamed him if he had.

Instead, the man put out his hand for Dick to shake. He reached into his suit pocket and pulled out a checkbook. "That is something I've been meaning to make right, Father." He wrote a check out quickly and handed it over. "This is what you've been giving us all these years, and I thank you for it, Father, but if you'd have come around to see us, you'd know we didn't need it. I've been saving it up to give back to you."

Dick took the check and stared at the number. "Was it all that much?"

"Yep."

"Well, I'll be."

Their food came and they ate quietly for a while. Michael was in a good mood now. He spoke constantly of his little boy and the boarding house he and his wife had run successfully for the past four years. He finally looked over at his father.

"You know, Dad." He wiped his mouth with his napkin. "Arvel Walsh came to see me a few years ago."

"No, I didn't. What did old Arvel have to say?"

"He said, be patient with your father. He said that you are the best man he knows in the world, but you are more hard-headed than any mule he's ever trained in all his twenty five years in the business." Dick blushed and stared at his plate. "He's the reason why I never gave up on you."

"Well, I'll be."

They talked well into the afternoon and then Dick waited for his son to finish work. He went home with him to the boarding house. He'd gotten a bouquet of roses for

Sal and candy for little Rick.

"Salvatora, this is my father."

He held his hat in his hand as he came through the door. Sal had never clapped eyes on her father-in-law, yet she knew him immediately. Her husband had his father's eyes.

"Ma'am." He bowed nearly to the waist. "Please forgive me."

She took him by the arm and brought him into her home. He was welcome. Little Rick had come out of his room, took one look at him and smiled.

"Rick, this is your grandfather."

"Capitan Welles, of the Arizona Rangers!" Little Rick held out his hand and his grandfather shook it. "Le conozco!"

"En Inglés, Rick, en Inglés." His father admonished him gently.

"No, no!" Dick smiled at them, "Es muy bueno."

The child led the old man into his bedroom where a shrine was set up in his grandfather's honor. Pictures and newspaper clippings, an Arizona Rangers badge, and other memorabilia adorned every wall of the room. Dick looked up at his son and had to look away. It was the first time in his life he wanted to cry.

■ ■ ■ ■

That evening they sat on the big front porch and watched the town go to sleep. Little Rick came out and kissed his grandfather's cheek. He'd not known such a thing for many, many years and it brought back fond memories. He watched Sal walk with the child back into the home.

"She's a beauty, Michael. They're both a pair of beauties."

Michael got a kick out of his father's new sensitivity. He decided to be a little bold. "In all these years, Dad, what was the thing that made you the most put off?"

Dick looked over at his boy. He was not angry at the question. It was time for candor.

He began to speak when Michael finished his thought, "was it my nonsense, or the fact that Sal was a whore . . ."

"Don't call her that."

"She was a whore, Dad, plain and simple. Hell, everyone knows it."

"I know but it's an ugly word. It's a demeaning word."

"Or was it because she's a Mexican?"

Dick sat back and lit a smoke. He breathed the tobacco in deeply. "It was everything,

Michael. It was everything."

"And, so, why the change?"

"Michael," he turned and looked his son in the eye. Michael looked like a young, fit version of Dick Welles, and the fact of it made what he was going to say that much more significant.

"I'm seventy years old, Michael. All my life, I've been fightin' to make something of myself. I had in mind that you'd be something too, something big, like Arvel Walsh's people. You, and what you've done, mixing with prostitutes, carrying on, mixing with Mexicans, that didn't fit into my plan. I was so ashamed of you, Michael. I just pretended you didn't exist. I've always held myself up to a high standard and I could not get beyond all that."

"I see." Michael felt wounded by his father's words.

"Then, I finally grew up, Michael. After seventy years on this earth, I finally grew up. Can you believe that?"

"And this foray into Mexico did all this?"

"Yes and no." He looked at the railing around the porch, studied it as if it held the words he wanted to use. "I almost found out the grand secret down there, if you get my meaning."

"Well, I imagine you almost met your

Maker at least a dozen times with the war and your rangering."

"Not so, Michael, not so. You'd think that, but I've led a charmed life. But down there, it came close. And there was something else. I swear, boy, I stared into the devil's own lair. I saw something down there that was unnatural, something beyond what decent folks should ever know. It was a wakeup call."

"So, you've learned to love Mexicans and whores and opium eaters?" His son grinned sheepishly.

"Well, it's not that simple. Let's call it an awakening. I guess old Arvel Walsh had a lot to do with it. I just don't know, Michael. I just don't know, but can we at least agree that maybe I've finally figured out it isn't my place to look down my nose at you because you've had problems or little Sal because she had to do things that she didn't want to do, for whatever reason, or that she has a different shade of skin than me?" He laughed at his own foolish words.

"Arvel told me a quote one time when we were on the trail, from some minister fellow, a Scotsman, I think. It was, 'Be kind, for everyone you meet is fighting a hard battle.' I think that's how it went." He felt foolish saying it.

"I'm not a philosopher, Michael. I leave that up to the learned class, the men like Arvel Walsh. But I know that you're my son and I'm damned proud of you. You're a good man and a good husband and father. You have a beautiful wife and she's a good mother, and you've got a fine son and he's going to be a good man. And, if you'll have me, I'd like to be a part of it."

"You're most welcome, Dad. You've always been welcome." Michael smiled and looked off into the distance, down the street at some activity. "Fighting a hard battle." He looked back at his father. "That about sums it up."

"For you?"

"Yes. I'll tell you now, Dad. If I could, I'd drink a whole bottle of that shit right this minute and be happy to do it."

Dick smiled, knowingly. "Your mother said it was all her fault. You got it in your blood from her side of the family; whole line of drunks and opium smokers."

"Like Uncle Al."

"Like Uncle Al."

"I used to think about him a lot when I was really low down. You know, your money and Sal is what saved me."

"Was it?"

"She used to take care of me. One day I

looked at her and told her I didn't want to live this way anymore. You know what she said to me?"

"What?"

"She laughed and said, 'You rich gringos can pick and choose your misery.' She said, 'I never wanted to live this way.' " He grinned at his father. "She'd just turned seventeen, wise beyond her years. She's always been so much wiser than me, than anyone else I've ever known."

"Out of the mouth of babes, eh, son?"

"Yep. And then I got my ass cleaned up and Sal and I took the money you sent me and we came here. No one knew what we were in San Francisco, at least not initially, and no one knew about Sal. She worked and worked and saved and took care of me to keep me on the straight and narrow, and, well, even though I'd drink a bottle of laudanum right now, I don't do it." He laughed cynically.

They sat a while and said nothing. Finally, Michael looked over at his father. He was an old man. He was old beyond his years and Michael knew that part of that age was his fault. He finally spoke, "I'm not so sure you're the ass that you paint yourself to be."

"No?" Dick blew smoke at the street.

"No. Arvel told me about how much nicer

you were than you let on. How you were the one who often held him back. I never used to believe it, but now I do. You aren't as much the hard case as you'd like to think." He laughed again. "He told me about how good you always were to Mexicans and Chinese and Negroes and how you changed your tune with his wife. He said you'd talk a big game but your actions never did match your words." He grinned broader. "The old coot couldn't keep his eyes off my Sal, by the way. He sure has a weakness for these Mexican gals."

"Oh, well, I can tell you, Michael, Sal and Maria could be sisters." He suddenly felt embarrassed. "You know, Arvel would never do anything like that, you know . . ."

"Oh, no, Dad. Didn't mean he would, and he wasn't crass about it. I'm just sayin' he sure loves Mexican women."

Dick smiled at his boy and then became downcast. "Well I sure let you down, didn't I, Michael?"

"No, Dad, you let yourself down. You missed out on a few years with Rick, and you missed out on the love of a wonderful gal."

He pointed with a nod of his head toward his bedroom where Sal was by now sleeping. "But, you've only let yourself down, and now it's time to make up for that lost time." He stood up and stretched, faced his father and put out his hand.

Things would be different from now on.

The next morning Dick Welles went to the bank and opened a new account. He deposited his son's check and added another thousand in the name of Richard Michael Welles.

Mother Superior rode next to the brother blacksmith from Bisbee to the Walsh ranch. It was a glorious morning and everyone was happy. Rebecca and Marta rode in the back, amongst their many N.S. Stein boxes. They tatted and talked and laughed the whole way. Marta could be periodically seen, lifting her head, breathing in the cigarette smoke, like a cat who'd just discovered her master preparing fish for dinner. The Mother shook her head slowly from side to side, a brief look of consternation on her face, but said nothing.

By late morning, they rounded a bend in the road and the ranch could be seen off in the distance. Rebecca was so excited and proud to show off her home to the little party. "There it is!"

Marta looked up from her work. She surveyed the land as if she were a potential buyer. A bell could be heard ringing off in the distance, announcing their arrival and when they finally approached the mule ranch, everyone was waiting for them. Like two princesses home from a long journey, their court stood in a proper receiving line to welcome them home.

Rebecca couldn't wait for the plodding horses to get there. She jumped out of the wagon and ran to her father, literally knocked him to the ground. "Daddy, Daddy!"

Arvel held her tightly, as if she were an overzealous puppy threatening to squirm out of his grip. He wrapped his arms around her and kissed her head, then her cheeks. He didn't try to stand up and they lay together for several moments as the others looked on.

Finally, Rebecca helped him to his feet. She held his hand and led him to the newly arrived carriage. "Everyone, this is my daddy."

Arvel shook hands with the brother and bowed while tipping his hat to the Mother Superior. "Ma'am, I am indebted to you."

Mother Superior blushed and looked down at the ground. Arvel Walsh, despite his years and present infirmity, was a handsome and gallant man.

"And this is Marta."

He beamed at the girl as he held out his hand to her. Marta shrugged up her shoulders, a new habit she'd acquired now that she was among human beings. She felt, was beginning to feel, more often humble these days.

She extended her hand and Arvel made a great bow as he took it and kissed it gently on the knuckle. He took off his hat and placed it over his heart. "You are much taller than I expected, my girl."

Rebecca stood, proud that the two were finally together. She felt not the slightest twinge of regret or jealousy. She loved them both, little Marta and her daddy and, just like with her mother, she was certain there was enough love to go around.

"Daddy, you might get a big letter from N.S. Stein." Arvel smiled at her, now focusing on the little girls' couture. "It wasn't Marta's fault, Daddy. I just got a little carried away." She looked to the back of the carriage at the many boxes.

"Oh?" He pretended to look concerned, but could not carry it off. He began grinning at his two little princesses. "Whatever it takes, my girl, whatever it takes to keep you two looking so beautiful is money well spent."

Rebecca turned to Uncle Bob and Pilar. "This is Marta."

They smiled at the child and Pilar could not help but think back to the day she'd first met Chica. This little child was obviously very much like that wild woman, but this time, Pilar didn't mind.

Rebecca could not contain herself and grabbed Pilar, pulling her down so that she could reach and kissed the woman on the cheek. "I've missed you, Pilar."

"And I you, my little one."

"You sure had us worried, child." Uncle Bob stood next to Pilar, beaming at the girl. "So, this is the famous Marta."

Marta smiled at the old man. She felt so queer. Evidently, the fine lady had told everyone all about her. It felt funny to be such a celebrity. She didn't fully comprehend the greatness of her deeds and could not believe that these decent folk wanted to give her any consideration at all. They were all so good. Good people. Chica was behind her and spoke up, "Marta, you remember this one?" The old man stepped out from behind one of the ranch hands.

"Old man!" She was pleased to see him. She looked up at Chica. "I knew you would find him! Thank you, Señora."

She ran up to the old man, not certain

what to do. He reached out and touched her under the chin.

"Old man, what is your name?"

The old man smiled. He knew now that the little girl would be all right. She was learning from the fine people, learning to be civil, learning to be a human being. "I am Ramon Jesus Santiago de la Garza." He grinned broadly. "But you can call me Old Man."

Everyone laughed loudly and the old man smiled.

"We are in El Mundo now, eh, Old Man?"

"Oh, yes, little one, we are in El Mundo for certain."

Marta looked back at Chica again. "Thank you."

Rebecca began looking about, searching for her grandmother and suddenly felt anxious that she might not be well. Before she could speak, Abuelita could be seen galloping up on a lathered pony, riding sidesaddle. She looked grand in her outfit and quickly slid off the horse and landed in their midst. She grabbed her granddaughter and spun her around. Rebecca looked down and introduced her to Marta.

Abuelita smiled, "So, we finally meet." She kissed Marta hard on the cheek, leaving a big wet mark and the former bandit was not certain what to do. Abuelita grabbed her with one hand and Rebecca in the other and moved deliberately toward the house. "Let's eat."

They got everyone to the table and had a grand lunch. The girls ate together and afterward Pilar ushered them into Rebecca's bedroom. A second bed had already been placed next to Rebecca's so that her new sister would be beside her. They prepared to change into riding clothes as Marta looked about the room, jaw agape at its loveliness.

"You can have your very own room, if you want, Marta, but I wanted you to stay with me for now, if that's okay." Marta stood, looking stunned. Her eyes moved about the room. She'd never known such a room. The maestro had a fancy, frilly room, but it looked like a bordello. This room was pretty and feminine and Marta wondered if, once she settled in, she'd ever want to leave it.

She looked at Rebecca's library with so many wonderful books. She picked one up and looked through it. Until now, she'd only known the Bible and an old World Atlas and the book about the man walking through hell with Virgil. Rebecca's books were a special prize, indeed.

"I want to stay in here, Rebecca, if you'll have me."

Rebecca had rummaged through her wardrobe and found two bathing suits. She gave the bigger one to Marta. She would be able to squeeze into her last year's suit. It would do and, anyway, they always stretched once they got wet. She handed the new suit to Marta who looked at it, uncertain of its purpose.

"We are going up to Rebecca's place."

"You have your own house?" The little bandit was confused and Rebecca smiled.

"No, it's a camp, an old Indian ruin on our land. There's a nice deep pool and we can swim. It was named after my daddy's first wife. She died."

She went out as Marta finished dressing for the ride. Marta wasn't used to her new boots but wanted to get them right without Rebecca's help.

As Rebecca waited for Marta she watched her father fumble with Tammy, getting ready for the afternoon's ride. He looked so old and frail to her now and she realized what he must have been through down in Mexico. She saw that he had to shuffle. He used to skip around like a young boy but now he dragged his feet and had to use his left hand to make his right hand behave. She watched him until he noticed her.

"All ready?" He still had the same wonderful smile, though. Nothing would ever make him stop smiling, she was certain.

"Daddy, you are not well." She looked as though she might cry.

"Oh, it's nothing, darling." He walked with her to the bench by the bunkhouse and sat down. He pulled her onto his lap and held her gently. "I'm getting better all the time."

"What happened to you?"

"A broken heart." She looked at him, confused.

"When I heard about you and Mommy and Grandmother, I just fell over, had a broken heart, and it made my face all crooked, made me all limp on this side." He showed her his hand, pretending to lose control of it and she smiled weakly. "But I'm better now. Not back to my old self yet, but much better."

She kissed him on the cheek and put her arms around him, squeezing him with all her might.

He became a little serious. "I'm awfully sorry this happened, Rebecca. I'm awfully sorry I didn't get you right away. God knows I would have traded places if I could.

I . . . your mother sure saved the day, didn't she?"

"She did, Daddy, but I never once thought you didn't do your best. I never ever thought you weren't trying."

By late afternoon they were at the deep pool. It had been well kept since Chica had come into their lives. She meant for it to commemorate the memory of Rebecca the wife, and Arvel's first child. She was also fond of it because it was where she fell completely in love with Arvel and where she guessed, by her best reckoning, that little Rebecca had been conceived.

They'd built a small cabin here and rebuilt the stone wall of the Indian cave dwelling. The girls ran inside to change into their bathing suits. They were splashing and swimming in short order. Rebecca began teaching Marta to properly swim.

"Shall we go for a dip, Old Girl?" Uncle Bob smiled slyly at Pilar.

"Old Man, you know I don't swim." She was working, preparing for dinner, as everyone milled about, reveling in the return home of their wonderful family, happy to be alive.

Arvel and Chica sat together, legs dangling in the pool and Chica whispered into his ear, "Remember what we did here the first time, Pendejo?" She smiled and gave him a wet kiss on the ear. "We made that one."

She pointed at her little girl with her toe. Arvel blushed and Chica threw her head back, laughing. The girls looked up. It was the first time Marta had heard her new mother laugh and it made her feel good, all fluttery in the pit of her stomach. She looked down at herself in Rebecca's bathing suit.

"I never swam in clothes before." She was pleased.

They were permitted to stay up as late as they wanted. Uncle Bob brought a guitar and they played and sang. Pilar made so many pan de muertos that Rebecca couldn't finish all of hers and gave them to Marta who'd eaten her share and was ready for more. She'd never tasted anything like them in her life.

Try as they might, they just couldn't stay up any longer and bedded down under the stars. Their daddy made up a big sleeping bag so they could lie down together. Marta looked over at her new sister. She listened to the happy voices of the adults nearby. Everyone was so happy and gay and they spoke of wonderful things. They said no bad words and no one was drunk or fighting or retching or screaming or crying out. No one was threatening or dangerous or mean. "It cannot always be like this, can it Rebecca?"

"Like what?" Rebecca was drifting, she half mumbled her reply.

"So nice and good and happy."

"Oh, it is, Marta." She snuggled down into the blanket and fell fast asleep.

Marta followed. She yawned and mumbled. "This isn't El Mundo . . . this is heaven."

Billy Livingston made it to the cool dark of the Bisbee Library on a sunny day. The old librarian was waiting for him; it was nice to be missed. She walked him to a quiet corner where she'd held a collection of the most recent editions of The Lancet, Nature, and the Journal of the American Medical Association. She noted that Dr. George had recently read them and asked the librarian to point out the articles that would likely be interesting to him. He smiled at her and sat down for a long afternoon of reading. He thought about Dan George's wound and decided he'd leave at five to check in on the family.

As he read, his mind wandered back to the events of the past days. He was a fortunate man because he was permitted to do things that reflected his talents. This he attributed primarily to Arvel Walsh. It was Arvel who brought him into this circle of friends and it was Arvel who was the glue that kept them all together. Without him, Billy would just be another eccentric genius, wandering the deserts of Arizona and Mexico. Now he was Billy Livingston the Healer, and famous throughout the land.

He was not getting younger and thought hard about Ging Wa's offer. He liked the young woman. She treated him as an equal. Certainly he was no physician and he appreciated his limitation in that respect, yet she always acknowledged his terrific powers of observation and his appreciation for science and objective medical research. She believed it was the basis for medical practice. She'd known so-called physicians with university training who could not judge good scientific data if it hit them over the head, often choosing silly home remedies and old wives' tale treatments, to evidence based on empirically proven methods.

Ging Wa needed help and Billy could definitely serve as a capable man-midwife without further training; he'd delivered many babies. He was also capable at tending to wounds and infections. And when he was not helping at Ging Wa's practice, there'd certainly be time to work in the library on research and this thought was very pleasing to him.

He thought about the fact that he was an aborigine, and this worried him a bit. He'd never want the George family to lose their standing in the community by having him around. They'd both overcome the stigma of Dan being an Indian lawyer and Ging Wa a Chinese physician. Dan and Ging Wa had both candidly discussed this. The majority of their clients was poor and was just glad for excellent legal services and medical care. They didn't see Billy's ethnicity as a handicap and would just as soon lose patients and clients who could not see him for his gifts, see him as a human being.

At just after five he walked up to the front door of the George home. He could smell dinner cooking and thought this wasn't a good time. He had slowly turned from the front door, quietly making his way down the steps when Ging Wa saw him through the window. She called out to him, beckoning him in. He hesitated as he did not want to disturb the family at their evening meal.

Dan George came out, towering over his small wife. "You come in, Billy. Supper's on."

They dined together and Billy enjoyed little Bob. When he'd finished eating he pulled the baby from his highchair and placed him on his lap, helping him with the rest of his meal.

"Will you work with us, Billy?" Ging Wa gave him her sideways glance, looking out through the long bangs of her raven hair.

Dan intervened. "Just bought the place next door, mate. It's yours if you'll come in with us. No strings attached."

Billy looked down at the baby on his lap. "If you don't think I'll be a burden. Don't want to tie you folks down. I know some folks might object to havin' a bloke like me working on 'em."

"Then they can, how do they say, sod off if they don't like it. Look at us, Billy. Do you think you'd put anyone off being aborigine any more than an Indian and a Chinese? Besides, we don't want 'em if they don't want us. We don't want or need their money, anyway. If they're too stupid to take advantage of Billy Livingston's craft, then, in the words of old Scrooge, 'If they would rather die, they had better do it, and decrease the surplus population.' "

"You are so bad, Dan." Ging Wa gave him a crooked smile. She looked on at Billy. "We want you with us, Billy, as long as you like.

As Dan said, no strings attached."

"Well then." Billy raised his glass, "I guess I'm in."

Chica settled in at home and prepared for the great celebration. In the year nineteen-hundred, on his eightieth birthday, Uncle Bob would marry for the second time in his life. Chica would make certain Pilar was beautiful and the old housekeeper would complain the entire time. She hated having so much attention paid her. She hated all the pomp, and she was certain she would jinx and, ultimately, kill Uncle Bob.

Uncle Alejandro had made the journey up north and it was uncertain if he would ever leave the mule ranch. The kidnapping of Rebecca and the trip south had taken its toll on the old bandit and he had trouble catching his breath most all the time. He was content to sit on the veranda outside of Arvel's room and watch the activities all around him.

Marta was most attentive to him. She called him Uncle and this pleased the old man. She'd bring him his food and drinks and constantly check to make certain he was comfortable and cool enough. He was so proud of his family of the North and enjoyed the fact that Uncle Bob, who was not much younger than he, was fit enough to take on the adventure of a marriage to Pilar, a woman several years younger.

Arvel had developed the habit of sitting for a few hours every evening with his Uncle Alejandro. He knew the man was dying, they both knew it, and Arvel wanted to be with him as much as possible until the end.

Arvel, on the other hand, was much stronger now and managed to walk easily with only the slightest limp. He could throw a rope with his right hand but was still too weak to stop a galloping mule. He left that to the younger men.

Alice stayed through summer. She no longer harbored any delusions about getting Rebecca back East, until one day, just as casual as you please, Chica started talking about it as if there was never any question. She brought it up at dinner and looked at the girls as they ate their meal.

"Abuelita, will you be taking Rebecca and Marta soon?"

The girls looked at each other, then at Chica, then at their grandmother.

"Oh, oh . . ." Alice was, for the first time in her life, speechless. "I didn't think you'd want me to now, Maria."

"Sí, they will grow up like wild beasts if they stay here. You take them back to Maryland and make them proper ladies."

"Oh, Mamma, do you mean it? Both of us?"

"Sí." She looked at Marta. "Will this please you, Marta?"

"I don't know. What is this place?"

"It is the land all the way back East. Where I showed you on the map, Marta. Next to the Atlantic ocean."

"Oh, yes. I know this place. This is where Abuelita lives."

"Sí, but you will have to learn many things from books. If I send you to this place, will you be good and help Abuelita and not be a bandit and look after Rebecca for me?"

"Oh, sí, señora. I will. I'll be good. I like to read books. Rebecca has shown me all of her books and I can read them. The old man taught me and I love to read English all the time."

"Yes, Mamma. She is good. She reads every book I give her with ease."

Chica looked at Abuelita. "Now you get two wild animals, not just one, Abuelita. Can you do this thing?"

"With pleasure, child." She beamed at the little girls. "With pleasure."

Chapter XX: Wedding Day

Uncle Bob insisted on a big celebration and Pilar finally went along with it. She'd never had a real wedding. Chica worked on her and had her looking downright pretty. Uncle Bob got himself a fine wool suit, high collar shirt and white tie. He'd also gotten a priest, the same one Arvel had found, to do the wedding mass. Arvel and Uncle Bob were not Catholic, of course, but the ladies were and it was important to them.

The old man had also made certain that all the customs were followed. They'd had the big lasso around them and the gold coins. It was thoroughly Mexican and Pilar pretended that it was all nonsense. She was overwhelmed by her two former bosses' consideration.

Bob also ordered hundreds of carnations shipped from California. He had the hands build a dance floor just outside the corral. Arvel found a second-hand generator from a defunct circus and had it shipped in from Tucson. He hired an electrician to run electric lights everywhere; around the house, around the corral, strung from the barn and surrounding the dance floor. It was going to be like Christmas in summer.

This was going to be an event to remember and it was all for Pilar. Chica ended up being Pilar's madrina de velacion; it seemed completely appropriate.

Uncle Bob chuckled at the memory of the day that Chica had first come into their lives. Pilar spat on the ground and declared that the young woman was no good. It was a strange transition and, over the years, the two became devoted friends. Pilar had learned to take Chica as she was; a little coarse, very unpredictable and still completely wild. She knew that Chica had a difficult time in her young life. No one ever knew or asked Chica about it, not even Arvel. Chica never talked about it and no one dared to inquire.

But Chica softened as well. She learned that refinement wasn't a bad thing. She wanted her little Rebecca to be raised right and always appreciated that Pilar's stability would assure it. And most important of all, Chica had proven to Pilar that she was the perfect mother and wife, completely and unquestioningly devoted to her family: her Rebecca and her Arvel and all the good people on the ranch. Chica lived to serve and nurture and protect her family and this was the quality Pilar admired most in the young woman.

Arvel stood as best man. They'd invited everyone from the expedition to Mexico and all who supported them in the rescue.

The pretty buxom redhead was the life of the party. She danced with all the eligible young men, white, Mexican and Indian alike. She grabbed Chica by the hand as she passed, gave it a squeeze and whispered something in her ear.

Chica looked at the pretty sandy-haired boy with blue eyes standing next to her. Things would be different between him and his mother from now on. Chica looked the woman in the eye. "It is time to live, Bonita, remember, it is time to live."

Hennessy was there and would not leave Arvel's side. He'd mellowed over the years and became one of Arvel's most devoted friends. All the nuns of the convent were there and Chica was able to present them with a hefty check to help in their ministry to the poor. She would never forget their kindness and the old Mother Superior's courage throughout the ordeal.

Dick Welles was there with his family and he proudly introduced everyone to his grandson and beautiful daughter-in-law. Little did he know that Michael and his family had been guests at the Mule Ranch for many years. No one had the heart to tell him.

Billy Livingston was in attendance with his adopted family and little Bob played on Uncle Bob's knee. Dan George offered the toast, as Arvel still felt too tongue-tied to speak clearly enough. He raised his glass and spoke in his clear, articulate voice; "To Pilar and Robert, may they continue to bring joy and happiness to each other and continue to bring joy and happiness to all of the good folks of this great land."

The hands provided the entertainment and everyone danced and sang along to the popular tunes while Will Panks and Raphael put on a fireworks display, Will's new family close at hand.

They celebrated late into the evening and through the night. Arvel saw Chica wander off alone, away from the glow of the electric lights. She was gazing off into the moonlit desert. He sauntered up behind her and put his arms around her waist, breathing in the lovely scent of her dark hair. Her cheeks were wet. She leaned back into his chest, pulled his arms around her and squeezed them tightly. She suddenly turned and looked into his eyes. "Is all okay, my Arvel, is all okay."

Epilogue

Joaquin went to the Bayonne post office to claim the boxes addressed to him. The clerk was a sullen little man who complained that the packages stunk of animal hides and were leaking rock salt all over his storeroom. Joaquin signed for the packages and got them home. He read with interest the scrawl, half English and half Spanish, recognizing at once it was from Chica.

The letter read:

> Dear Joaquin,
> Here are two head for your Russian man. Do not open these boxes in front of any children or weak man or weak woman. They will make them fall over, I think. Ha Ha. These heads belong with the other hijo de puta I made for you many year ago. The one head, it don't matter which one, is Sombrero del Oro,

the worst bandit of Mexico and brother to the first head. The other is his servant. Please to send these to the travel show. You may have all the money it make. I do not want the money, I just want to make the man look like stupid fools. Make sure many gringos see them.

    PS-Rebecca got stolen by Sombrero del Oro, but she is good now. You know, once you open the box, what happened to the bandit. Dead, dead, dead. Ha Ha.

Love, Maria

ABOUT THE AUTHOR

John Horst, (1962-) was born in Baltimore, Maryland and studied philosophy at Loyola College. Among his interests are the history and anthropology of the old west.

The employees of Thorndike Press hope you have enjoyed this Large Print book. All our Thorndike, Wheeler, and Kennebec Large Print titles are designed for easy reading, and all our books are made to last. Other Thorndike Press Large Print books are available at your library, through selected bookstores, or directly from us.

For information about titles, please call:
(800) 223-1244

or visit our Web site at:
http://gale.cengage.com/thorndike

To share your comments, please write:
Publisher
Thorndike Press
10 Water St., Suite 310
Waterville, ME 04901